An Eloquent Caper

By

Randall Probert

An Eloquent Caper

by Randall Probert

www.randallprobertbooks.net

email: randentr@megalink.net

Second Edition

Cover Illustration
by Ralph Sarty

ISBN: 978-0-9852872-4-5

Published by
Randall Enterprises
P.O. Box 862
Bethel, Maine 04217

Foreword

This novel is based on the true life story of one of Maine's most colorful poachers—who wishes to remain anonymous. Besides being a poacher, Jason Smith was also a storyteller, a good husband and father.

Jason's life, as portrayed in the novel, starts in the lonely town of Washburn, in northern Maine. There, his saga begins after his father remarries and moves his family with him from crewcamp to crewcamp, as he made his way in the lumbering business.

The legendary game warden, Earl Landean, is fictional and his character is created from early accounts of other game wardens.

Duluth Wing is a real person. . .and many thanks, Dude, for the history of Flagstaff, Bigelow and Deadriver villages. His association with Mos Jalbert, during Mos' early years, is fictional.

Mos Jalbert is fictional and he characterizes those wardens who have chased Jason through the last thirty years. The last scene where Jason and Mos meet on Jason's last night-hunting caper is fictional, but their stories are real.

CHAPTER 1

The Infamous Jason

It was the beginning of September, and in northern Maine that usually meant the beginning of autumn. The foliage hadn't started to turn yet, but the night air was cool. Just right for sleeping. But try as he might, Jason couldn't sleep. The real reason was that he was trying to decide what he would do for the rest of his life if he sold his woods operation and retired.

The anxiety was keeping his mind from relaxing. But he chose to blame his wife Jerri for making him quit drinking a week ago. "It's for you own good, Jason. You ole fool, you ain't as young as you once were," she had said.

Twice during the night though, when he thought Jerri was asleep, he had gotten out of bed and sneaked out to the garage for a small "nip." *What was worse—this or taking sleeping pills,* he asked himself to clear his own conscience.

But even that didn't work. He knew he would sell out and he hated to admit that the years were creeping upon him. It would be a big change in his life. He tried thinking about a sexual fantasy to quiet his mind, but that soon changed to something else and eventually he was back to thinking about retirement. He tried thinking about his days when he was poaching and that brought Mos Jalbert, the local game warden, to his thoughts. He chuckled as he thought of the last thirty years and all the capers he had pulled and gotten away with, and how ole Mos had chased him through the years. There wasn't a hint of criticism in his laugh. Instead, there was one of friendship and admiration for Mos. After all, he was only doing his job.

His thoughts were interrupted then as a coyote cried a

solitary howl in appreciation for the deer remains Jason had taken out back and left in the orchard next to the salt lick. A screech owl hooted off in the far distance. Jason could just make out is clamorous cry.

There was a cool breeze blowing through his window and even though that helped to relax him, he still could not sleep. He had laid down the law to his wife right after they were married. “Woman, if you’re going to domesticate me, at least let me sleep with the window open.” In time, even Jerri had grown accustomed to the window being open and on numerous occasions had the bed covers soaked with rain or covered with snow. But it was her husband’s tangible link with the outdoors and she understood and respected his need.

The heavy truck traffic had started and even though it was still dark out, his wife would be getting out of bed soon to make his breakfast and send him off to the woods. “Come on, Jason, time to get up,” she said as she rolled the blankets back.

The only reply was a non-committal moan as he rolled over onto his back and relaxed for the first time since the night before. In his mind, he had finally accepted the fact that it was time he left the woods to those who were young and more fit. After all, he had spent most of his entire life in the woods—from the day he was born. Travelling from one woods camp to another with his father and now he had his sons to carry on the tradition and the family name. Jason had left his mark in the woods, as well as on the land, in more respects than one. Now it was someone else’s turn.

He lay there in bed on his back, looking at the ceiling and thinking how strange it was that he could see the stars in the late night sky from his bedroom. Just then, Jerri came in, turned on the lights, and said, “Come on, Jason, or you’ll be late. Breakfast is ready.”

Slowly, little by little, he inched out of bed and put on his work clothes and stumbled out to the kitchen. “What’s the matter, Jason, are you sick or didn’t you sleep good last night?” She asked.

"I'm okay. Just laid awake for awhile, that's all," he mumbled. She didn't push it any further, but she knew that wasn't all. She knew her husband well enough now to know when something was bothering him. She let it alone and served him his breakfast.

When he had finished eating, he got up and said, "I haven't got time for coffee this morning and don't bother putting up a lunch for me either. After the crews get to work, I've got to go to Millinocket and see someone about some equipment," he said, but not quite all the truth. No need to tell her until he had it done.

Once outside, with the cool morning air on his face, he began to slowly feel better. The sun was just starting to brighten the horizon and by the time he got to the woods, it would be daylight and most of the crews would probably already be there.

* * * *

Instead of going back to bed like most people probably would have done, Jerri figured that as long as she was already up, she might as well start making some mincemeat from the neck of the deer Jason had brought home two days ago. She skinned the hide back, cut the head off, stripped the meat off, ground it up and set it aside. Next, she diced some apples, and mixed in some raisins and spices with the deer meat. Then she took a new bottle of brandy and added just enough to the mixture to add flavor and took a sip for herself. There was nothing more to do with the mincemeat until later in the day. She always liked to let it set for awhile before putting it in the canning jars. "Needs to be aired out," she would say.

She took another sip of brandy and turned the television on. Before she sat down to watch the morning news, she decided the brandy was pretty good and had another sip. The news was just a continuation of the previous day and of little interest.

As the effect of the brandy started to work, Jerri's head dropped lower and lower, until her chin was resting on her chest.

She fell fast asleep. If she had known beforehand that the brandy would have the effect on her that it was about to, she would have never taken that first sip. She started to dream that she was in Houlton and talking to an Indian woman. The Indian woman was saying, "Do you know you're married to my husband?"

In her dream, Jerri answered, "What?"

"You are married to my husband," the Indian woman repeated.

"I doubt it!" Jerri said. Then Jerri looked at the Indian woman's kids; she had six of them with her and each one looked exactly like her husband Jason. She exclaimed then, "My God, you can have him! Take him and go!"

The phone rang then and Jerri woke up. The first thought that was in her mind was that Jason had never told her about his first wife. Then slowly she realized that she had been dreaming.

* * * *

Before starting the engine in his pickup, Jason took out his rifle, saying, "Won't need this today," and started back towards the house with it. He stopped and turned back towards his truck, saying, "No, it wouldn't feel the same if I didn't have it." But as he got to the garage door, he said to himself, "Oh, gee-hokey, I won't be shooting anything today anyhow. Hell, I'll leave it." With that, he put it in the corner of the garage.

By now, the first rays of the sun could be seen peaking over the horizon. Jason lived on a high hill that overlooked the town of Patten and as he backed out of his driveway, he was instilled with the picturesque setting of the town in the hazy daylight with a few puffs of white smoke coming out of some of the chimneys. It was a scene he had seen hundreds of times and each one was more impressionable than the other.

He didn't know why, but instead of heading towards town, he drove north. For some unexplainable reason, he wanted to drive by the warden's house and see if Mos Jalbert was at home. What did it really matter if he was or not? He wasn't going to shoot anything this morning. He'd left his .308 savage in the garage; maybe it was only an impulsive instinct.

Mos only lived a couple of miles up the road from Jason, so he really didn't waste much time. He drove by and sure enough, Mos was home. Instead of turning around, he decided to go a little further and cut across the Owlsboro Road to Shin Pond. He had done this same thing many times before. It was usually with the intention of killing something on his way to work. More often than not though, ole Mos had seen him go by and figuring that Jason was up to no good, had followed him.

It didn't take Jason long to figure out that if he wanted some fresh meat and didn't want a run-in with the warden, then he would use a little reverse psychology. He would drive by Mos' house only on occasions when he had no intention of shooting anything, thereby hoping to confuse him.

Well, this morning was only out of habit that had been formulating for years. Jason stopped near the mouth of the road and backed into the woods. He killed his motor and waited to see if the Ole Fox had seen him go by this morning.

After awhile, Lucas saw Jason sitting in his truck and naturally thought that something was wrong, so he went outside to see. "What's the matter, Jason? You got trouble?"

"No, just playing games with Mos to see if the Ole Fox comes out," Jason said.

"Why do you torment him so, Jason? You know, sooner or later he'll get ya."

"Well, he has you know. Three times in the last thirty years. Not bad considering what I've taken home for groceries. Besides, it's become more of a game between the two of us now more than anything else. I mean him no ill feelings. He has a job to do and in fact, I've come to respect and appreciate what he does."

Lucas scratched his head and as he turned to walk back to his house, he said, "Yeah, maybe. But you have an odd way of showing it." Jason laughed a deep-hearted laugh and knew what Lucas was talking about.

When Mos didn't come, Jason continued his trip to the woods and headed west on the Owlsboro Road. "Must not have been up this morning," Jason mused.

Traveler Mountain was clearly visible this morning as the sun reflected against the ledges. The top of the mountain was white with snow already. *Won't be long, I guess. Maybe it's a Godsend that I'm calling it quits after all,* he thought.

He was in no particular rush to get to the woods this morning. He was sure that if the crews got there first, they could start work without him. Besides, this was his favorite part of the day, except maybe on those rare occasions when he'd go night hunting on foot. Then that was without question the best he could ask for. In the morning, everything seemed so peaceful and clear. The birds were usually the first to awaken and their singing was rather enjoyable. Later in the day as it started to warm, road dust would fill the air. If you happened to be behind a log truck, the dust would be so bad that it would sift through the truck cab and soon blanket everything inside. No, the mornings with the cool, clear air were definitely the best.

He had been fortunate this morning and had made it to the Huber Road in T6-R7 before the big log trucks had started to roll. Now he had about twenty-five miles to drive through the woods to get to the base of Beetle Mountain to where his crews were working.

Just before reaching the Soper Brook Bridge, there's a long, straight stretch in the road. Just beyond the bridge, Jason could just make out a dark spot in the road. As he got closer, the dark spot turned around to face him and he then realized that it was a small cow moose. Instinctively he started to slow up, so not to spook it, and at the same time, he reached for his .308 savage that he always carried for just such an emergency.

"By Jesus Christ all mighty, I took that son-of-a-whore out and left it in the garage. Damn! Yes, sir, and it's a brown one and no calf. That means she's dry. The best hunk of beef I've seen all summer and I left my rifle home!"

The cow just stood in the tall grass along the road as Jason drove by and he said, "This is your day, ole lady. If it had been yesterday, you would have been in my freezer by now."

He stopped at Mitchell Pond, got out, and just sat on a rock, overlooking the water. There was a beaver swimming out in the middle and it was carrying a poplar branch. "Sign of an early winter," Jason said, "getting in his feed-bed this early in the fall."

He looked around him and then up at the ridge behind the pond and saw several giant white pine and spruce trees towering above the others. "God, how things have changed," he said. "I can remember cutting on top of that ridge. Now look at it. Look at how much it has grown back, just like man was never there. Yup, man can spend his whole life in the woods, cut down every tree he comes to, and scar the hell out of the land and when he's done and turns around, he'll find he's closed in again with new and stronger trees. I'll admit I don't understand everything people say about God, but I do know one thing for sure and that's there is something much greater than man himself that can rebuild a forest and heal wounds of the modern-day lumberman."

As he patiently watched the beaver swimming, his thoughts were drawn to the drastic changes he had seen in his life in the woods business. The ax had been replaced with the two-man crosscut saw and then eventually that had been replaced with the poignant, foul-smelling, noisy chainsaw. The early models had been so heavy and cumbersome that it was used primarily to fell the trees. Only later and if one dared, it was used to limb a tree. Now, saws are made so small that they can be held by one hand and they're faster and more powerful than the early models. Only in the last few years have the chainsaws been replaced with mechanical harvesters and mechanical delimbers. In some crews, the chainsaws are now obsolete.

The workhorse had been replaced with lag-tractors or crawlers, and when they were replaced with the rubber-tired skidders, everyone said they wouldn't be practical because they'll roll over so easy. "Just wait 'til you get on a side hill." But even on the side of a mountain, they proved to be more efficient and more dependable than either the horse or the crawler.

Jason had worked on possibly the last log drive in the state—it was along the East Branch of the Penobscot. Now log-drives are against the law. "What gawd-damn nonsense is that?" Now the tall trees were hauled to the mill, tree length, instead of dimensional or four-foot pulpwood on trucks that could haul better than 100,000 pounds. "Some change from the horse-drawn sleds," he moaned.

The day was wearing on and he knew that he had to get to work. He left Mitchell Pond and his reminiscing of the past. He still had several miles to drive yet before he reached his wood yard at Caribou Brook. But again, there was no hurry, so he poked along at a leisurely pace and simply enjoyed the ride.

Near the turn between Beetle Mountain and Caribou Ridge, two small deer stepped into the road. As Jason came around the turn, he slowed and laughed a hearty laugh and said, "Go on, you're safe today. I don't have my rifle." After watching the two deer amble off and back into the woods, Jason began to wonder if even if he had his rifle if he would have shot them. A few years ago there wouldn't have been a second thought. He would have had them both. But for some reason, he was watching these two with a different perspective. It was odd how he had never taken the time before to notice. Was he changing his outlook on life, or was he just getting old and slowing down? He didn't feel old and he could still do a day's work. "Maybe I'm changing," he said aloud. Then he grinned a happy smile that seemed to start from his heart and work its way to the surface.

By the time Jason got to the yard, all the other crews had arrived and had gone to work. Each morning, he routinely walked around the cuttings and stopped to talk with each crew to survey their site and to see if they had any problems with their equipment. No one was working on the side of the ridge now; it had all been cut. But he decided to walk around the perimeter and look things over from the top.

It was an excellent September day. The sun was bright but the air was still cool. From the height of the land, he could look down on most of the cutting area. "I can remember when crews with only a horse and a two-man saw were doing the same as these foul-smelling machines. The only difference is that I would have fives times as many men, lumber camps, and a cook. Now the men return home each day and sleep with their wives. I've seen an awful change in the woods in my days."

He sat down on a stump and just let his mind begin to wander. For some strange reason, he could see in his mind a young French fellow from New Sweden as he went sailing through the air and screaming like a loon until he hit the trees.

It was back in the horse days when he was cutting a right-of-way in the Pleasant Lake country. He was working for an Irishman named Jim Ryan. Well, on this day, Jason had felled a huge beech tree. The trunk was hollow and the top was all branches. When it fell, it doubled a small hardwood tree to the ground. Well, Jesus Christ all mighty, the next thing Jason knew, he looked up and this little French fellow, Timothy Martin, well he climbed on that spring pole and had his arms and legs wrapped around it. Martin hollered, "Cut it!" Well, Jesus Christ, one of those fellows cut the top of that tree and that shot Martin screaming like a loon and flying right through the air and over the tops of some hemlocks.

Well they had heard some branches break and Martin was laying on the ground, with his face cut up pretty bad. Jim Ryan took one look from where he and Jason were standing and said, "Ooh, Jesus, what ta fool. Ooh, the son-of-a-whore. Ta pooor boy. Ta, he's nothing but a gawd-damn nut—ta hell with him," the big Irishman said as he spat a mouthful of tobacco juice on the ground. Jim, Jason, and mostly the whole crew went down to see how Martin was. He lay on the ground, unable to talk or scream; all he could do was moan. His face was flattened with a huge lump over one eye and five or six teeth missing.

These memories got Jason laughing so hard while slapping

his knee that he almost rolled off the stump and onto the ground. He said aloud, mimicking Jim Ryan, "Ooh, Jesus, ta poor boy," and laughed some more

He slid back on the stump and the thought of another caper came to mind that had happened just days after Timothy Martin and the spring pole. It was while working on the same right-of-way.

Back in those days, the roads were still grubbed out the hard way and it was Jason's job to clear the brush and stumps. Crawler tractors were in use in those days, but most of the crews didn't have much faith in them. They'd say something like, "nothing to keep the gawd-damn thing from tipping over." So consequently, Jason pulled most of the stumps out with a team of horses. "I like horses, too," he'd say. Well, there were a bunch of Dewely brothers from Caribou working that year. George was a pretty good worker along with his brothers, Forest and Beecher. But Sherm was foxy. He'd lug water and such, and then he'd get off to the side, lay down and sleep. There was also a crew of Frenchmen working there from Van Buren. They were good workers, too. They could cut as much wood as any crew in the woods. Well, this one particular day, as these Frenchmen were working their way along the right-of-way, they came to a huge yellow birch that had blown over. If you have ever been in the woods much at all and seen one of these huge trees that had gone down, you'd know how Sherm must have felt as he saw the nice shelter the roots had made when they were pulled out of the ground. It was a hot day and the roots provided a cool, shady spot. So naturally Sherm took advantage of it and laid down for a nap.

Now these Frenchmen being as good workers as they were, it didn't take no time at all to cut through the tree with a two-man cross-cut, but they didn't know that Sherm was sound asleep behind the roots. Well, when the tree was cut through, the stump rocked back and fell into place where it had been with Sherm under it.

The two Frenchmen stood there for a moment appreciating the job they had just finished when one of them said, "Hear that, you?" It came again, a weak muffled "help." The two Frenchmen were a little spooked cause they knew no one else was around and they didn't quite know where the noise was coming from. They ran back towards the camp and met Jim Ryan, the Irishman, and told him about the strange voice. Ryan had been looking for Sherm and not being able to find him, went back to the yellow birch with the Frenchmen. Ryan looked around and listened but he couldn't hear anything. Just as he was about to walk off, he heard, "Heellp." So faint was it that he wasn't quite sure or not if he had heard anything. He turned around and there by his own feet, sticking out of the ground was the tips of Sherm's own shoes and again he heard, "Heellp, heellp."

"Jason," he hollered, "bring the team up and pull this stump off this Jill Poke!" That's what he called ole Sherm. Jason hooked on and just as he had the stump almost pulled back, the chain slipped and it fell on top of Sherm again. Eventually, they got the stump off and Ryan stood there shaking his head, saying, "I'll surely kill ya." Sherm took one look at Ryan's face and he knew the Irishman meant it. He wasn't hurt as bad as the crews might have thought because he jumped out of that hole and got clear away before Ryan could grab him. He chased Sherm for a ways, but gave it up. "Yeah, you Jesusly nut, I'll get ya next time." The words came spitting out in both Irish and English. He hollered down through the trees, "Let this be a lesson to ya, boy — no more sneaking off!"

Jason got to laughing so hard this time that he actually did roll off the stump and as he picked himself up, he was still laughing and saying, "Let this be a lesson to ya, boy!"

The sun had warmed up some by now and like ole Sherm, he found some shade in a spruce thicket behind him. There was a natural dugout and a bed of spruce needles. He had always enjoyed the fresh smell of spruce and today as he lay there looking up through the boughs at the clear sky, he said to himself,

"I've seen the best of it. By Jesus, yes. The woods, the hunting, and the best wife a man could ever want." With that said, his eyelids slowly closed and with them, everything of the present was erased as he drifted back in time to the days of the lumber camps and the shooting of moose and deer to feed the crews.

* * * *

Jason Smith was born March 10, 1929, to Milton and Mildred of Castlehill. He was a squawking eight-pound baby. "There, son, what are you going to call him?" Oscar asked as he slapped his son's shoulders. Without any hesitation, Milton replied, "Jason."

"Why on earth would you want to name him Jason?" Oscar asked.

"After Stonewall Jackson." No explanation, just Stonewall Jackson.

"But why in hell name him after a southern rebel?"

"Because he needs a name and reputation to live up to. I want him to grow up with principles and to be as stubborn as a jackass so that no man can get the best of him. Oh, yeah, I hope he can shoot, too," he laughed.

So there it was, the prologue to Jason's life. He shortly started to live in accord with it. He was proving to be a strongwilled lad. One might call it stubbornness, but he knew what he wanted and wouldn't settle for less.

During the first two years of his life, Mildred, his mother, smothered him with love and attention. She never complained when he woke her up in the middle of the night and then kept her awake until dawn. She would always sit by his crib and rock him so that he would not wake his father who had to be up early every morning to go to the woods. His father never begrudged him, either, for his squawking or for his wife having to spend all night by his side. Milton relished in the love he saw between his wife and his boy.

Mildred had been to see the doctor and he had told her that she had a chronic case of tuberculosis and that she probably wouldn't live for more than a year. It wasn't until the last days of her life when she could no longer take care of Jason or his father. It was too late for any hope of a cure.

The night she died, she had asked Milton, "Take our son with you wherever you work. Don't let him be alone." When Milton offered to bring Jason to her in her last hours, she said, "No, I don't want him to watch me die. I don't want him to suffer with the memories of watching me. Take care of him, Milton," she pleaded and those were her last words.

At first Jason, even at the early age of two and a half, was distraught with grief because of his mother's absence. He wasn't yet old enough to understand what death was, so his father had tried to explain that she had only gone on a long trip.

His grandmother was doing her best to take her place and he would even laugh and play with her, but it wasn't the same. As with all youngsters at that early age, they become restless and inquisitive, and Jason was no exception. Little by little, he pulled himself out of his shell and began to find new and exciting interests.

Milton also felt the loss of his wife and her last words were constantly echoing through his head. He decided for the present and until things seemed to change some with his personal life, he decided that Jason would be better off living with his grandparents while he was away working. The woods and crew camps were not exactly an ideal place to bring up a youngster without any help. The fall potato harvest was in and Milton had hired-on in the woods, out in the backcountry with no way out until spring. He said goodbye to his folks and gave Jason a hug, and without saying anything further, he was gone.

Each spring after the snow was gone and the log drives were over, Milton returned to the farm in Castlehill to help with the spring planting. As soon as the fall harvest was in though, he would leave for the woods. There he stayed until the following spring. This went on for about three years and he met another woman. They were soon married. That same year, Jason started school, which in time would prove to all those who came to know Jason, that they were in for a complete and new education. "No, no, Jason. Do it this way," a distraught teacher would say.

Jason's reply would be, "Nope, Grandfather says this way." No amount of encouragement or threatening could change his mind. He was already proving to be as stubborn as his namesake. One day after the harvest was over, Jason's grandfather said, "How about you and me go bird hunting today, boy?" He asked as he drank his morning coffee.

"How can Jason go? He has school," his grandmother said.

"Nonsense. He'll learn a good deal more while hunting birds than he ever will in that school building." This really made Jason light up. In fact, the next day when his teacher asked, "Where were you yesterday, Jason? Were you sick?"

Jason piped up, "Nope. Granddad and I went bird hunting. He says I'll learn more from him than I ever will in this school building." His teacher was so shocked with his rationale that she rushed right over to the Smith farm that very afternoon to have a talk with Jason's grandparents.

After that lecture, Jason never missed another school day unless he was so sick that he couldn't walk.

Jason had a good life growing up on the farm with his grandfather, and his Granddad enjoyed it as much as Jason did. When he wasn't working, you could always find the two together. If for something better to do, they would walk along the edge of the potato fields and look for animal tracks.

By the time Jason was ten, his father had put together a woods crew of his own and had gotten a contract to cut wood in Crystal on the Poorman's Retreat Road. So Jason left the security of his grandparent's farm and started his trade at an early age.

The best thing about it was that there wasn't any school there or damn little of it. This was his father's first job on his own and he was finding it difficult to always find enough money.

Being close as they were to town, the men would often times want an advance on their wages. Then there were food supplies to buy and the unseen necessities. When the meat supply would get low, his father would often go out at night and foot-jack a deer.

In those days, they didn't have the powerful flashlights that poachers have now, so he would take an old kerosene lantern and painstakingly so not to break the glass globe, wrap tinfoil around the globe with a small hole torn through to let the light out. This was his spotlight. But as crude as it may sound, it worked.

Milton never was greedy. He only shot what was needed. But as Jason could remember in later years and as he retold the stories, it was just like New York City. You went out there and snapped on a light; there were so many deer that you could take your pick.

Milton never considered himself a poacher. He just took enough and always tried to make sure that it wasn't a doe. But the stories started to circulate and rumors were going through the camps and on one particular night, Milton asked Jason to go with him. Milton had strained his back on a log that day and now he needed Jason's help to drag a deer back. Gleefully Jason grabbed his jacket and hat, and ran after his father. "Now, boy, if you're going with me, stop that running and you'll have to be quiet or you'll scare the deer away."

They found their way to the edge of a large apple orchard where Milton had found a sheltered place behind a couple of small spruces. He set his rifle down and took the lantern from Jason. He lit it and said, "When I say it's okay, turn this knob and hold the lantern up like this and sweep it across the orchard, but move it slow. If you pick up a deer eye, hold the light on it while I shoot."

Jason was so nervous that all he could do was nod his head. In the dark, Milton wasn't sure if he understood or not, but there wasn't enough time to explain it all again.

The lantern was going with the shield covering the light hole, and Milton very quietly walked around the spruce trees and started across the middle of the orchard. Just then a deer blew and stomped the ground to alert the other deer of danger. "Okay, now, son."

Jason turned the knob like he was supposed to and held the lantern up high and started so sweep the orchard. He couldn't believe his eyes. There were deer everywhere. Just then, a rifle cracked down at the lower end of the orchard and then another directly across from them and then another at the other end of the orchard. "Gawd all mighty, boy, douse that light and let's get the hell out of here! The wardens are sure as hell going to be all over this place in no time. Those gawddamn fools!"

It didn't take them long to hike back to camp. "Hope everyone of them gets caught," Milton spouted. Jason was nervous at first when everyone was shooting, but afterwards, he felt a sense of exhilaration and the excitement of the chase.

This was Jason's preamble to hunting for food, a necessity of life, and to the excitement of the game. This night would always be alive in his memories for the rest of his life and would forge his cunning reputation. Jason had tasted the nectar, and now he wanted more of it.

As it turned out, the fellows who had done the shooting were locals and not from Milton's camp. He put the word out that there had better not be any more hunting near his crew camps or anywhere near his lumbering operations. This he naturally assumed was the unspoken law among all crew camps—you don't poach in another man's breadbasket.

After the experience of that night, Milton was reluctant about letting Jason do any more hunting, whether it was in the daylight or in the dark. "But why?" Jason would demand.

"Because I said so," his father would answer. He realized that night how close they had been to being caught and the danger from the bullets of the other poachers. So for the rest of that fall, Jason worked around the crew camps doing chores and hating every minute of it. But not all were bad times or spent pouting. He mostly enjoyed listening to the men talk about their work. Each night they would brag about the large tree he had to fell. Seems as though to Jason that the trees kept growing from night to night. At least in their stories one might think that it was an impossible task to lay one flat on the ground.

During December, a small schoolhouse was opened at the intersection of the Retreat Road and the Island Falls Road. This meant that Jason had to go to school. "But, Dad, I have work to do here. Who's going to do it if I have to go to school?"

"We'll manage; you need your learning," his father would answer. So on the first of December, Jason was up early with clean clothes and a new pair of boots. There were no buses in those days. If the roads were not cleared of snow, the kids were expected to walk. The distance wasn't great, but it was the agony of the walk, to spend all day sitting in an uncomfortable chair, doing something that he didn't like. Actually, he only had to walk a little less than a mile either way.

After about a week, Jason and another friend, Thomas, had to stay after school. The rest of he pupils were allowed to go home because someone had thrown a wad of wet paper at the teacher. "Who threw that?" the teacher demanded. No answer. "Who threw this?" she demanded and stood up. "Unless someone speaks up, I'll punish every one of you."

Jason had not thrown it, but he didn't want to see everyone in trouble either. He stood up and said, "Miss Cooly, I did."

Before Miss Cooly could answer, Thomas stood up, knowing that Jason had not done the dastardly deed and not wanting his friend to take all the blame, said, "No, I done it."

For a brief moment Miss Cooly stood there with her hands on her hips and then said, "All right, I'll punish you both. One for throwing the wad of paper and the other for lying. You both will be staying after for two hours, cleaning this room."

When the two hours were finally over, Jason and Thomas started the hike towards home. They hadn't gone far when both boys came to a stop. "Did you hear that, Thomas?" Jason asked nervously.

"Yeah, what was it?"

"I don't know but it came from over in those bushes," Jason said. He turned his light on. The clicking sound came again.

"Up there in those branches," Thomas said. When Jason put the light on the branches Thomas had pointed towards, there sat five plump partridges. While Jason held the light, Thomas found a stick and killed all five. Jason took three of them home with him and Thomas took the other two.

When Jason walked through the camp door, his father asked, "Why so late, son?"

Jason immediately held up his hands and said, "Me and Thomas went hunting after school." That was a good lie and this way he wouldn't have to explain the real reason he was late.

By the end of December, the snow was too deep to continue school and expect the kids to walk through it, so once again the doors were closed. Jason happily stayed home at the crew camps.

That winter he learned to drive a team of horses. His granddad had taught him back at the farm in Castlehill, but driving a team in the winter, through snow and over ice, required an experienced hand. He learned that he had to be the eyes for his team and watch that they stayed away from icy slopes and weak ice along the brook. His team was only as good as he himself would become.

It was hard work and for a ten-year-old boy, Jason tried to do his share. He wasn't allowed yet in the deep snow or in an area where choppers were felling trees. Most of his teamwork was comparatively light.

In January, the food supplies were getting low and the snow was too deep to get out for fresh supplies. So each morning, the crews were fed biscuits, deer meat, and black coffee. For supper, they had potatoes, gravy, deer meat, and usually apple pie for dessert. This was Jason's favorite meal. He couldn't understand why some of the men were grumbling.

There were still plenty of potatoes in the sawdust shed and there was no end to the deer in the choppings. Once in awhile, one of them would shoot one that had been eating some of the gray moss that grows on spruce and fir trees and the meat would generally taste like the moss. When the supply of deer was as ample as this, it was thrown aside if it had a strong taste to it.

During the second week of January, the weather took a change for the better. It warmed up some and rained off and on for two days. The men didn't seem to mind getting wet because they knew that as soon as the weather turned cold again, everything would freeze up, and they'd be able to walk on the frozen snow instead of trying to wade through it. This also meant that someone could take a team out to town for food supplies.

Since everyone was busy in the yards, Jason was the only one available. "Jason," his father said, "I want you to harness up the small browns and go to town. Give Mr. Fenmore this list and tell him I'll be to town in the spring to square up with him."

Jason lit right up like a kerosene lantern. His father had given him a job to do and he would be the boss until he returned with the supplies. After breakfast that morning, he very smartly harnessed the small brown pair and hooked up to the small dray his father had built with sides to it for hauling supplies into camp during the winter months.

The frozen snow was strong enough to support the small team and once Jason got to the Patten Road, the snow was packed and frozen as hard and smooth as a New York boulevard.

The Patten Road was the same as the Island Falls Road. The only difference was the direction you were traveling in. If it was towards Patten, then it was the Patten Road, and vice versa.

He met some of his schoolmates along the way. They were playing on newly formed ice ponds. But Jason didn't have time to stop and talk or do fool kid's stuff. He was a man now, with responsibilities. There was no time for fooling.

He was disappointed with the attention or the lack of it,

when he got to town. No one seemed to notice that he was driving a team of horses by himself and that he was only ten years old. Disappointedly, he went to Mr. Fenmore's and loaded on all the supplies his father wanted. "Tell Milton not to worry. He can square up with me in the spring. Say hello to your ma for me," Mr. Fenmore shouted as Jason started the team back towards the Poorman's Retreat Road, now on the Island Falls Road.

After the January thaw was over, it started to snow again. Every day at first, then it calmed down to only about twice a week. But that didn't slow the work any or damper the men's spirits. If anything, the work was easier now. With a good crust under the new powder, they could sail along through the snow.

With the spring thaw came rumors and stories of famous log drives. Most of the rivers, though, were no longer used for driving lumber. But in places throughout the state, like the East Branch of the Penobscot and the Kennebec River, the drives were still in full swing.

The crews had mostly gone home by now. Only a skeleton crew was left to load the trucks. But these could not be loaded until the mud had dried up or the trucks would never get out of the woods. So day after day, Jason wandered around the camps, looking for anything to do to keep busy. He would watch as the remaining men worked on building a contraption called a jammer. If it worked without any snags, it saved a lot of time. Two logs were stood up with a third one in the front, fastened together with blocks and tackle, and a pair of horses would pull tension on the rope and lift the log up towards the blocks and then lowered onto the truck bed.

It actually saved a lot of time and work as compared to loading with Kent-dogs. But it, too, had its drawbacks. Occasionally one of the uprights would slip on the rope, catch or break, and the log, if it fell on anyone, it would either break a leg or kill the poor fellow. Jason watched and decided even though it meant a little extra effort, he would prefer to roll the logs off the decking boughs with Kent-dogs to the truck beds. He never did get comfortable working around jammers, and if the opportunity would allow, he'd sneak off to another part of the yard.

There were times during this lull while they were waiting for the mud to dry that he would find a sunny spot and daydream about working on a log drive. He had never seen one or even been near one. All he knew of the drives, he had learned from listening to the men talk around camp. They made it sound like a glorious time with a lot of camaraderie and good times, especially around the campfire and cook wagon at night with the men telling yarns and sipping whiskey.

The log drivers had, through the years, developed a certain mythical aura about the drives. This was understandable as those who successfully completed a drive could be found in some tavern or the center of attention as he retold his daring feats on the river, such as how he danced out on a logjam and by himself dislodged the jam. Then not being able to make it ashore in time, had to ride out the river on one of the logs. Or how he had jumped into the icy waters to save someone from being crushed by the boom of logs. If the truth be known, probably he had fallen in and had tried desperately to drag himself out before he was crushed.

But regardless of the truth behind those stories, Jason was glorified by them and wished that someday he too could take part in the drive before they were non-existent.

* * * *

Once the logs had all been hauled to the mill and the yard was cleaned up and the camps were closed, Milton moved his family back to Castlehill for the summer to help with the summer planting. But before the spring planting was finished, he had gotten another contract at Pickett Mountain in Hersey.

Jason and his stepmother stayed on the farm with his granddad while Milton went to Hersey and then into Pickett Mountain Lake. The road systems weren't that much and before he could even think about hauling in supplies, building crew camps, and cruising the Emerson woodlands, a road had to be swamped, cleared, and bulldozed.

When the camps were finished and the food supplies were hauled in, Milton went back to Castlehill to get his wife and Jason. Still, he couldn't think about cutting any wood. Even though the camps were built, there were still roads that had to be cleared and brushed out for the horses, horse hovels, and storage sheds for the hay and grain.

Milton had hired a local man called Homer T. He never did know what the "T" stood for, only that everyone called him Homer T instead of just Homer. Homer T was a handy man in most fields except the marketability of the wood. So Milton told him what had to be done before the crews were brought in and he could have Jason help him. It the meantime, Milton cruised the woods, laying out the hauling roads and marking the trees he wanted cut. The landowner had hired Milton with the understanding that he was to cut only the hardwood and no softwood at all. The mill in Patten was at the time paying good money for good veneer logs to be used for making plywood.

So Homer T and Jason built the horse hovels, which were by today's standards, crude structures. But it kept the wind and rain out. When the hovels and sheds were done, they went about making crude furniture for the camps and even dug a well and piped the water into the cook camp. Once the water was running, it had to be kept running. There were no faucets or storage tanks. Gravity fed the system and made it easier for Marg, Milton's wife and chief cook. This would also eliminate extra work for Jason since it was his chore to fill the watering tubs and buckets each day.

But it wasn't all work. On Sunday, Milton would take Jason fishing on Pickett Mountain Stream. The stream was small, but downstream a ways from the camp, a couple of beaver had dammed the brook. The trout fishing there was exceptional. Jason wasn't aware of or even knew what was meant by a legal limit. He naturally thought that when his pack basket was full, then that was the limit. None ever went to waste. What couldn't be eaten that day was canned and stored in the mud by the spring.

Milton expected to hire about fourteen men that winter. "Homer T, we'll need two more camps. I've decided to get more men." That would give him four three-man crews, one man to swamp additional roads as needed, and one man as yard tender. That also meant more horses and additional hovels and hay sheds.

During the month of July, Jason was busy helping Homer T with the additional buildings. Milton was still busy running survey lines and marking the prime yellow birch trees. These had to be the best possible because they were being turned into aircraft plywood to be used on the military aircraft that were going overseas to fight against the Germans and the Japanese. There were a lot of nice white spruce and pine, but on the Emerson grounds, all he could cut was yellow birch and an occasional rock maple.

Because of the war, Milton was having difficulty finding enough men. He had only six locals and the other eight were Indians from down river. By the beginning of September, the camps were completed and everything was ready to start work.

Homer T was the yard tender and Jason was his assistant. There were no pulp loaders or cranes to do the heavy work. It was all done with the Kent dog. When two men became efficient with the tool and could work with each other, a lot could be accomplished. But during that first day, the hours dragged by. At night after supper was eaten and the men had a chance to clean up, they would all gather in the cook camp and Milton would turn the radio on for the seven o'clock broadcast. The announcer always started out the same. "Good evening. Everything is going well." He was speaking about the war effort in Europe and what America was doing to prepare for enteringthe war.

For the rest of that night, most of the conversations were centered around the war. The general feeling towards the

Germans was mutual. Each bragged about how many of the enemy he would kill if he were over there fighting.

For the better part of Jason's life, he had grown up with the words of war echoing in his head without really understanding what it was all about. All he could figure out was that the Germans were preparing for a big war in Europe and that it wanted a superior breed of people to administer the affairs of the world. It really wasn't making a whole lot of sense to him, so he went to bed.

That following Sunday, Jason took his .32-20 rifle from the gun rack and with a pocket full of cartridges, he headed towards the choppings to shoot a deer. Milton had always told him, "Son, never gut-shoot a deer. If you do, he'll only run off and die, and you'll probably never find him."

"Where do I shoot him, Dad? In the head?" Jason asked.

"Well, that would be a good place, if you can. But just behind the front shoulder or the neck is good, too."

No one worked on Sunday and he could have his pick of the deer. He followed the main hauling road into the first chopping and stood still, surveying the land. Nothing at all moved. He went to the next chopping and found the same. Then he went to the next and even in the last chopping. There were no deer.

Disappointed, he started back for camp. He hoped to show the new crew that he could shoot a deer and that he was a man. He hadn't gone far when movement in the corner of his eye caught his attention. He stopped and turned only his head. He saw a small lamb deer eating the tops of raspberry bushes. Slowly, he pulled his rifle to his shoulder, aimed, and fired at the brisket. The deer fell to the ground and as Jason was jacking another shell into the chamber, he saw another deer start to run. Instinctively, he pulled up and fired, and the deer went down. He was so excited that he forgot to jack another shell in and started to run down towards the second deer. Just as he came into sight of it, it jumped to its feet and ran off. Jason was dumbfounded. He knew he had hit it. Just then he looked down and saw a small puddle of blood. "She ain't going far," he said to himself. He walked over to the lamb and it lay pretty still, so Jason knew he had this one. He laid down his rifle against a tree and reached in his pocket for his knife. "Oh, gee-hokey, I left the damn thing back at camp." He picked up his rifle and ran back.

"Dad! Dad!" he shouted. "I got one! I mean I got two!"

"What do you mean you got two? What did you get?" his father asked.

"I shot two deer, Dad. Two of them!" he said excitedly.

"Well, that's good. We have one to eat and we have some to give away. You got your knife?"

"I left it at camp. I'll go get it," he said as he ran off.

The lamb was still warm by the time they returned.

"Where's the other one, son?"

"It dropped over there," he said as he pointed in the direction, "but it got up and ran off when I walked over to it. I don't think it went very far. There's a pool of blood where she was laying."

They dressed the lamb off and turned it over so the cavity could drain. Then Milton went over to look at the ground where the doe had been. He ran his fingers through the blood and then along the ground. He then smelled his fingers. "Ayah, just what I thought. You paunched her, son. We may find her and we may not. How'd you happen to gut shoot her?" his father asked.

Jason told him the story and added, "I guess I was so excited that I hurried my shot and didn't look where I was aiming."

"Well, never mind. We'll follow her trail and see." They started off and at first it looked promising. There was blood on both sides of her trail, but the further they went, the less blood they found until it was all gone. "She stopped bleeding, son. I think you lost this one. This is why I told you earlier to never gut-shoot an animal. Most generally, it will only run off and die several days later. Remember, son, we shoot deer for meat and not for the sport of it. Come on, let's pick up the lamb and get her back to camp."

Jason would always remember that experience, and from

it, he learned a valuable lesson. Although in the years to follow, he would more often than not go night hunting for the sport of it and the thrill of the suspense. But that was only if he was low on venison and the meat was never wasted.

To the people in that particular community, when people talked about meat, they were not speaking of beef. It was deer and moose venison.

Things were going just fine at the Emerson camps at Pickett Mountain Stream until one Sunday afternoon when Milton told Jason, "Son, there's a school opening tomorrow in Hersey, just this side of Campbell's place."

With shocked disbelief, Jason dropped his water bucket and said, "What's that you say?"

"You heard me right, son. Tomorrow you go back to school."

"But Dad."

"No *buts* about it. You go to school and that's that."

The next morning, Jason was up with the crews but instead of his work clothes, he had on school clothes. He had to be up early because it was a four-mile trek to school and there weren't any buses.

Jason had a determined will about him. He had to have in order to live up to his namesake. There were some areas of study that Jason was bored with and consequently, he did rather poorly. But there were other areas where he did very well. It was only a matter of applying himself. Jason found that he liked this school better than the one in Crystal. There were more boys his age and fewer stuck-up girls. The four miles he had to walk each way wasn't really bad either. It only made him late getting home.

After the leaves had fallen, Jason started carrying his father's shotgun, hoping to shoot a partridge or two. Game wardens weren't around much in those days. Leastwise, not much in the daytime during the fall months. But the mere mention of "game warden" would make some men nervous.

One night, Homer T wanted some fresh meat and at the supper table one of the crew said something about seeing a game warden poking around a stream. Well, Homer T was so shaken that he dropped his coffee cup on the table and it broke.

"What's the matter, Homer T?" Milton asked.

"Nothing. You say the warden was around today?"

"Yeah. One of the men thought he had seen him."

That's all it took to convince Homer T he shouldn't go hunting that night. The word "game warden" in itself was legendary throughout the crew camps and in all parts of the woods. Their grit and boldness was talked about among the crews and stories were told from camp to camp. Their reputations preceded them wherever they went. Homer T at that moment didn't care about listening to anymore stories. He only knew he didn't want to get caught and pay a fine. No, he would stay in camp tonight.

Jason remembered these stories and he understood that he needed a license to hunt partridge and that he wasn't old enough to have one. Before he got to the clearing, he would leave his shotgun behind a large yellow birch tree and then pick it back up on his way home.

School was going pretty well. That is until one day when Jason wanted to take one of the extra teams instead of walking the eight miles each day. It was December and the snow was deep and the walking was slow and tiresome. It was Sunday evening and the crews had drifted back to their camps and the cook camp was now quiet. Jason had put this off for as long as he could. He wasn't exactly sure how his father would take it.

"Dad, if you want me to go to school, give me the black team to travel back and forth. The snow has plugged the roads."

"You lost your head! Christ, I only have two teams and you want to take one to school!"

"If you want me to go to school, give them to me or it's the end of school for me," Jason replied.

"Well, if you like the black team so much, you can start driving them in the morning."

"Okay. Anything's better than that." So that was the end of school for Jason. He was now doing a man's job and he expected to be treated equally. And he was. He swung his weight on the job and nobody gave him any extra help that the other driver's didn't get. There were even times when he was too stubborn to ask for help, like if he had trouble rolling a large log or unhooking a twitch chain.

It was a rough winter for an eleven-year-old. The snow was deep and the ground was festered with large boulders, making it extra difficult to work around.

One sunny Sunday morning in late February, Homer T and Jason decided that they had enough of moose and deer venison and they wanted fresh trout. Pickett Mountain Lake covered a large area, but most of it was too shallow and muddy to support trout. Homer T knew of only one spot where they might find a school of fat trout and that was in the center and about two-thirds the way up the lake on he west end. There was an area where gravel covered the bottom and not mud. He always believed the bottom was clear because of a spring that kept the silt off the rocks.

They took a frying pan, cooking utensils, and a slab of salt pork. They found some line and Homer T had a pack of fishhooks. He made a crude but efficient ice chisel in the make-believe blacksmith's shop a month ago. The edge was honed so it was as sharp as a razor and because of its weight alone, would just melt through the ice.

"Homer T, can I take my rifle along?" Jason asked.

"What for? Aren't you tired of eating deer and moose meat?"

"Yeah, I am. Just an idea, though," Jason murmured.

When they had their gear together and packed securely in their packs, they strapped on their snowshoes and headed up along the stream towards the lake. "Are these snowshoes handmade, Homer T?" Jason asked.

"Yeah, Tilly Palmer from Moro made them. He lives not to far from here. He has a little shop set up in a shed and he makes a few pair each year. These are the best shoes you'll find anywhere."

"Who did you say he was, Homer T?"

"Tilly Palmer. He guides occasionally with me and my brothers, Harry and Luther at the camps at Hall's Corner on the North Road," Homer T said.

"Guess I don't know him."

They weren't long hiking to the lake and when they stepped through the bushes that fenced the lake around the shore they were looking directly west towards Traveler Mountain. Katahdin set off to the left a little. Each was capped with snow against an indigo blue sky. "That's some view huh, Homer T."

"Sure is. Won't see this setting in any city."

Once at the other end, they cleaned the snow off and chiseled four holes through the ice. Even though the chisel was sharp, the progress was slow and tiring. The ice was forty inches thick. The ice and slush that was cleaned out of the holes was piled up at one corner of the hole and a hardwood branch was stuck in and soon frozen. The line was secured around this and any breeze coming across the ice would catch in the branch and provide a natural jigging motion to the bait.

Homer T chiseled the first two holes and then said as he handed the chisel to Jason, "Your turn. Each man must cut his own ice."

Jason didn't have as much strength as Homer T, even though Homer T was not a very large man. Bit by bit, Jason cut through the ice and soon his baited hooks were in the water. "Let's go ashore and get a fire going," Homer said.

They put together some birch bark and dry pine branches, and in no time at all, they had a blazing fire. On top of that, Homer T threw in some dry wood and then some green wood to make some hot coals to cook on.

"Jason, go check the lines while I get some wood." The snow cover on the ice was wind-packed and the walking was easy. The bait was gone from the first line and at the next, he pulled in a trout that would go about a pound. He picked up two more trout at each of the next lines. After the lines were all baited again, Jason picked up his trout and walked back to the fire.

“I’ve made us some tea. Be ready in a minute,” Homer T said.

“Good. I’ve got three trout,” Jason replied.

“Just right for the frying pan. Better clean them before they freeze.” When Jason had finished cleaning the trout, he hung an alder branch through the gills. Homer T poured them each a hot cup of tea. Then he sat on the bank of the shoreline, sipping his tea, reminiscing in his mind of his life as a lumberman and guide. He had enjoyed a good life. He never had much money, but he had always managed to get by. He looked out across the ice-covered lake and thought about how lucky he was to be sitting there enjoying the fresh air, high in the mountains with some good company. “No, sir. No city slicker would ever understand.”

“What’s that, Homer T?” Jason asked.

“Oh, nothing. Just talking to myself. Hey, we’d better go check out lines again.” They got two that trip and when they returned to the campfire, the three trout that Jason had put on the alder bush were gone. “Did you take the fish, Homer T?” Jason asked.

“No, but I think maybe I know what did. Look at those tracks there,” he said as he pointed towards the base of the alder. “See those small tracks and this is the trout being pulled behind.”

“What animal is it, Homer T?”

“Mink. They’re big fish eaters. I’ll clean these two and start frying them. Why don’t you follow the tracks and see if you can find that rascally fellow.”

“Okay,” he said as he went off after the fish-eating mink without further ado.

Homer T cleaned the trout, and then cut up some salt pork and started that sizzling before he dropped in the fish. When that was done, they had a hearty meal of salt pork, trout, pan bread, and hot tea. Homer T laid back against the root of a cedar tree and said, “Jason, I’m going to shut my eyes for just a second. Why don’t you go check the lines again.”

Jason brought back four more trout this time. As he was

resetting the last line, something had grabbed the bait and went with it. Jason let it go with the line until just before it came to the end. At just the right moment, he pulled sharply and set the hook.

Homer T was still asleep and snoring fiercely, so Jason had to holler at him to wake him up. "Homer! Hey, Homer T, look at this one!" he said as he held up the trophy for Homer T to see.

Homer T jerked awake and at the same time said, "Well . . . that must be the granddad of all trout. How much does it weigh, do you think?"

"Don't rightly know, but it's as long as my arm. We'll have to take this one back with us or nobody will ever believe us," Jason exclaimed.

Before the day was over, they had filled one pack basket and part of the other. "Let's do this again, Homer T. I like fishing through the ice."

"It's not always this nice out, though," Homer T said as he shouldered his pack and started for camp. That night for supper, the crew enjoyed fresh trout as Jason retold his yarn about following the mink to a hollow stump and waiting with a club for it to stick its head out of the hole. All enjoyed the change from venison, but in the morning, they could expect deer steak and biscuits again.

Jason's stepmother, Marg, had frozen some of the fresh trout. She smoked the rest with alder bark and then canned them. She was an excellent cook and all the crews enjoyed her cooking and they often told her so.

March tenth rolled around and to Jason's surprise, the whole camp had secretly planned for his twelfth birthday. In those days, it wasn't unusual for someone Jason's age to go to work to help support the family. But it was generally some minuscule job like stocking shelves or sweeping floors. Jason, on the other hand, had willingly assumed the work and the responsibility of a man. When his father gave him the alternative of going to school or driving one of the teams, Jason had become a man. There were times because of his young years that he would need help. But more often than not, he was too stubborn and too proud to ask. He would rather stew with his own anger and difficulties than to admit for one second that he could not do something.

So, that was how it was on that night of his twelfth birthday. He was accepted as one of the crew. He was a man who drove a team of horses in the woods to earn a living. Homer T had taken Jason out cruising for some new timber later that afternoon so Milton and Marg could get things ready for the surprise.

Gifts in those days might not, according to today's standards, be anything but ordinary. But to Jason, a pair of socks or gloves or the work Marg had done in repairing a pair of work trousers were all deeply appreciated. One of the Indians, known only as Joe, had hand-carved him a new handle for his Kent-dog. Another crewmember had spliced his driving reins. But what meant the most to Jason was the unmistakable fact that he wasn't forgotten and that he was appreciated and accepted as an equal. Yes, this had been the best birthday celebration that he had ever had.

After he had all his gifts, he walked over to Marg and put his arms around her and kissed her. "Thanks, Ma, for everything." At the same time, he looked at his father and noticed that he was smiling pleasantly to himself and there was just the glow of a twinkle in one eye.

Milton could not have been more proud of his son if he had just been elected President of the United States. No father could ever be more satisfied with what he saw in Jason than he. Silently and to himself he wished that his mother could somehow be there to see her son. She too would have been pleased.

* * * *

Even though that winter had a higher than normal snowfall, the work in the woods had not been hampered. In fact, all the crews had done exceedingly well. It was better than Milton had first anticipated. He had hoped to have the yards cleaned up and the logs all hauled to the mill by March fifteenth but there still remained about thirty thousand feet to haul yet. On the twentieth, the man from Emerson's office showed up with a bodyguard and a suitcase of new money.

It was a slow process, paying off each man. Milton had to keep a weekly tally sheet for each man and how much wood he had cut or hauled. There weren't any computers or calculators, so it all had to be done by pencil and paper. Even after the lodging expenses were deducted, each man was paid well for his winter work. After Milton had calculated his own earnings and found his profit margin was better than he thought, he gave each man, including Jason, a nice bonus.

"Men," Milton bellowed over the loud chattering, "I want to thank you all for seeing it through this last winter. I can't remember when I worked for a better bunch of men. For any of you that would like to stay on, we'll be starting up again on the first of June.

With a hearty laugh, most of the crew said they would return in June. But first things first. Once their belongings were packed, they struck it out for town and the first bus leaving for Bangor. There were priorities and then there were things that could be taken care of later. First, after a bath, shave, and a haircut, each man wanted to get drunk. In a way, you couldn't blame them. Life all winter in a woods camp kind of makes a fellow woods-queer. Most bosses, and Milton included, didn't go along with any tomfoolery in camp. So each man had a good drunk coming to him to release the pent-up frustrations and to relax. Next, before they even had a decent meal, most men found that they needed a warm body beside them in bed—a woman. The easiest place to find such a woman would be on the waterfront in Bangor.

Most generally, as it was, by the time they returned to work in June, most had lost all their hard-earned money and really had no place to go except back to the woods. If the money wasn't spent on women and liquor, there were a lot of pickpockets to lighten your billfold.

Jason stood in the background, listening to the men excitingly talk about what he was going to do first once he hit town and how many women it would take to satisfy him. The drinking really didn't appeal to him, but he was just beginning to be aware of his sexual cravings. He didn't fully understand what was happening to him, but occasionally these cravings kept waking up and nagging him. So whenever anyone started talking about women and a good time, Jason paid close attention without trying to appear to be too interested.

Homer T left most of his stuff at the camp because once the spring fishing was over he would be back. The trips to Bangor no longer held any interest for him. His first love was guiding and sitting next to the campfire at night, telling his stories to his sports. Whether they were just stories or not, it didn't matter—everyone seemed to enjoy listening to them.

Milton and Marg had been talking for a month now about what they would buy with their money. It became a yearly ritual to buy something that they needed and could not normally afford. They limited themselves to just one article. Marg wanted curtains for the camp, a new cook stove, and a wringer washer. Milton wanted a new rifle, not that there was anything wrong with the old one. He just wanted a new one—a Marlin .45-70. He needed a pair of snowshoes, some new work clothes, and an axe. These were not luxuries but necessities, the same as a new cook stove and a wringer washer. They would buy these because they were necessary. He and Marg finally decided to put away any extra money left over and someday maybe buy a Model T Ford car.

With the men gone and all the lumber hauled, Milton, Marg, and Jason packed their clothes and went to town. The crew camps had been left on the Poorman's Retreat Road, so they stayed there until they were ready to move back to Pickett Mountain.

Jason was up early every morning and could usually be

found fishing on the nearby brook. In the afternoons, he'd walk to town or hitch a ride if he could. Most people were happy to give him a ride. It was unusual to find someone his age that seemed so mature and at the same time have such a jovial attitude about everything. But Jason was shrewd. He never let on that he had a pocket of money. Everyone assumed that because of his age that he was penniless like the other boys. *So be it*, he thought, *if they give me a ride because they think that I can't pay.*

He bought new work boots and clothes and his auxiliary item was a .32 special Winchester rifle and two boxes of cartridges. That night he was eager to try out his new rifle. He waited until it was dark and the full moon was just peeking over the horizon. "Be careful, Jason. Stay in the shadows," his father said as he walked out the door.

It was a warm night and there was just enough of a breeze to keep the flies away. It was difficult to stay in the shadows because the moon was so bright. The night air looked much as the early morning hours just before daylight. Eventually he found his way to the same orchard his father had taken him to when the whole town seemed to be there. He realized there wouldn't be any apples yet, but he was figuring that the deer would be after the clover and grass.

He sat quietly one the edge of the orchard in what little shadows there were. It wasn't until after midnight when the first deer appeared. They kept coming and soon there were deer everywhere. Jason's heart pounded like a drum. He didn't want a wet doe or fawn, so he looked for a lone deer standing off to one side. It wasn't long before he saw what he wanted and it fell to the grass and was still before the echo from the shot died away. Cautiously, he walked over and there lay a small spike-horn buck and the antlers were in velvet. He was careful not to paunch it or break the diaphragm before he was ready.

Once he was done, he slung the deer on his shoulders, picked up his rifle, and walked home.

* * * *

When the crews came back in June, every man that was there during the winter returned. The money was good and the food was excellent and their pockets were empty.

It was 1941 and the war effect was in full swing. President Roosevelt was building the supply channels to Europe and Russia and the demand for aircraft plywood was greater than ever. All that summer, Milton cruised the woods, looking for veneer logs. "The best," he would say, "Those guys who fly need the best." He was concerned and trying to do his part in helping defeat the Axis powers. He selected only the best and when those were cut and *only* then would he turn to the less perfect trees.

Again Emerson said no softwood. Because of the war effort, there was little or no call for spruce or pine. So it was left standing until there was a market. He hired another four men from Quebec and Homer T built another cabin. These four men from St. Jacques, Quebec were workers. The other men, not to be outdone by the foreigners, worked even harder. Each was trying to outdo the other.

The yards continued to fill up and Emerson had to employ two additional trucks to make up the difference. They were cutting trees so fast that Jason began to wonder if and when they would run out.

Life at camp had changed some too with the addition of the four Frenchmen. They were all quite musical and on occasions they'd play a tune or two for the camp.

Jason's job was still the same. He even drove the same team of blacks. One day, he twitched for one of the French crew. One of the men, Alex, had felled a huge silver birch. When the tree was topped off, it measured twenty-six inches at the small end and it was twenty-four feet long. The red-heart in the center was non-existent. To a true lumberman, this was a beautiful piece of wood. Jason looked it all over and tried to visualize how it would look sawed into boards and used in making furniture and stuff. But it would also make some excellent aircraft plywood, so he decided that the boys flying those machines needed it worse than he.

That winter he turned thirteen and Milton and Marg had only a family celebration for him. He was just another man in the crew camp and not of particular interest anymore. The year before had been different because of his age and the work he was doing.

At the spring breakup, each man again received a bonus along with the winter's wage. This season, Milton and Marg had a larger profit margin even from the previous year. Homer T took his money, tucked it away, and put together all his gear to take with him this year. This year, after the camps were shut up, they would not be returning to them again in the summer. Instead, they would go deeper into the woods towards Pleasant Lake. They would build another set of camps and live there until the woods were gone.

"What time in the summer, Milton?" Homer T asked.

"We're going back about a mile and a half. We have to build another complete setup, cruise the woods, cut new roads, log landings, and twitch trails. Be just you, Jason, and me for a spell until the camps are ready. Probably we ought to get started by June first. It'll take us awhile to do everything," Milton said.

"Same crews coming back next year, Milton?"

"Not sure. The war's building. Won't surprise me none if some of the boys go over. Might have to go to Canada for men this year. They're good workers as long as we can keep 'em from getting homesick and going back."

"I'll plan on being back then the first of June. Where will I find you?" Homer T asked.

"Look for me at Emerson's office in the mill. I'll be there off and on until we move back to the woods. You going to guide again this year, Homer T?"

"Yeah, but first I want to visit my brother, Luther. You know he lost his family in a fire and he was burned quite badly."

"Yeah, I heard about that. How's he doing?"

"Last word I got was that his burns had healed but the scar in his mind is bad. He can't forget what happened. Blames himself mostly and he's lonesome."

"Tell him that Marg and I said 'Hi.'"

"Thanks, Milton. Guess I'll be on my way now. The last truck is about to leave," Homer T said.

"See you in June," Milton replied.

Marg took their extra money and this year she was determined to buy them a new bed. "Milton, I've had it with sleeping on this old thing. We're getting a new bed and that's that."

How could he object to that even if he wanted to.

Jason used his money wisely. He bought some more work clothes, 3 boxes of cartridges, and a fishing rod. The rest he squirreled away with his other savings. There would be a day when he'd look back and be thankful that he had been so thrifty.

It was the summer of 1942 and the only topic people were talking about was the war against the Japanese and when we'd beat the Germans. Jason wished he'd been a little older so he could join the army and go fight the bastards. But even though he was mature for his age and could certainly fill a man's shoes, he was still only thirteen. Everyday in the newspaper, the front page was covered with articles and photos of what was happening to England and to President Roosevelt's promise for continued support. "Why in hell doesn't he just declare war on them, Dad, and get us over there so we can kick ass and stop all this fighting?" Jason asked.

""I'm not sure, Jason. Maybe he knows more about it than we do. We've got to support him and his decisions though and maybe someday we'll understand," his father answered, even though he wasn't really sure if he understood. But at least it gave Jason something to think about and he saw the concentration on his son's face as he sat there thinking.

For the most part of April and May, Milton was busy working with Emerson's field man, deciding where best to set up the crew camps and where the best yellow birch and rock maple were. With the increasing war effect, there was a greater demand than ever for aircraft plywood and Milton's contract for the next year had been doubled. That meant double the crew and none of the men were coming back this year except Homer T.

"Jason, tomorrow you and I are heading for Canada to find a crew to start up in June. Marg, you'd better stay here. We'll be about a week." They were two days getting to Fort Kent, where they were told that their best chances would probably be in either Claire or Edmundston, New Brunswick.

It was mostly French there, but Milton had grown up on the banks of the Aroostook River in the heart of French speaking Maine, and he could speak French fluently. He signed up twenty-nine men. Half of them were to start the first of August and the other half would start in September. Now he needed a woods boss and the only place to find one suitable to handle French-speaking men was either in Allagash or St. Francis.

It was at the general store in Allagash that he met Jim Ryan. He was a short, square-shouldered, French-speaking Irishman. It was one hell of a combination, but by his mannerisms and attitude, Milton knew he had himself a good man. "Hoo, Jesus," he would say. It was comical to listen to him talk, especially in the evenings when he was telling some story. It was an Irish brogue with a French accent. It was even worse when he got excited.

Jim agreed to be at the campsite by the first of June. Milton, Homer T, Jim Ryan, and Jason would start building the cabins, hovels, and sheds with the crews all set to arrive in August. Milton and Jason stopped over in Washburn to spend the day with Jason's granddad before returning home.

* * * *

Homer T arrived at the plywood mill on the day he had said he would be there. All their gear and tools that they would need to complete the camps were loaded in the back of a Model T

Ford. Jason had his .32 Winchester beside him on back, just in case. And it was a good thing too, because right where the main camp was to be built was the nicest brown cow moose you could imagine. Since there wasn't a young'un with her, Homer T said, "She must be dry. It'll be good eating." With one shot behind the head, she dropped where she had been standing. For the rest of that day, Jason worked on cutting the meat and storing it in a cooler that Milton and Homer T were working on at the spring.

Once the main camp was up and finished, Milton went cruising, and left the camp building to Homer T and Jason. As he cruised out different sections of the woods and laid out the twitch trails, he began to wonder if the Irishman from Allagash was going to show up. The first of June rolled by and no word from him. "Damn shame. He would've made a good man," Milton muttered to himself.

That evening when he got back to the camp, the jovial Irishman was sitting on the floor in the corner, telling Homer T and Jason about his walk from Fort Kent. Apparently, Jim's wife didn't think much of the idea of him leaving and being gone for months. There had been a bitter argument and when Jim had walked off towards his truck, Mrs. Ryan grabbed an axe and did a number on it. It was so bad that Jim couldn't get it started. Fearing for his life, he grabbed his pack and jumped out of the way. "You leave, Jim O'Ryan," is how she always called him whenever they were having one of their discussions, "and you'll have to walk."

"Then I'll be walking. If you think for a second that I'll be staying here with you, then you've gone loco in the head, woman," he hollered back.

"Then be off with you, but if you come back in the spring, I won't be here," she said.

"I'll be gone and if you aren't going to be here come spring, then I'll be back."

That was Jim Ryan's reason for being a week late. He had walked over a hundred miles, carrying his belongings with him.

Jim worked with Homer T and Jason, building camps while Milton cruised, laid out roads, and marked the choicest trees with bright red paint. Those of the lower quality were marked with yellow paint.

By the first of August, the camps and sheds were completed and the French crews had showed up a day early. "Jason, tomorrow morning, I want you and Homer T to take a truck into town and bring back those supplies. You'll have to make three trips, so get started early. Go to the house and bring Marg, her new bed, and things on your first trip. Jim, tomorrow I'll want you to get the crews started on cutting the right-of-ways. Emerson will be here tomorrow and I'll have to spend the day with him."

Earlier, Homer T and Jason had hiked down to Pleasant Lake, caught a mess of trout, and fried them in salt pork. Along with the fish, they fried potatoes for supper.

Normally Jim Ryan was a quiet man and even-tempered, but there were those occasions like when that fool Tim Martin climbed on the spring pole and hollered for someone to cut it free. "Ta, he's nothing but a gawd-damn nut," he had muttered. On the next day when Sherm Dewely was caught under the yellow birch tree, he hollered, "Eh, he's just a gawd-damn jill-poke."

"Let this be a lesson to you," he hollered after Sherm as he ran through the woods. He knew the lumbering business and everyone knew enough not to cut him any slack. Even though he was short, his square shoulders made up for what he was lacking in height. He became known as the big Irishman who speaks French.

The French were a colorful lot and most every evening they'd get together in one of the camps and someone would always play a musical instrument while another one would step-dance to it. Tim Martin used to play a variety of songs, both French and English, on a squeeze box until the day he was shot through the air like a potato on the end of a stick.

After a couple of weeks, some of the men said they had to go home because of a death in the family. Four or six fellows would leave for a few days and then come back. This went on constantly until there was so much snow that the roads were plugged. Jason thought this was a little strange after awhile with so many people dying and all. Then it came to him that maybe all they were wanting was to feel their wife's warm body beside them and lose themselves in a sexual fantasy for a couple of days. His yearnings, too, were becoming more and more prevalent. But what was he to do, stuck out there in the woods, away from everything—especially girls. He decided that next spring after he got his winter's pay, he'd remedy that even if he had to go to the waterfront in Bangor. He'd have himself a woman.

September rolled around and the rest of the crews from Canada arrived. It was like a small town there in the middle of the woods. Marg still had her radio with her and each evening they would all gather in the main camp and listen to Roosevelt speak to his country. "My fellow Americans," he would start off saying, "all is going well with the war effort in Europe and across the Pacific." Then he would relate the day's events about how the Russians were doing and how the Japanese seemed to be pushing further and further ahead in the Pacific. "But the day is coming," he'd say, "when we'll march across Europe and push the Germans into the awaiting jaws of the Russians. And we'll sink every Japanese battleship on the ocean and carry the war to her front doorstep."

The next Sunday morning, Milton said to Jason, "Get your rifle, son, we need some camp meat." Jason gladly grabbed his .32 and a handful of cartridges. One thing you didn't do in those days was a lot of target shooting. Once it was sighted in, that was enough. "Don't waste your cartridges on something you can't eat," Milton said one day. They walked up to the head of the lake across West Brook and then each of them took a different trail. Jason had only gone a short ways and saw a calf standing broadside. He dropped it with the first shot. Immediately, he heard his father shoot and figured he must have gotten the cow. He dressed his off and walked back to see how his father was doing.

Milton had shot a large bull and not the cow. "Black as the top of the stove and look at that rack!"

"Twenty-four points," Jason said.

"What did you get, son?"

"A calf."

"Good, we'll keep that one. Should be better eating than this big fellow. One to eat and some give-away meat. We'll give it to Homer T and let him take it to town when he goes out next time. His family could use it," Milton said. They walked back to camp, hitched up a team and dray, and went back after the bull and calf.

The next morning, Homer T put the moose meat into the back of the Model T, without even trying to hide it. It would see him through the winter. That night, he stripped some meat off the neck and fried it with some potatoes.

"Will you be back again, Homer T, before spring?" Luther asked.

"Doubt it. We have a bigger contract this year and we're a little further in the woods. I'm not sure if we'll even be able to keep the road open to get the wood out."

The trip back to camp seemed to go faster and easier than coming out. Although he enjoyed seeing his brother, Homer T always enjoyed getting back to camp. These were his real friends. Milton and his family were like family.

"How was your trip out to the clearing?" Jason asked.

"Good."

"Know that calf I shot? You couldn't even cut the gravy. It was so tough. It was the meanest piece of meat I ever did see," Jason said.

"Strange, but the bull was really tender."

"Oh, you're just joshing me. If either of them would have been edible, it would have been the calf."

"Maybe so, but I'm telling you like it is," Homer T said.

There wasn't any snow on the ground yet and it was the first week of November. The Emerson man had made a special trip in to see Milton and wanted him to go out with him to the clearing. "Sure, sure thing. Jason, tomorrow noon you bring the Model T out to town and pick up the supplies at Fenmore's store. I'll meet you at the mouth of the mountain road at dark. After I finish with Emerson, I'm going to do some hunting in that area," Milton said.

"Okay, Dad."

Well, by dark the next afternoon, Jason was at the mouth of the mountain road but his father wasn't. Instead, Warden Steed was standing there looking as stern and conscientious as ever. "What's up, Warden?" Jason asked.

"Is Milton Smith your father?"

"Yeah, what's up?" The only thing Jason could think of is that Steed had caught his father with an illegal deer or moose and had him in jail now.

"Then you must be Jason?" Steed asked.

"Yes."

"Your father has been in an hunting accident and has been taken to the Island Falls Medical Center."

"What happened? Is he okay?"

"He'll be fine. Someone shot him in the hip by accident," Steed said as he pointed to his own hip.

"Who did it? Who shot him?" Jason asked.

"I'm not sure yet, son, but I will and when I do, he'll regret the day he pulled the trigger," Steed said.

"I best be on my way to Island Falls then," Jason said.

"I think it probably would be better if you went back to camp and told your mother and take your supplies in. I've got to go over and see you father anyway, and I'll tell him that you've gone back. He'll be sore and stiff tomorrow, but the next day you could probably go over and get him. Just take it easy on these rough roads."

"You're sure he'll be alright?" Jason asked again.

"Yes, he'll be fine. He walked out of the woods by himself. He's tough, son. He'll make it."

"Maybe you're right. I guess I'd better get back to camp. Thanks, Warden."

On the way back, Jason couldn't help but think how accommodating the game warden had been. Steed wasn't like the rumors he had heard. He had gone out of his way to tell Jason about his father. Then if all the stories told about Warden Steed were wrong, then what was it about that man that seemed to instill the fear of God into people? He had said that he would find out who had shot his father and that person would have ole hell to pay. He honestly believed that Steed would do it and God help the fool that pulled the trigger.

* * * *

In those days, it was a long drive from Hersey to Island Falls. The roads were rough and Warden Steed had to stop once and fix a flat tire. It was out of his way and he was using his own vehicle, but there was a hurt man and it was his job to find out who the culprit was and prosecute him.

He walked into Milton's room without knocking, pulled a chair up backwards, and sat down to face Milton. "How are you doing, you ole poacher?" Steed asked with a chuckle in his voice.

"Sore as hell! If it hadn't been for my pocket watch, that damn bullet would have really hurt. As it was, it was deflected away from any bone and came out the cheek of my ass. Hurts to sit up."

"If you feel up to it, would you tell me what happened?"

"Well, I had my dog with me and I was walking down this woods road while I waited for Jason. I saw this deer feeding on the side of the road, so I up and fired. It was a small spike horn. Well, it ran off but I didn't figure it would go too far. Just then, Seth LaDonte stepped out into the road and asked what the shooting was about. I told him I'd just shot a deer and that it had run off. I pointed him in the direction. Then Seth said that he and the boys had wounded one earlier and were following it. I told him that maybe this one was wounded. But I doubted it because it was feeding. Just then, there were several shots and I told Seth, 'Tell your boys to stop shooting or they might get my dog.' He did and I started back down the road and there was more shooting. One of the bullets struck me. Seth hollered, 'Stop shooting, boys. We got Milton!' The boys never even came out to see how I was. Ole Seth said, 'I guess you're not hurt too bad, are you, Milton? You can make it out all right, can't you?' I said, 'Yes, if you bastards don't shoot me again I can.' They all left then and went home, and I walked back to the road. The bastards never even gave me the deer."

"What time was that? Can you remember?"

"Hell, yes. When the bullet struck my watch, it broke and stopped at thirteen past three."

"I've told your son what happened the best that I could and sent him back to camp to tell Marg. He'll be out the day after tomorrow to get you."

"Thanks, Steed," Milton said.

As Steed started to leave, he turned around and said, "Oh yeah, Milton, don't let me find any meat that's gone to waste this winter." He left then without waiting for an answer.

Two days later, Jason left the Farrar camps with the Model T and his .32 Winchester. At the Pickett Mountain Stream crossing, he slowed up to cross the loose planking and saw a nice eight-point buck just a short ways upstream. He cranked the window open and stuck his already loaded rifle out the window. The buck never even looked in his direction and Jason squeezed the trigger and the buck dropped in the water.

He dressed it and washed the cavity with water, then loaded it on behind the Model T. He didn't like having to haul it clear to Island Falls and back, but there wasn't time to go back to camp.

Warden Steed came to his mind again as he drove along.

Jason had never met Steed before yesterday and his opinion of him was formed from listening to the other men talk. Some thought he was a sneaky, no good son-of-a bitch while others held him in high esteem. He did know that the man was to be feared if you were poaching. But what Jason had witnessed the other day when his father had been shot was more concern than anything else. He was beginning to respect Warden Steed with an awe of admiration and reverence.

As he neared the height of land at Bear Mountain, four men dressed as the typical sport with plenty of money, stepped into the road. Everything they had was new. Even their rifles had that bright, shiny look to them. "My rifle has shot more deer than all those rifles have together," he muttered to himself as he looked at his weatherworn .32 Winchester. He stopped next to the tallest of them and at the same time, he noticed a tent pitched under some spruce trees.

The tall fellow, Brian O'Neil said, "Jesus, that's a nice deer."

"Yeah, it's a pretty nice buck," Jason answered.

"Anymore like that around?" Brian asked.

There was a twinkle in Jason's eyes and he decided he would have a little fun with these city folks. "Matter of fact, there is. You're right in the middle of some of the best deer country around."

The New Yorkers all looked surprised and Brian said, "Well, where in hell do we go? We thought we had made a mistake camping here. The mountains are so steep and all."

"Well, by Jesus, that's where you're wrong. It's steep all right, but there are trails that go right around that mountain. All anyone has to do is walk up and sit down. Pretty soon something will come along that trail and if you can shoot that thing you're carrying, well it's almost a sure thing."

After Jason had helped his father into the Model T, he told him about the four out-of-staters and the wild goose chase he had sent them on. They both roared with laughter so much that it was difficult to control the Model T.

By the time they returned to Bear Mountain Pass, it was late in the afternoon and the four sports had heard them chugging up the road. They were waiting beside the road.

Jason stopped and said, "Thought you'd be hunting up on the mountain. What are you doing here? It's prime hunting time you know, just before dark."

"We did just like you said and sure enough, they came walking right up to us. Come on over and see for yourself," Brian said.

"You go ahead, Jason. I'm too sore and stiff to get out."

Jason walked to their camp and there were two of the nicest bucks and a doe that you ever laid your eyes on.

"It's just like you said. We walked up there and it wasn't no time at all before they came walking around the peak on that trail you told us about," Brian said.

"One thing I don't do is lie...at least on purpose," Jason added.

"The only thing that's ever been on that mountain is eagles," he told his father later.

It had started to rain a little and their tent was leaking. "Where do you stay?" Brian asked.

"Oh, we have a set of lumber camps back in about four miles."

"Suppose we could go back with you? We'd pay if we could stay in one of those camps."

"Sure. Load your stuff in the back of the truck and hop on." They had brought practically everything with them except for the kitchen sink. They had some of the best sipping whiskey that money could buy. They had canned ham, chicken, and all kinds of vegetables.

The next morning, the four sports walked, or rather, stumbled out of their cabin. They'd missed breakfast and Marg wasn't about to serve breakfast again. She had a hard and fast rule. If you missed the first calling, there wasn't a second. They'd gotten pretty drunk on scotch and rum the night before.

"What'll you take to help us get another deer?" Brian asked.

"Shouldn't be too hard."

"Are there any deer up here?" Brian asked.

"Oh, a few," Jason answered.

"If you can help us get another deer, we'd pay you of course."

"Okay." It wasn't anything to shoot one, but Jason was still up to a little devilry. He could have shot a nice buck the minute he stepped into the cutting area where he had been working three days ago. But he didn't. Instead, he went back to work with his team. He'd shoot one just before dark. This way he'd get paid twice for that day.

Sure enough, just before dark, he spotted a huge buck standing behind some bushes. He judged where the front shoulder was and squeezed the trigger. It ran a few steps and dropped. Once back at camp, he told them about how he had seen it early in the morning and how he had chased it all day. "Yes, sir, by gee-hokey. I ran him so hard that he just ran out of energy and quit. I'd walk up the ridges, jog down them, and run like hell across the flats and open spaces. I got him though."

They believed every word of it. The crew on the other hand, even though they were French, got the gist of what Jason was up to and most of them had to leave the cabin in order to keep from laughing and giving him away.

The next morning turned out unusually warm, so the four had to pack up and leave so the meat wouldn't spoil. Before they left, Brian gave Jason one hundred dollars and what was left of their food and rum. There was probably another hundred dollars worth of food. The wheels were grinding away in his head and it wasn't hard to figure that during the deer season each year he could make as much money guiding and selling deer as he would working all winter in the woods. So that was the beginning of the commercial hunting for Jason. He had a taste and now he wanted more.

The four sports had gotten a ride out with one of the

hauling trucks. They were no sooner out of sight and Warden Steed appeared in the middle of the camp yard. I mean, he just appeared from nowhere.

Jason turned and saw him and immediately his heart jumped up into his throat. He knew, he just knew that he was here to take him in for selling that deer.

"Hello, Jason. Is your father here?" Steed asked.

"Yeah, he's inside," Jason stammered. He understood now what the men had been referring to when talking about Warden Steed.

"How are you feeling, Milton?"

"Not bad, considering. What brings you out this way, Steed?"

"Just wanted to see how you were. If you want, I can arrest one of them for shooting you or I can take the whole bunch. One of them is guilty."

"No, Christ, no. They're nice people. It was just an accident," Milton said. "Just tell 'em to watch what they're shooting at next time."

"I've talked to them once and I will again by gawd."

Before Steed left the crew camps, he had one of Marg's special meals. It was moose meat, he knew, even though it was smothered in onions. But it was good and he never let on that he knew the difference.

Jason came in before he had finished eating and wanted to know how he could become a registered guide. Steed dug his notebook out of his back pocket. It was the same one that held his invitations to court and other forms that he used on the job. He found what he wanted—an application for guiding.

Jason filled in the information and then Steed asked him some questions about hunting laws and the woods, and asked him to take a compass course from the camps through the woods to Pickett Mountain Lake. That was easy. He didn't need a compass. He knew the way blindfolded, but he wanted to impress Steed that he could use a compass.

After everything had been completed, Steed said, "You know, Jason, even though you're a guide, that doesn't give you the right to shoot the sport's deer for them or sell them for that matter."

The afternoon had slipped by fine until now. Now Jason was convinced that Steed knew about him killing that six-point buck for the fellows. And he probably knew about the money, too. The rumors he had heard about Steed were seeming more factual than just rumors now. He swallowed hard and said, "Yeah, I know."

Milton wasn't one to just sit around while the others worked. Each day he forced himself outside to walk around the camp yard. He'd try to work some in the tack shed, mending harnesses and sharpening saws and axes. The work caused severe pain in his hip, but he was afraid that if he stopped altogether that his muscles would stiffen and weaken to the point where he would really be crippled.

Two weeks went by before he finally made it to the woods. He was pleased and at the same time, surprised at how well the job had carried on. Jason had shouldered a lot more responsibility along with the Irishman, Ryan, and Homer T. Nowhere, he decided, could he ever have found a better crew.

Thanksgiving came and with it came a new snowfall. The French crews had all decided to stay over the holiday and work. Thanksgiving in Canada was just another day for them. Marg had planned a special meal for that night. Instead of venison, she had bought a couple of turkeys and had made giblet gravy.

That morning, Jason was out of bed early. When he saw the new snow, he grabbed his .32 Winchester and struck off for the woods. There were tracks everywhere, but they had all left the choppings before daylight. Jason found a large track and started to follow it. He knew it would be easier if he had chosen a smaller track, but he wanted a large set of antlers.

For awhile, the buck was oblivious to Jason following and spent a lot of time browsing and pawing in the leaves for beechnuts. "Buck," as Jason began to call him, was heading more or less west, towards the West Brook swamp where he'd probably hold up in a fir thicket for the day.

"I'll outfox him," Jason said aloud. "I know where he's going and I'll be there waiting." He left the track and headed straight for the swamp, where he calculated ole Buck would come down out of the hardwood. He had figured close but he went too far. As he stopped to look the area over, he saw something move out of the corner of his eye. Instead of turning around in one quick move, he stood motionless for several seconds, listening. He heard it—the unmistakable crunch, crunch, of a four-legged animal walking on leaves. He turned his head just enough so he could see it and then even slower, he turned his body at the same time as he brought his rifle to his shoulder. Ole Buck sensed something sinister, stopped, and lifted his head to sniff the air. The air was filled with the repugnant smell of man. The ole buck had one chance and took it. He made a graceful leap to the right, towards some cedar and spruce trees.

If he could make it to these, he'd have a chance. Right then, Jason squeezed the trigger and felt the recoil in his shoulder as the deer staggered but didn't fall. The bullet had grazed the brisket without any serious damage. There was plenty of blood on the snow, but Buck was still running. Jason walked over and looked at the blood and picked up a piece of bone. He knew it was from the brisket and he hoped that if the deer wasn't followed right away, it might lay down and bleed to death.

Jason sat down and began to think of the turkey dinner he would be eating that night. When he figured he had let Ole Buck alone long enough, he picked up his track and began to pursue. Tracking was easy now. There was a good blood trail to follow. "You'd have to be blind to miss this one," he said to himself.

Buck hadn't laid down at all and the blood trail was getting fainter. Another ten feet and it was gonc altogether. Buck was running like there was nothing wrong. He had to outwit the ole deer if he was to get 'em. Tracking him would only cost him time and be to the deer's advantage. No, he decided to head for the brook and walk along it and try to cut him off. Surely he could get there before the Buck, considering that he was wounded and all. But that wasn't the case. As Jason walked downstream along the bank, he saw where Buck had crossed before him. On the opposite shore, the dirt had been pawed away and there was blood on the snow again. "Good, he's bleeding again. He'll have to lay down soon and rest." But that was only wishful thinking. The bleeding stopped shortly and Buck regained his stride. "Where are you going now, ole Buck?" he asked into the wind.

He had no choice but to follow. His stride had lengthened, quickening his pace. His only hope now was to tire him, causing him to make a mistake. But ole Buck was a strong deer and as smart and cagey as he was strong. He had taken Jason up a hardwood ridge and then jumped off the downward slope into a bunch of small fir trees.

Jason had been hurrying so fast that he never noticed that the tracks he was following had turned around. When he came to the end, he stopped and scratched his head. He walked back along his own tracks, but he had carelessly obscured Buck's in his haste. He made a wide circle and then another, and another until he finally came across the deer tracks behind a clump of fir. "You're a wise ole son-of-a-whore, Buck, but the battle isn't over yet." Little did he know then that it would have been best to leave Buck alone and head for camp. But no, he continued to follow at an even faster pace now than before.

He was obsessed now with taking that deer. So obsessed that he wasn't paying any attention to the direction he was traveling in or that it had clouded over and was beginning to snow. His pace was fast but he stayed on the deer's tracks and twice more, before the sun was overhead, the deer had backtracked and jumped off to one side. He had crossed the swamp at the head of West Brook and was now re-crossing it and heading for higher ground—straight for the top of Mt. Chase.

Jason knew the mountain was too steep and rugged for a deer to cross and decided to outwit him by going around the ridge towards the east and try to catch him coming back down. When he came to the East Branch of West Brook, he laid down on the gravel and had a drink of water and then looked for a vantage spot to wait for Buck. He soon found just what he wanted; a small pinnacle between two sloping valleys. There he sat down and waited.

He waited so long that he began to wonder if he had made a mistake in assuming that Buck would come this way. He was hungry and had worked up a sweat by the fast pace he had kept up. Now the cool air was making him stiff and cold. He stood up to stretch his legs and get the circulation back. But he forgot all about his stiffness and how cold he was as soon as he saw Buck at the stream, where he had earlier stopped to drink water.

Buck was sniffing the ground where Jason had laid. Just then, Jason's foot slipped and a rock was jarred loose, rolling off the pinnacle. It didn't make much noise, but there's a saying that goes, "When a pine needle falls to the ground, an eagle will see it, a bear will smell it, and a deer will hear it." Ole Buck heard the rock all right and without hesitating to see where the noise had come from, he took off on a run. Jason fired one shot, but he knew that it was useless before he even saw the wood fly from the tree beyond where Buck had been standing.

So, the chase was on again and Jason was mad at himself for being so careless. He was running now, paying little or no attention to where he was going. He was tired and he was beginning to stumble in the snow.

Buck had led him on a merry chase in the swamp at the head of Pickett Mountain Lake, and was now going in circles, trying to confuse his pursuer.

Jason stopped in frustration and realized that daylight was almost gone and if he expected to get back to camp by nightfall, he had better leave immediately. "So long, ole Buck. You've earned the right to live." *But which way do I go? Where am I?* he thought. He knew if he headed east, then he would sooner or later come to the Pleasant Lake Road. *But would there be enough daylight?*

When he got to the shore of Pickett Mountain Lake, it was dark but he knew where he was. He followed the shoreline until he came to the outlet. Then he followed that to the road. But there was still two and a half miles to camp.

* * * *

Back at the camp, Marg asked, "Jason, where have you been?"

"Chasing a deer through hell and back," he replied sourly as he hurried to his room to change his clothes. The whole camp yard smelled like turkey and all the fixings. Everyone was eager to sit down and eat their fill. The story of Jason's ordeal with the deer had spread like wildfire through the camp. Once the meal was over, the Irishman, Jim Ryan, stood up. "Jason, me boy, we hear you had quite a chase today with a big deer. Tell us about it."

Jason was proud to be so readily accepted by the other men, especially at his young age. He was even more buoyant with the prospect of telling his story to the others. He had listened for so many years of Homer T, his father, and others telling their exciting capers and now it was his turn. He relished in the heat of attention he was getting. He retold the story from the time he fired the first shot to finally finding his way back to the Pleasant Lake Road.

Down at the end of one of the tables, a Frenchman by the name of Louis Paquette said, "Hey, mon ami. Tell again the story about the deer il cheureux qui afait une imbecre de tai." He retold the part again of how ole Buck had doubled back and stepped precisely in his own tracks and then jumped a good thirty feet off the trail behind some fir trees. He left out the part about him walking in the buck's tracks and had no way of telling if he had re-stepped in his own tracks. But the story was a good one and by making out that the huge buck was actually clever added a little esteem to the story.

By the time everyone had gone back to their own camps for the night, Jason was actually glad he hadn't killed the deer. Storytelling was a lot more fun and he had a knack for it that everyone seemed to enjoy, including his father and Marg.

During that winter, Jason felt a little remorse for the deer, knowing that he had only wounded it and wondered whether or not he would make it through the winter. Everyday, he kept a vigilant watch in the works for a wounded deer or one that might look a little more poorly than the others. "Working on your conscience, son?" Milton asked one day.

"Yeah, I guess it is. I wonder every day whether he's made it or not."

"Well, it's good to see that you care. It's one thing to shoot an animal for subsistence and use it. But it's wrong not to care if one is wounded and left to suffer and finally go to waste. I think you can see the difference, Jason, and I'm glad. Let this be a lesson to you—always make sure of your shot and don't let anything go to waste."

For the rest of his life, Jason would remember those words. And those words would unknowingly forge his reputation as a hunter. But to the local game warden, he would be known as a poacher.

On Sundays, Jason started snowshoeing in the area where he had first seen the deer in hopes of finding him still alive. It was on his second trip into the swamp that he spotted a few drops of blood in the snow. It was Buck. No other deer could have a track as large as this one.

He spent the rest of the day making trails through the swamp and chopping down cedar trees for him to feed on. By morning, the snowshoe trails would harden and the deer would be able to walk on them. Each weekend for the rest of the winter, he would go to the swamp and make new trails through the trees and to new food supplies. He felt that he owed ole Buck that much and hoped to clear his conscience. For the next several years while he worked at that camp and then in Emerson's camps, where he would become woods boss, he never hunted in that swamp again. He told his crews that under no circumstances were any of them allowed to hunt there. When one of them would ask why, he would simply say, "Because I said so."

Jason was fourteen that winter and for his birthday, the crew gave him a book, "The One-Eyed Poacher" by Edmund Ware Smith. How little did he know then that this book, the characters, and the capers in the story would correlate so much with his own life.

He accepted the book graciously with thanks but was not very overwhelmed with the gift since it would require reading. He had learned to do that in school but that was for kids. He was a man now, doing a man's job. But one rainy day three weeks later, too wet in the woods and the yard to do much, he laid down in his bunk and picked the book up. He read all that morning and then Marg said, "Lunch is ready, Jason. Aren't you going to eat?"

After he had finished his lunch, he went back to his bunk and read some more until it was finished. He had never heard of anything so amusing or so interesting before, especially from a book. The trickery and deception used and exploited to outwit the game warden and the precarious situations that the one-eyed poacher found himself in. He didn't know if there was any truth to all this, but it surely made for some enjoyable reading. As time would have it, Jason would read and reread this book until he had about worn the print from the pages. Often times during his own career as a poacher, if he'd happen to find himself in a dubious position, he would ask himself, "What would Jeff Coongate do in a similar circumstance?"

* * * *

That year after the spring breakup when the logs were all hauled to the mill and the crews were all paid for their winter's work, Milton asked them to wait in the yard outside. "I've got something to tell you, boys." Everyone went out and was standing around chatting with one another while waiting for Milton.

"Men, I have some good news. The man from Emerson's office said we could start up again as soon as the ground dries up. I expect to be working full force by the first of June. If any of you would like to stay on, I'd like to have you. This will give you about six weeks to go home to your families, to the waterfront in Bangor, or to do whatever you like. If you plan on showing up in June, would you sign your name on this ledger so I'll know what to expect." They all signed on again, every damn one of them.

"What about you, Jim? You going home for a spell?" Milton asked.

"Yee, Jesus! I don't know. I hate to think what's waiting. Maybe by luck she'll be gone. If not, I'll come back before June," the burly Irishman said.

Jason went to town alone this year. He got a room at Pike's Boarding House and got a hot shower, a shave, and a haircut. Next he bought some new work clothes, boots, and cartridges for his .32. Although he had been planning a trip to Bangor, his father had asked him to be back in two days. Bangor was out and so was any prospect of a warm body.

He spent his last day roaming around the town and talking with friends that he hadn't seen for awhile. For lunch, he bought a hot dog and soft drink, and was eating outside. Just as he was about to take his first bite, two young ladies stepped right in front of him and began to giggle.

"What's so funny anyhow?" Jason growled.

"Nothing," one of the girls said.

"Then what are you laughing at?"

"Nothing. It's just that we haven't seen you around here before. Are you from out of town?" the girls asked.

"Well, in a way. I live in the woods in Emerson's camp on the Pleasant Lake Road. I work for my father, driving a team of horses."

"What's your name? Mine is Jerri Hanley."

"Jason Smith."

"Are you the same Jason...I mean, Milton Smith's son?" the girl asked excitedly.

"Yes," he replied matter-of-factly. "Why? Does that upset you?"

"No, no. It's just that we have heard stories about you, that's all," the girl stammered. "Look, we've got to leave now. Ma's calling. She's across the street." The girls left and Jason ate his cold hot dog. It would be about five years before he'd see Jerri again, but he wouldn't forget her.

Jason returned to the camps the next day and the Irishman, Jim Ryan, had also just gotten back. "What are you doing back so soon, Jim?" Jason asked.

"Ooh-wee, that gawd-damn woman; she broke her promise. When I left last summer, she said she wouldn't be back. She never could tell the truth. She was there and had never left. So I did."

Homer T didn't come back until June, so that left the three of them—Milton, Jim, and Jason—to repair the camps. This year Marg wanted a root cellar built beside the kitchen camp. While Jim and Jason dug the hole, Milton twitched in some cedar logs for the walls and roof. When they were finished, Milton stood back and said, "A keg of beer would probably ice over in the summer, it's so cold in there."

There was one week left before the crews would return and all three men were busy either shooting moose or catching fish. Marg wanted her new root cellar filled before things got so busy that no one paid any attention to it.

Since Jim wasn't much of a fisherman, he went moose hunting with Milton while Jason cleaned out the fish holes in Mud Lake and Pleasant Pond. Marg kept busy for the next several days, cutting and canning moose meat and fish. "If you men don't get in here right now and help me with this, you can forget all about eating because you won't want anything when I finish with you!" she said in exasperation.

If she had been living out in the settlement, Marg would have been busy picking and canning dandelion greens and fiddleheads. "Fiddleheads! Hey, you guys," she said in surprise. "We haven't had any fiddleheads for years. How 'bout tomorrow you three go find me some so I could can them."

Later that afternoon, Marg had made a venison meat pie and had set it on the back porch to cool before they had it for dessert that evening. But during supper, there was the most ungodly sound coming from the back porch and all of them jumped up from the table. "Jesus Christ! What in hell is that?" Jason shouted.

"Watch your language at the table, Jason," Marg calmly reminded him.

"Must be an ole boar bear come out to get an easy feed. You got anything out there he can get into, Marg?" Milton asked.

"Yes! My mincemeat pie!"

"Jason, get your rifle. Jason?" He was too late; Jason had already left and was now racing back across the camp yard with his rifle in one hand and cartridges in the other. But the bear had heard the confusion inside and took off towards the woods, carrying the mincemeat pie between his jaws.

"No sense chasing him now, son. Better wait until morning unless he comes back tonight." The ole bear did come back that night. Marg always put a little rum in her mincemeat and the bear had taken a liken to alcohol and had come back for more.

Jason was sitting in an easy chair beside the cook stove, sound asleep when he heard the scratching on the back door. He awoke and slowly pulled the hammer back. Just then the ole bear stood up on his hind legs and raked the screen with his front paws. With one swipe, the screen was gone and the bear was trying to crawl through the opening. Jason never had time to get out of his chair or even aim the rifle. He just pointed it towards the bear and pulled the trigger. The bullet caught the bear in the middle of the throat, sending him sprawling backwards onto the ground. Jason made sure that the bear was dead. Then he had to tell everyone about the fracas before he could go to bed.

The next morning, he and Homer T skinned the bear and threw the hide on the back of the Model T and drove to town. There was a twenty dollar bounty on bear back then if you turned the hide over to the town clerk. After he put gas in the truck, he had eighteen dollars in his pocket. That's almost as much as he was making a week working in the woods, if he had a good week. An idea started to form in the back of his mind. *If I could kill a bear each week, I could get an extra twenty dollars a week. That would be eighty dollars a month. If I sock it away each month with my winter's pay, it wouldn't be long before I can buy myself one of these lag tractors to twitch out the wood instead of using the horses. Some of the crews have 'em and I hear them say they are less troublesome than a team.*

These thoughts were active in his mind and he lost all concept of everything else, including Homer T.

He soon discovered that it wasn't that simple to shoot a bear each week. He was usually busy from the time the sun came up until it went down again. That left only Sunday and it was illegal to hunt on Sunday, even for an ole bear. But Jason justified it by saying he was doing it for the greater cause and for the good of everyone. Probably the game warden, if he had known about Jason's activities, would not have shared the same philosophy.

The idea of maybe the game warden catching him made him apprehensive. Then one Sunday, Warden Steed stopped at the camps to ask about two people who were supposedly fishing Pleasant Lake. Jason thought this was only a ploy to spy on him. But regardless of the warden's real reason for being there, Jason stopped his Sunday hunting and instead, only went out after supper during the week.

He didn't know exactly why this should trouble him more than shooting a moose or deer at night, but it did. Maybe because it was for the money, whereas the moose and deer were to feed the crews. Maybe that was the difference.

That fall, he shot another ole boar bear and the two cubs that were left behind when an outsider had shot the sow. He didn't make as much as he planned, but he put his money away with the rest of his savings. "Someday," he said, "someday."

By Christmas that year, word of Jason's exploits with his rifle had reached the settlement and rumors were circulating, making him sound as notorious as "The One-Eyed Poacher" in Edmund Ware Smith's book. These rumors eventually got to Warden Steed and he wanted to put a stop to Jason's poaching ways before it was too late.

Steed had been in town just before the holiday and had overheard a conversation that Milton, his family, Homer T, and the infamous Irishman would be staying at the Farrar camps this year. With everyone gone, he decided that this would be an opportune chance for a youngster to go hunting. He didn't want to arrest Jason; he only wanted to put the fear of God in him.

So on Christmas morning, Steed and his wife Molly were up early. "We'll have the tree tonight after I get back."

"Where are you going on Christmas morning?" she asked.

Steed told her of his plan to snowshoe cross-country from upper Shin Pond and over Robert's Mountain. "I don't want to arrest him, dear. I only want to scare the living hell out of him to keep him from becoming a poacher."

He left the warm security of his house before the sun was up and was over the top of Robert's Mountain before nine o'clock. He figured that if Jason was going to hunt that day, he would do it somewhere in the choppings where the deer would be feeding.

It would be abortive if he wore his snowshoes while hiking through the woods if he hoped to accomplish what he had in mind. He found a well-used deer trail leading in the direction he wanted, so he removed his shoes and walked in the trail, leaving no evidence that he was there.

It was a cold day and Steed was getting cold. He was already hungry. It was into the afternoon before he saw Jason. He was carrying his rifle and was plainly looking for a deer to shoot. Every footstep was made without making a sound and he was walking into the wind. *For a young fella, he sure knows what he's doing*, Steed thought.

Steed crouched down behind a clump of spruce trees and waited until Jason was well ahead before he stepped out to follow. They hadn't gone far when Jason pulled his rifle to his shoulder. Steed thought he was about to shoot, so he stepped off the trail and hid behind a huge rock maple tree. Jason lowered his rifle and relaxed, but remained where he was, watching.

He could see deer all around him but he didn't want to shoot a doe this time of he year. He might be a poacher, but he had ethics. Eventually he saw what he wanted and put the rifle to his shoulder.

Steed also saw the buck and knew Jason was going to shoot it. He waited just long enough until he figured that Jason must have sighted him in and then he let out a blood-curdling bellow, "Hey!!" The bellowing sound was coming at Jason from all directions, as the sound echoed throughout the valley, making everything vibrate. Jason pulled the trigger but the bullet was about fifty feet over the deer's head.

The deer took off running and so did Jason. He had no idea who had hollered or where it had come from. Right now, he didn't much care. He was getting the hell out of there and away from whoever it was.

Steed stood in his tracks, laughing as he watched Jason run through the woods. He had scared him, but the game wasn't over yet. He went back and picked up his snowshoes and went to the Farrar camps.

Milton was out in the yard when he approached. "Hello, Steed. What brings you out this way on Christmas?" he asked.

"I had a tip that there might be a bunch fishing on the lake today."

"Are they?"

"No. Bad information I guess."

"Come in and have some coffee and a bite to eat while you're here."

"Thanks, I will," Steed said.

Milton had heard the shot and was on his way out to the woods to give Jason a hand with the deer when Warden Steed suddenly appeared in the camp yard. He knew that there was no possible way that Steed could not have heard the shot. *But what was he doing here?* He had walked in from the direction where Jason had shot. So if he wanted Jason, he wouldn't be here. *What was he up to?* Milton kept asking himself.

Marg put the coffee pot on top of the stove and fixed Steed a plate of leftovers. She also was wondering what the game warden was doing out here instead of being home with his family.

Jason had run as if the wrath of God was on his heels. He didn't care. He only wanted to get away, but every living thing seemed to be filled with this awesome roar. He ran head on until he was out of breath. He stopped and looked behind him, but there wasn't anything there. After he had collected his wits about him, he circled back through the woods to the office camp where he slept. He opened the back window and crawled in. He hid his rifle under the mattress and then went to the cook camp where he knew his parents would be.

He opened the front door, walked in, and closed the door behind him. He was in the middle of the room before he realized that there was a third person there. When he recognized Warden Steed, he stopped dead in his tracks and his heart jumped in his throat.

"Hello, Jason," Steed said.

"Hello, Warden," Jason replied. His legs were suddenly like pieces of cold iron. His mind was telling him to walk over to the table and sit down, but his body was not responding. All the while, his father and the warden kept talking.

Ever so slowly, he began to move towards the table. As he sat down, Steed looked at him for only a second and then turned his attention back to Milton. Jason sat there dumbfounded. *Why doesn't he say something? Just tell me you caught me and I'm under arrest,* Jason thought. *Why do you just sit there? It's not like you don't know anything.* The silence was worse than if Steed had arrested him. The apprehension was working and Steed had a difficult time keeping a straight face.

Finally, after his coffee was gone and he had eaten his fill of mincemeat pie, he stood up and said, "Marg, you make the best mincemeat pie that I've ever had. You'll have to give me the recipe sometime for my wife. Thank you." He walked over towards the door and opened it, then stopped and turned towards Jason, "Oh, yeah, Jason—Merry Christmas."

Not until Steed was over the top of Robert's Mountain and down over the other side did he dare to stop and get it out of his system. He laughed so much and so hard that his sides were hurting and he had to sit down on a log to catch his breath. By bellowing at Jason just before he fired at the deer, he had saved the deer's life and kept Jason from violating the law. He had punished him more than any court could have done by letting Jason walk in on him at the cook camp and by not saying anything.

Jason, on the other hand, didn't think it was so funny. *How did Steed happen to show up here on Christmas instead of staying home with his family? And why did he just sit there and act like he didn't know anything? How did he know I was going to shoot an illegal deer? What was his point of just sitting there? It was him who had hollered. Maybe all he wanted was to scare the hell out of me.* These thoughts were stuck in his mind as he watched Steed disappear into the woods. "Jason, Merry Christmas," he had said. *Sure*, Jason thought.

When the atmosphere had cleared, Jason asked his father, "What brought him this way on Christmas?"

"Well, I don't know exactly. He did say something about someone who was supposed to be fishing the lake but he never went near enough to see. It was good talking to him though. For a warden, he's not a bad fellow. Wanted to know how my leg was where that son-of-a-bitch had shot me," Milton said.

Jason told his story of how he had almost been caught and how Steed had hollered at him. "It scared the living hell out of me," Jason said.

"Maybe that's all he was here for. Did you think of that? Maybe that's what he meant when he said 'Merry Christmas.' Could be he did that to keep you out of trouble." Milton mused and chuckled to himself. "Not a bad fellow, that Steed."

Jason wasn't so sure now. He had gained more respect for the man but he couldn't forgive him for scaring the living Jesus out of him. But he was irked and at the same time, awed with his untimely appearance. *Or was it untimely? Do you suppose he came here to do just that—to scare the living hell out of me? But why go to such extremes on Christmas day? And how in hell did he know that today of all days, I was going to shoot that deer?* He was beginning to understand a little now why some of the crews had talked about the warden in such a mystical way. It was uncanny how he knew what he was up to and how he happened to be there at the exact moment. These thoughts were in his mind as he walked across the camp yard towards the office and his room.

He cleaned his rifle and oiled it well. He put it back in the rack and there it would stay for the remainder of the winter. He had developed a deeper appreciation for the meaning of game warden, and their devotion and zealous dedication of their work —especially Warden Steed. He didn't behold any grudges. After all, he was only doing his job. "But does he have to enjoy it so much," Jason asked aloud. Yes, Jason had a deeper respect now and a better understanding. In an odd sort of way, he even kind of liked Steed. Even if he was a warden. There was something about him that Jason found intriguing.

Jason lay down on his bed, thinking that if he continued poaching, Steed or some other warden was bound to catch him sooner or later. The logical answer was to stop poaching, but to Jason that would be worse than...well, he didn't know worse than what. Just that it would be. "I've got to have some sort of knack," he said to himself. "Everyone has one of some sort." But he didn't know yet just what his would be. He had a reputation already at his young age, but if he didn't find that knack, his reputation would become infamous and sooner or later he'd end up in jail. "I'll have to work on it," he concluded.

But what he didn't realize was that he already had a knack. At least, he was subconsciously developing one. The crew all enjoyed listening to Jason tell his stories about chasing a deer, how he'd let a moose go, or how he'd laid on his stomach while watching a bear cub. He had a knack for telling stories and talking to people, and this ability would someday get him out of more scrapes and messes than he could ever realize. This ability to tell stories, especially if they were his own, and of course they were all true, would forge a legend and image that was even more illustrious than his poaching.

* * * *

Spring came and with it, the usual mud season when the crews are let go until the ground dries. The wood yards were still full this year at the spring breakup and now that meant the logs could not be hauled to the mill until June.

There was to be another change, too. The camps were to be torn down and they would be moving further back to the head of the lake at Emerson's site. Anyone who wanted to return in June had that option and all but one man would return. But Milton needed more men, so again he and Jason went to Fort Kent and then into Quebec for the help. Marg was busy moving back into their temporary lodging on the Poorman's Retreat Road in Crystal. Homer T helped her; he didn't go to Matagamon to guide this year. Last year turned out to be a babysitting job for a bunch of snotty-noised rich bastards who thought they knew it all. Except on the last day. After Homer T decided he wouldn't be getting a tip from these jokers anyway, he decided to have a little fun. The last night of their week's fishing trip, Homer T purposely set up camp on Birch Point, knowing full well that there was a dump-rummaging old boar bear nearby.

He had it all planned out, even to his escape. After they

arrived and everything was unloaded from the canoes, the city sports stretched out on their bedrolls for a nap. This gave Homer T his opportunity to set the stage of his dastardly deed. He went into the woods to fetch some dry wood for his cooking fire, but first he removed a can of bacon grease from his pack. He was quite awhile in finding what he wanted, but eventually he did—an old rotten log had been turned over and was ripped apart. Only a hungry bear that was looking for grubs and ants would do this. He scouted around and found a well-used trail that the bear was using and put a spot of bacon grease on a rock. From there all the way back to the campsite, he put a little grease here and there on the bushes just so the bear wouldn't get lost. The sports were still asleep but still all the same, he stole quietly to the canoes and turned them over and spread a generous amount of grease on the canvas bottoms on all the canoes except his own. Next he buried the empty can of bacon grease amongst the remaining food supplies, knowing that the bear would eventually follow his nose from the canoes to the food supply.

After supper, Homer T turned in early and hoped the sports would also. But instead, they sat around the campfire while they drank the last of their whiskey without ever offering Homer T any. *Well, that's all right you flatlanders. I'll have the last laugh.* Homer T knew the bear wouldn't come into the campsite as long as they were up. He hoped the bear was lurking nearby, waiting for his cue.

It wasn't until after midnight that the sports finally had enough and went to bed. The alcohol was working and soon they were snoring heavily. Homer T grabbed his pack and bedroll and placed them in the canoe. He pushed off and started paddling along the shore. He hadn't gone far when a thought occurred to him. Why leave? At least not yet. He patiently waited about fifty feet off shore and it wasn't any time at all before he saw a shadowy figure at the canoes. The bear licked the grease off all three canoes and then as if in anger, took his paw and swiped the bottoms of each, tearing a long gash through the canvas and cedar ribs. The bear was still hungry and he could still smell the aroma of bacon grease in the air. The bear walked beyond Homer T's vision, but by the sounds, he knew that the bear was rummaging through the food supplies. He wondered if those flatlanders would even wake up from their stupor. He paddled off, laughing out loud. "The next time you come to Maine, maybe you'll bring your manners with you." He laughed some more.

The next morning at the dam, he pulled his canoe ashore and went about looking for a ride into town.

"No, Marg, this is okay. I'm not guiding this year anyway," he said.

The United States was building more planes each day and the demand of aircraft-worthy plywood kept increasing. Emerson had moved the camps to the head of the lake because he wanted twice as many men as Milton had last winter and there just wasn't enough room at the old site. "Milton," the Emerson man had said, "your contract is twice the size for this coming year. That means twice the men and a larger area for the camps."

Emerson had employed another contractor—Farrar—to set up camps nearby and Milton was to be woods boss at the Emerson camp. There weren't as many men from the surrounding area as the war effort was increasing every day, and new and younger men were being called in to fill the ranks. Jason was still too young to join up but that was his secret desire. He never said anything to his folks because he didn't want to upset them. But each day he would dream of flying one of those small fighter planes that was made from the wood he was cutting, and fly right into the heart of Germany and single-handedly win the war. Thoughts of being shot down or dying never entered his mind. Only after that was over, he would fly his plane across Asia and fly right into Tokyo. For the time being anyhow, he was doing what he could and that was cutting down the best the land had to offer of yellow birch and getting it to the plywood mill in Patten.

Jim Ryan never bothered to go home at all that year. "What's the use," he'd say. "She'll only scream and cuss at me. No, might as well stay right here by gory." Jim was a good man in spite of his drinking. He conversed fluently with the Canadian crews and they in turn respected him. He was a good woodsman, too. As fine as Milton himself.

With twice as many men now, Milton was concerned about groceries. He had a storage room and a root cellar and ice hauled in from Patten that first year. It took a pile of food to feed fifty-six men and Marg needed extra help, too. Often during that first summer at the new camp, Milton would send Jason out with his .32 Winchester to get meat. He got moose meat, not deer. "But what about the Game Warden Steed? What if he catches me?" Jason asked.

"Don't worry, son. I believe he might take a different view where we're using it to feed the crews. It he shows up, I'll take care of it."

The men needed more than a steady diet of moose meat. It was delicious and no one seemed to mind, but Milton wanted the best for his men if he expected the best from them. So he sent Homer T and Jason out to the settlement to pick up a bunch of live pigs and truck them back to camp. It was two days later when they finally got back. The tailgate of the truck had fallen off and the pigs all fell out and ran off. Jason and Homer T only rounded up half of the lot by nightfall and decided to stay put in hopes that their squealing and grunting would bring the others back.

Once back at camp, the pigs were butchered. Some of the meat was salted and some was put on ice in the root cellar. Jim Ryan and another man from the crew smoked the bacon and ham. They used beechnut wood chips to flavor it.

Jason kept on killing moose. What wasn't used immediately was canned and put in the root cellar. It was by now becoming pretty much a game to Jason. He never knew for sure if Steed knew what he was doing. But just in case, he was careful. Always watching the trail behind him and sometimes firing his rifle into a stump, he would wait to see if Steed would ever show up. He was also developing his knack. He never told anyone exactly where he was going or what he was going to do. And he never admitted to ever shooting a deer or a moose in closed season. If one of the men asked, he would just grin and walk off. He always had an answer to any question that was thrown his way. “Better to keep ’em on their toes,” he’d say.

* * * *

After that first winter at the new camps, it became evident that they would be there for some time. Emerson had wanted white birch and beech cut along with rock maple and yellow birch now. The hillsides and ridges were covered with the finest of hardwood that could be found anywhere.

Milton could foresee some of the changes coming and after that first winter he had ordered, with his boss’ approval, that some of the camps be torn down and replaced with permanent housing. “If you expect to drive a horse hard all day, then you’ve got to feed it and take care of it. Well, you’ve got to do the same with the men and I’ll take care of my crews,” Milton said.

That first summer, there were three new camps built to replace the three temporary ones. They were still log camps with rough, wooden floors, but compared to the ones they replaced, they were like palaces. Each camp had two bedrooms with two men to a room. The bunks had springs and mattresses instead of coarse horse blankets spread over pine needles. There was running water, even though there wasn’t any hot water. It was force fed from a spring high upon the hillside. There was a roofed-in porch also so the men could sit out in the evening air in the summer.

These camps were the first of their kind in the area and because Milton provided such comfortable housing, he had his pick of the best crews available. Men from all over were waiting to hire on. This kept the men who were already working, producing their best. If not, they each knew there were plenty to replace them.

The next summer, three more new camps were built and during that following winter during a slow spell, two more were built. That next summer, six more were built to bring the total to fourteen. Also that summer, Milton had gone to an army surplus auction and bought a diesel generator. Marg now had electric lights in her cook camp and the yard outside was always lit until ten o'clock each night. Each camp also had one light fixture. At night, it looked like a small city set off in the wilderness somewhere. Actually, it was as if you looked at it in a phenomenal sense of understanding. It provided to a certain degree, most everything that could be found in a settlement. There was even some small-scale entertainment. That is, providing the Frenchmen brought along their musical instruments.

The following spring, Jason was eighteen. He was bound and determined that he was going to Bangor and splurge like the men who make it an annual affair to the waterfront. He was old enough, he decided, to drink and have fun like the others. But mostly he wanted to feel a warm body beside him in bed.

So one day when his father said, "Jason, this spring I want you to run some lines for me," Jason replied flatly, "No! I've worked like a man for the last seven years and this year I'm going to Bangor with the others. Each spring I've stayed back and worked for you. Not this year...I've earned a break."

"Well, if that's the way you feel about it, I guess you can. Maybe it s time you saw something besides lumber camps. Only my hope is that you're not disillusioned."

Jason warn't sure what his father had meant exactly, but regardless, he had said in his own way that it was okay. The big day came when the men were paid for their winter's work. Like always, it was in cash with crisp, new money. Before getting on the train for Bangor, Jason went to the bank and deposited all his money except for one hundred dollars. On that, he figured he should be able to have a grand time.

He was with a merry lot and they sang and told stories the whole trip. It was evening by the time they arrived and the first thing on the agenda was supper, then drinks, and then women. He had seen and experienced the big city, gotten drunk, and slept with a warm body.

He wasn't disillusioned exactly. In fact, he really didn't know what to expect when he left. Just now, he knew he wanted to get back to what he knew.

As Jason got older and became more experienced in the woods, he began to naturally assume more and more responsibility and took a great load from his father, whose main job was now shuffling papers and doing the business end of the operation. This also caused him to be on the road more and more. Jason and Jim Ryan together would oversee the woods. What one didn't know, the other did.

It was during the winter of '48 that Jason, who was almost twenty, was described by many as meeting his waterloo or the cessation of existence or activity. He had fallen in love and wanted to marry.

In retrospect, probably the musical French crew could be held accountable for this dastardly deed. The reprehensible stories that generated from their ability to sing and dance had reached the settlement. In fact, it was this tomfoolery that helped make life there at the camps a part of the legend that would later surround the life of the early lumberman. Well, the girls that Jason had casually met in town several years earlier had heard of the going-ons and one warm Saturday evening in February, they decided to go in and see for themselves. The girls were nervous at first and went to the cook camp to find Marg. She made the girls feel comfortable and asked if they would like to stay for supper and then the singing and dancing later on. She knew full well what the girls sole purpose for being there was.

When Jason walked into the cook camp that night for his usual supper of baked beans, fried moose steak with gravy, and biscuits, he wasn't prepared for visitors, especially girls. He immediately recognized Jerri Hanley, whom he had met when he was fifteen. He hadn't seen her since. He had a difficult time to keep from tripping over his own feet. For someone who was as adept at storytelling as he was, he was finding it exceedingly difficult to find anything to say at all. He made an abortive attempt and when he failed, he withdrew himself and listened to the others chatting.

He could very vividly remember talking to Jerri and her friend five years earlier and just as he had decided he wanted to know her better, she had made up an excuse and ran off. Now she was here, sitting at the same table as he was, and he couldn't think of anything to say. Seeing her there, that night, had sparked the same fire he had felt then. Only now it was burning, not a wisp of a flame.

After supper, Jason went outside. The moon was full and it was casting shadows on the snow. He walked over to see Homer T at his own cabin. "Hi, Jason. Come on in," Homer T said.

"You got a minute, Homer T?"

"Sure, what s the problem?"

"Me. Tonight at the supper table, I just sat there like an idiot with those girls there. I wanted to talk with them, but I just couldn't."

"Oh, that's normal. Maybe you like one a little. Just relax and be yourself."

"That's easy for you to say. How can I relax when I want to be friendly and talk with her, but I can only blurt out words that don't make much sense?"

"Well, you just pretend you are talking to one of us and talk about what you know. Once the fellows get to playing and dancing, ask her to dance. Seems to me that she's come all the way out here for something," Homer T said and chuckled.

Jason waited until after the music had started and then waited a bit longer before he dared to venture back to the cook camp where the entertainment was. Everyone was having such a good time that no one really seemed to notice him. That is until Jerri spotted him. "Hey, Jason, I thought maybe you weren't coming over."

"Oh, gee-hokey, I was just talking to Homer T," he replied. That broke the ice. He felt better now and warn't so nervous.

They sat together and talked about everything under the sun. He even got up enough courage to ask her to dance. After it was all over, Jason graciously said goodnight and then the girls spent the night in his parents' camp. The next morning, Jason eagerly offered to drive them into town.

Each Sunday after that, he would borrow his father's truck and drive into town and call on Jerri. He was in love. He was a felled man, chopped off at the knees like a giant pine, tumbling face first. In later years, Jason would say that Jerri deliberately went after him and that he didn't do the chasing. To his friends, he would describe this event in his life as, "I looked up and she was coming through the skylight. I said to myself, 'Well, there's a hunk of beef.'" This, he only repeated in the company of friends and never so loud that Jerri would inadvertently overhear. He only did it in a loving, caring text.

That December on Christmas Eve, Jason and Jerri were united in wedlock. The night before was a monumental occasion. Homer T, Jim, Milton, and some of the crew gave Jason a party. It was a chance to change his mind and tease him and give him a hard time.

They started off drinking beer and then switched to rum later on. Finally by two in the morning, Jason went to bed. When he awoke four hours later, he was in worse condition that when he went to bed. He was sick and his muscles were sore. It was agreed that it might be best if the wedding ceremony be in the morning. This would give those who had to drive back out to the settlement plenty of time before dark. So begrudgingly, Jason got himself out of bed and cleaned up. The thought of food was repulsive. Time seemed to drag on and on. When he was ready, Jason stepped out into the morning sunshine and was completely surprised to see how many had showed up for the occasion.

For their honeymoon, Homer T had given them the use of his cabin on Matagamon Lake, and Milton had given them his truck to use. His parents gave them the best gift of all—their blessing, in the deepest sense of the word. They didn't have much money and in Milton's own words, "We're dirt poor, son. I only wish we could have done more for you and Jerri. Jerri, we hope you will be happy. You're like a daughter to us. Go now and have a nice time." That meant more, especially to Jerri, than anything anyone else could have ever said.

They stayed at Homer's camp for two days before returning to work and life in the lumber camp. Jason had saved a little money, but because of the times and low wages, he could not afford to lose much work. The following March, some of Jerri's friends gave her a bridal shower. It was a little late, but the thought was behind it. Jason was working in the woods that day and couldn't be there.

Jerri adjusted to life in the woods very readily. Her job was to help Marg in the cook camp from which she did earn a little money. She put this away in their special savings.

That September, Mark was born and Jason was the proudest man around. He had a son. Before his family was complete, he'd have two more sons and three daughters. But for now, his world revolved around Jerri and Mark.

One day, almost a year later, Jerri decided to put Mark in the baby carriage and go for a walk. She was tired of just hanging around the camps with no time for herself. So she tucked Mark in with his blanket and as a second thought, she went back to the camp and placed Jason's .32 rifle in the carriage alongside Mark. "Just in case we see a bear," she told her son, not that he really understood.

It was about a three-mile walk to the lake by way of the old campsite, Farrar s camp. But she wanted to sit on a rock and feel the sun in her face and listen to the water splash on the shore. It was a beautiful day. There were no flies or humidity. Once she made the turn by the old campsite, it was downhill all the way to the lake. As she turned to go down towards the lake, she met a log truck coming back up. The driver recognized her, slowed up, and poked his head out the window. "Nice day, Jerri. You might want to be careful. There s a big bull moose up ahead."

"Thanks, Leroy," she said as she pointed to the rifle. "I'll be all right."

"Yeah, I bet you will," he replied.

By the time the story had gotten back to Jason, it had been fabricated, so naturally he thought that Jerri had taken their son out to poach a moose. Well, he'd have none of that and he'd tell her so as soon as he finished work. He wasn't having a poaching wife. If it was meat they were needing, he'd do the poaching.

Jerri adjusted very easily to camp life in the woods. She enjoyed Marg s company and she thought the world of Milton and Homer T. It wasn t long before she had another baby. They had a girl this time.

With the end of the war, people had more idle time on their hands and there were more automobiles around now. People were forever coming and going from the Pleasant Lake area and the Emerson camps. The access road had to be improved to support the weight as the trucks were being built bigger and heavier.

"Things around camp are changing, Homer T," Jason would say. "It's not the quiet life that we once knew."

"No, it ain't, that s for sure. Those damned automobiles are the fault. If those people had walked in here instead of riding those fancy buggies, I guess we d see a difference. People of today are just plain lazy," Homer T cursed.

It was true though. If people had to walk from the settlement all the way to the lake, there'd probably be few that would even venture off the road. But at the same time, this kind of made life in the lumber camp a little easier, too. If fresh food was needed, it was only a matter of driving into town and back. It only took a half a day now.

The lumbering business was in full swing now. They were cutting as much white spruce now as hardwood. Seems as though there was a building boom going on the west coast and there was a shortage of building material. The boom hadn't reached the east coast yet.

One clay in 1952, Jason tied his team of horses to a snag near a cool stream and sat on a rock in the shade. He had been pondering for some time about buying one of those clunking steel crawler tractors. They were greasy and foul-smelling but some of the crew down river were using them and getting more wood than the crews using horses. He knew his father, and he wasn't sure if he'd allow it in the woods on his job. *But all the same*, he thought, *I ve got to be thinking about moving Jerri and the kids out to the settlement and that means they'll need a house. That takes money*. He was paid piece work, it only seemed logical then if he bought that crawler he would be earning more money. Besides, when he wasn't twitching out logs, he could bulldoze roads and it would be paying for itself.

It was settled then. He untied his team from the snag and walked them back to the hovel. Jerri was walking across the yard and he called out to her, "Hey, Jerri! I m going to town and I might not be back until tomorrow." That's all he said.

He'd been saving his money since he was eleven and now as he stood before the teller's window watching Mrs. Odgerson count out his money, he was pleased with himself with being so thrifty. He didn't quite have enough, but the bank was more than willing to loan him the rest.

The next day, he rode into the camp yard on a brand-new yellow John Deere crawler with an arch.

His father was only mildly surprised and a little doubtful if Jason could get enough work out of it to make it pay. The others laughed and said, "What are you going to do, Jason, pull it with a horse?" Then they'd laugh some more.

Before the day was over though, the laughing had stopped. The crews had started work shortly after the sun was up that morning and by six o'clock that night, Jason had cut and twitched as much wood as the best crew had gotten all day. Yes, the laughter had stopped. Jason's foresightedness had paid off. Now he was broke and owed the bank some money. "We'll have to eat more fish and venison," he said.

At only fifty dollars a week working piece work, Jason had to find a substitute job in order to pay off the loan at the bank. It wasn't long before the other crews began to see the advantages of the crawler and by the time the snow was waist deep, Jason had his answer. Nights after supper and on weekends, he would open twitch trails for the horses and plow roads and the camp yard. On several occasions, he would have to stop work and push one of the log trucks out of an ice hole or out of a ditch. This extra work made him tired, but by spring breakup, his crawler was paid for.

That spring, Jason loaded his wife and two kids into his father's pickup and went out to the settlement. It was time he found a house, a place to live for his family. There was a small house on the way to town and the rent was reasonable. He and Jerri didn t have much in the way of furniture, but friends and relatives helped out.

While he was out in the settlement, he heard a rumor that Warden Steed was getting done; he was retiring. "Nonsense," Steed said one day when Jason saw him in town. "Why quit doing what I like?" But the rumors kept circulating all the same. Before going back to the head of the lake that spring, Jason planted a large garden and then went hunting to ensure that his family was well provided for. He still remembered the apple orchard on the Poorman's Retreat Road and the clover field adjacent to it. He asked a friend if he'd mind dropping him off later and then picking him up later. "Sure thing, Jason. I'd be happy to do it. Only thing, I want one deer for myself," Larry Bottel said. Larry was a renowned poacher and storyteller, too. In fact, he could probably just about best anyone in a good yarn.

Larry dropped Jason off that evening right at sunset.

"Good thinking, boy. Steed will be eating his supper about now. I'll be back after I hear your shots. Remember, two deer." The moon wasn't full yet but it was bright. Jason had no sooner stepped to the edge of the green field when he saw a nice, lone deer at the other side. Since it was alone, it was probably a buck.

He sighted down the barrel and squeezed the trigger. The deer dropped. He didn't rush right over. Instead, he waited where he was and before long, another stepped out into the clearing. He shot that one and then walked down and gutted them both out. He had no sooner finished when he saw headlights coming up the road. *Hope that's Larry and not Steed.*

They threw the deer in back and Larry said, "Come on, Jason, we d better get out of here." He held his nose to the wind, sniffing like a dog. "He's coming. Smell it?"

"Smell what?" Jason asked.

"His cigar. It's in the wind. Come on, we d better get, unless you want to spend the night in jail." They left and never did see anything of Steed or of anyone else for that matter. Jerri canned that deer and Jason went out alone the next night. This time he went to the Hatt Farm in Crystal. He shot a lone deer and naturally figured it was a buck, but this time it was a wet doe. *Won't be as good eating*, he said to himself, but neither did he let it go to waste. Jerri was all set now. She had her garden and a root cellar full of deer meat. That next winter would have been extremely lonely for Jerri if it were not for their two children. She kept busy looking after them, making quilts, and mending clothes. She missed Jason, especially when the early years of any marriage can be difficult if forced to live apart. But it never, ever entered her mind to ask her husband to quit the woods and do something else. Jason was doing what he knew and liked, and that was fine with her.

Jason missed his wife and the comfort of a warm body beside him at night. But he pushed himself harder than most men would have. His crawler was paid for and he didn't have any major breakdowns yet. Now he needed money to buy a house for his family. The temporary home for his family was fine for this winter, but he wanted them in their own house by next summer. So consequently, he rarely came out of the woods to see his wife and kids. He worked around the clock, cutting trees and bulldozing new roads. It had paid off. By spring, he had earned enough money so that he and Jerri were able to buy their own house. The day Jason and the crews were paid, Wally Chapman rode into the head of the lake purposely to see Jason. "Jason, I want you to come work for me this summer at Bowlin Pond."

"You drove all the way in here to ask me that?"

"Yes. I came to see you and ask you to come work for me," Wally said. "You have a reputation of giving a man a day's work for his wages and besides, I could surely use that crawler of yours. I'd be willing to pay you extra for it," he added.

"I don t know. I'll have to think it over. I'd kind of hate to leave my father. Besides, Jerri and I were figuring on buying a house this spring."

"Tell you what, Jason. I have a crew of camp carpenters at Bowlin camps and they're yours if you want help in building a new house."

Jason groaned over that a bit and then said, "Can't give you an answer right now. I have to talk it over with Jerri first."

That's okay. I'll be staying in town for awhile at the Burmingham Boarding House. Can you give me an answer by the end of next week?"

"Yeah," Jason replied, pondering it over in his head. On his way home, he had already made up his mind. He would go to Bowlin Pond, but he and Jerri could not afford the material to build a new house even with Chapman's carpenters. He had heard of a crew camp for sale in town that the C-C men used while building the American Thread Road and the road to Matagamon Lake. It was bigger than the usual woods camp and these were supposed to be insulated and wired for electricity.

He bought the C-C camp the next day and told Wally Chapman that he'd go to work for him at Bowlin Pond. "Good. How are you going to move the C-C camp to your lot?" he asked.

"I'll have to hire a truck somewhere."

"Nonsense. I'll send one of my own out along with the carpenters to help you set it up," Wally said.

"Thanks. I could use the help." When the building was moved and set on Jason's own lot, he sat down one evening to relax and appreciate his new home. It wasn't much yet, but it was his.

Before leaving for Bowlin Pond, he made sure Jerri and the kids were provided for. He planted another garden and shot two deer. This time he took his own pickup and left Larry Bottel to home.

"Hey, Jason, you going to get a couple of deer this year like we did last year?" Larry asked Jason one day when the two met in town.

"I've already got them, Larry. Had to hurry up cause I'm going to work for Chapman next week."

"Have you heard about Steed? He s getting done."

"No, I haven t heard a word. Seems as though that was going around last year too," Jason said. "You starting rumors, Larry?"

"No, not me. That's the gospel truth," Larry stammered.

"When Steed gets done, he'll just do it without saying anything to anyone. Besides, why are you in such a hurry to see him retire? He's a good man for a game warden." Jason thought back to that Christmas greeting several years back.

"Could be we d get another one that was younger and full of piss and vinegar."

"What's with you? Gone soft for the warden?" Larry snapped.

"No, I m just saying that he does his job, that's all. Why fix something that ain't broke?"

* * * *

The wages were better at Bowlin Pond, but Jason missed the crews at Emerson camp and Homer T and Jim Ryan. Chapman's crews were hard workers all right, but they weren't the merry lot that the French were that he was so used to.

Jerri got a job as cook that first fall at Chapman's until his regular cook returned from a family emergency. "I don't want to be stuck back here, Wally and not be able to get out to my own home. If your man hasn't come back by the time you have to plow the roads, I'll have to leave."

"We have a deal then?" Wally asked.

"Yeah, as long as you agree to those conditions."

"Good, it's settled then. When will you be ready to move in?"

"Tomorrow morning," she replied.

"I'll send one of my men out for you," he said. As he was about to leave, Jerri said, "Don't say anything to Jason. I want to surprise him."

One day in October while Jason was out in the woods working, Wally hollered down from the camp roof to Jerri, "Hey, Jerri, you like to hunt?"

"Yes."

"Well earlier this morning I saw a flock of partridge down there by the thicket," he said as he pointed in the direction with his hammer.

"What'll I do with the kids?" she asked.

"Where are they now?"

"Sleeping."

"I'm about finished here. I'll watch them for you."

"Okay, thanks." She found Jason's shotgun and grabbed a handful of shells. She had no idea what they were, only that they were for the gun she had. Jerri had never done much hunting, but she knew enough to walk softly and keep a watchful eye.

Years ago, someone had dumped some garbage near where the thicket now grew, because now in the middle was an apple tree. There beneath it were five partridge. The first shot took two that were close together and the other three flew up into a near tree. Very calmly she reloaded, and one by one began to shoot those. Just as she had closed the action for her final shot, the last remaining bird flew directly at her. Methodically she pulled up and pulled the trigger without aiming. The bird dropped to the ground behind her. By now, Chapman was outside and had witnessed the last shot.

"That's some fine shooting, Jerri."

"Thanks," was all she said. She picked up the birds and walked back to camp.

The regular cook returned before the heavy snows came, and Jason took Jerri and the kids home. It was a cold winter that year and Jerri would spend most of her time filling the stoves with firewood.

By the end of February, the snow was too deep for Jason's crawler and even most of the crews had gone home. The men found that it was just too troublesome trying to wade in the stuff and expect to cut any wood. Jason stayed on only to keep the roads open with his crawler. "Jason," Wally hollered, "down along Grand Pitch there s a bunch of tall pines. If you think you can get a team of horses out there, drop 'em and twitch them to the riverbank. In the spring, we'll just push 'em in and drive them with the rest of the logs."

"How do you expect the horses to wade through this stuff if we can't?" Jason asked.

"It's all down hill from the Pitch. The team should be able to handle one log at a time. I'll pay you extra if you can get 'em all," Chapman said.

That afternoon, Jason strapped on his snowshoes and beat trails through the pine thicket and packed a road wide enough for the horses. Then he went back to camp and got two five-gallon buckets. "What are you dong with those, Jason? Freezing down your road?"

"Yeah, I m going to try it," he replied.

It was long after sunset before he had finished. In two days with the cold nights, he would have a frozen road for the horses. It was solid enough to drive a truck on.

Those were not the giant pines that he had dreamed about, but they were magnificent. It only took seven or eight logs to make a thousand linear feet. Actually the way Jason had laid out his trails and frozen road for his team, he had made the job relatively easy, especially since Chapman had agreed to pay him extra.

That spring, one of Jason's lifelong dreams had come true.

There was extra water behind Matagamon Dam this year because of the heavy snow and the wood roads had broken up early. Chapman had no choice but to river drive all his wood to market that year. It would be the last river drive ever on the East Branch.

Jason's job, after all the logs had been rolled into the river, was to follow the drive and push logs off the shore and break up jams. He wasn't long deciding that the drives were not as glamorous as he had imagined. No matter how careful he was, he was constantly getting wet. As long as he kept working and walking, it wasn't too bad. But when he'd stop for lunch and then again at the end of the clay, he'd almost freeze. To top that off, since he had to follow the drive, he was always the last to the chow line and by then it was usually cold.

But his spirits and enthusiasm were not dampened. He enjoyed the hard work, and the camaraderie was unique and very special for Jason. Sometimes in the evenings if all had gone well during the day, Jason would tell stores of shooting moose or deer during his years at the Emerson camps. One night he told the story of the time his father had taken him to the orchard on the Poorman's Retreat Road when everyone in town was there that one night.

He intentionally left out about the time Steed had scared the living hell out of him that Christmas morning. He never forgot that experience and from that day on, he never took Steed for granted or any other warden for that matter.

About halfway through the drive, the weather turned off cold and the fog hung low over the river. It was late in the afternoon when it happened. Jason was way behind the drive on this day. The water had dropped, probably because someone had closed the gates on Matagamon. Well anyway, the pine logs were hanging up on rocks and fetching up in the bend in the river. Jason was working that side of the river alone on that particular day. There was a rock island not far from shore on his side of the river just before the river took a sharper turn to the right. Two long logs had fetched up lengthwise and others were jamming behind them. The water was still like ice if you were to fall in. Jason saw an easy way out of the jam by stepping on some rocks. He put one foot on the first rock and jumped to the next. He landed with both feet squarely in the center. The rock started to move and a head about the size of a dog's stuck up from the side. Jason gave a war whoop and jumped off into the icy water, exclaiming, "Jesus! Jesus! Jesus!"

Wally Chapman was just coming up behind him in a canoe, when he saw Jason jump off and scream something about Jesus. "What the hell has gotten into you?" Chapman asked.

When Jason turned around, he was as white as a sheet of paper. He grabbed the side of Chapman's canoe. In his hysteria he tried to explain to Wally. "There's the gawd-damnedest sea monster that you ever laid eyes on." When Wally turned to look in the direction Jason was pointing, he said, "Why, Jason, that's nothing but a snapping turtle."

"Maybe, but it's the gawd-damnedest...gawd-damn, it's coming this way! Jason picked up his Kent-dog and with all his strength, swung at the back of the turtle. The turtle turned and started for deeper water. Jason swung again and broke his Kent-dog in two. "Let it go, Jason. He won t hurt you now. Maybe after that attack, he might live; you don t know."

"Holy gee-hokey, Wally! I never witnessed anything like that. No way cow-in-jennings!"

"It's only a snapping turtle, Jason."

"Well, maybe so, but that son-of-a-whore didn't have to give me such a fright."

"Get in, Jason. The water is coming up. Someone must have opened the gates. The logs will clear themselves. We might as well catch up to the others," Wally said.

"Promise me one thing, Wally. Don't, for Christ's sake, ever say anything to the men about that turtle."

* * * *

The drive had ended and every muscle in his body was sore and stiff. He was cold and he was hungry. All the men boarded the train for an easy ride home, but when they got to where the town of Davidson used to be, the train had to stop because the crews were working on the rails. They walked from there to Stacyville and hitched a ride to Patten.

Jason had just sat clown to supper with one of Jerri's well-prepared meals with all of Jason's favorites, when Larry Bottel burst through the kitchen door gasping, "I told you. I told you he was getting done!"

"What in hell are you stammering about?" Jason asked.

"Steed. Steed's all done. He retired while you were on the river. Some gung-ho young fella has taken his place. And he's made the comment that he'd give the poachers here a desultory sample of hell. That's not all either. You know where he's living? Two houses below mine. Only two houses, I tell ya! Oh, Jason," he said as he lowered himself into a chair with dismay. "Oh, Jason, he's out to get me and I'm a poor man."

Jason didn t want to insult his friend but he couldn't help it. He roared with laughter and pounded the table with his hands until his sides ached. "What's all the worry about, less you think he's smarter than you, Larry. Sounds like a challenge to me. What's the critter's name?"

"Mos...Mos Jalbert."

* * * *

Mos Jalbert. His name rang through Jason's head, and every muscle in his body became as rigid as a two-by-four plank. There was a nauseous feeling in the pit of his stomach as panic rapidly crept over. The very mention of his name meant that he might be lurking and watching, concealed behind some bush.

Jason opened his eyes and instinctively looked for some place to hide. Then reality swept before him as he slowly began to realize that he had fallen asleep and must have been dreaming.

He sat down again on the stump and mopped the sweat from his forehead. *Wow, that was some dream.* He realized now where he was and that he had only been dreaming about his own life. But he looked cautiously around him for Mos, just in case he hadn't been and the ole fox was there.

After he had regained his composure, he stood up and looked out across the woods operation and the men and machinery below him. He had only been asleep for an hour, but he had experienced an entire life span in that time.

He walked down off the ridge to where some of the men were drinking coffee. "Any of you seen the warden around this morning?" he asked, feeling somewhat paranoid after that dream or perhaps a little guilty of trying to call Mos out this morning by driving by his house.

"No, we haven't," they answered.

"I'm going back out. I've got an appointment in Millinocket this afternoon." There was still several hours before his appointment and after leaving the woods, he drove straight to the lake road that he first traveled with a team of horses. He didn't know why he was going there, only that area had been so much a part of his life.

As he crossed over the gulch at Bear Mountain, he could envision the hunters from New York as they stood beside the Model T as he told them they were right in the heart of deer country. He laughed and drove to Pickett Mountain Stream. The camp yard had grown back to trees and no one would ever know that here once stood a prosperous little lumbering community.

At the turn where the road divides to the sawdust pile on the Pleasant Lake Road, he stopped. He didn't get out, but sat quietly as he looked about. This was the Farrar campsite. There were only trees there now. The era was gone and forgotten. It was sad, now; not even a single camp was left to mark the spot and somehow say *we were here*.

At the Emerson campsite, he shut his motor off and stepped out. The clearing was still here, but years ago, someone had bulldozed the camps over and buried them. The water pipe was still in the brook and so was the rock dam he had built to create a deep enough pool to keep the trout alive. The apple tree that Homer T had planted was still alive. A bear had torn some of the branches from it, but it still had fruit.

He stood at the edge of the clearing next to the brook and slowly looked around. He was filled with sadness and his flesh was covered with goosebumps as the campsite came alive in his mind. He could see his father, Milton, as he walked the team of horses to their hovel. Homer T was talking to his stepmother, Marg, and the Irishman, Jim Ryan, was swearing at one of the French crews. Voices came from the cook camp as the men ate their supper and the air was filled with quiet and music as the little Frenchman played his guitar. He stood there, filled with vibrations of his past life; times that had once been so important to him. It was as real to Jason right then as if he had been moved back in time. Everything that has ever existed has created its own unique vibration and if these vibrations could be caught, then the recipient could view the past. This is what was happening to Jason. He had returned to this spot many times before, but had never felt the over-empowering wave of emotions.

He wiped the tears from his eyes and got back into his pickup and drove to Millinocket. The deal was struck and all Jason had left was his crawler and a bundle of money.

He wasn't happy but he was relieved. "But what do I do now?" he asked out loud. He drove home and his wife, as always, was waiting with a smile and had his supper ready. He waited until they had finished eating before he told her the news. "If that's what you want, Jason, that's fine with me." That was all she had said.

He told her of his dream and how real to life it had all seemed and about the emotional wave he had felt at the head of the lake at the Emerson camps. She told him about her dream of him having another wife and six kids. They both laughed and then Jason went into the living room to watch the evening news on TV.

Jason couldn t relax. He kept worrying and wondering if he had done the right thing. He wanted a drink of rum or anything for that matter, but he had promised Jerri to slow down. *Not to quit but to slow down.*

He went outside in the fresh air and came right back in again. He sat down at the kitchen window and stared at the lights.

"Jason," Jerri said in a reassuring voice, "why don't you get your rifle and go get a deer tonight?" That was music to his ears.

"Yes, by gee-hokey, maybe I will."

CHAPTER 2

Mos Jalbert

It was the same night that Jason had difficulty in falling asleep from worry and anxiety about his future if he sold out. Mos long ago had developed an extra sense or an awareness about things, which allowed him to sleep peacefully at night. He'd drop off to sleep beside his wife Renee and then without physical warning, he'd get out of his bed, put on his uniform, and leave.

There were other times when someone would try to sneak into the yard with intentions of vandalizing his state vehicle only to be caught by the shirt collar by a vice-like grip. Well, on this same night, Mos had lain awake all night, thinking about the next day.

Unlike Jason and his anxieties, Mos knew it was time to say he'd had enough and it was time to retire. He had spent the last thirty years as a game warden and had loved every minute. But now he would retire and he was happy about that. He lay awake not from the worries and anxieties about his future, but he was looking ahead to the happy times he'd have to spend with his wife and their grandchildren.

As Jason was stepping outside into the morning air, Mos was just sitting down to the kitchen table by the window with his first cup of coffee. He was pouring his second cup and instinctively looking out the window just in time to see Jason drive by. He laughed out loud and his wife asked, "What's so funny?"

"It's Jason. He just drove by. He's probably trying to sucker me out like he's done in the past. The ole rascal thinks I'll still fall for that game." At first, Mos had taken the baited hook. But after a few times, he learned that whenever Jason drove by his house on his way to work, there was no need to worry about him doing any poaching. It was the mornings that he didn't see him that he later learned that he had to worry.

Mos called him the ole rascal without any vexations towards him. Instead, it was with a mixture of friendship and understanding. Jason was an unyielding poacher and it was Mos' job to apprehend violators of the law.

He watched Jason as he drove out of sight. As he drummed his stump of a thumb against the table, he remembered the day when Jason had saved his life.

"What time do you have to be in Augusta, Mos?" Renee asked.

"Ten o'clock, but I'll be back for supper." Yesterday he had loaded all of his equipment and state property into the back of his pickup so he wouldn't have to do it in the morning. He kissed his wife goodbye and left. There was nothing unusual about being out at this time of day and everyone waved as he met them on the road.

The interstate between Sherman and Augusta is a lonely stretch of highway and when travelling it alone, it becomes very easy to concede to the hypnotic effect of the highway itself and the sound of the tires on the pavement. And once in this state, the mind can play games and confuse the person by creating illusions in the mind. As Mos drove along, he was aware that he was developing a bitter attitude towards the warden service. But try as hard as he could, he could not stop the negative thoughts.

It's just as well that I'm getting done now anyhow," he said. "They've taken the fun out of the job and made it a job. There was a time when I couldn't wait until I could go back to work the next day or instead of taking the day off, I'd work it right through. Nobody ever said anything. But God, now they'd hang you for it. Look what we've become. Now we're hiring women to catch poachers. What in hell do women know about hunting and fishing. Female wardens will just cause discontent with a man's family. Sure glad I never had to work with one. I can remember not too long ago when I might be gone for a week or more, patrolling some river or back country. Now the head hanchoes would rather I be right next to the gawd-damn radio every minute like I was married to it. And the equipment that we get now! More like tinker toys. Useless! I don't know what the reason is, but you take a game warden that's a damned good man in the woods and knows how to catch poachers, and once you put him in Augusta behind a desk, it's just like someone turned off a lightbulb. The frigging town eats their brains out. Seen it happen time and again. It's not enough that we fight with the poachers, their lawyers, incompetent prosecutors and judges, but now it's like the supervisors are always trying to mess with the wardens. It's like they'd really want to take us to court. At times we're fighting our own people. Yeah, I'm glad that's over. I should have done it years ago.

But that wasn't quite the truth. This was only the negative part of his mind talking. He had enjoyed his thirty years as a warden and he got as much out of it as he gave. The local people had come to respect and like him, too; even the hardcore poachers. With them, it had become more of a game than anything else. He earned his reputation though and that, nobody could deny him. At fifty-five, he was still doing more than most men at thirty. The fresh air and the miles and miles of stream banks and woods trails he had walked along during the past thirty years had kept him in good health. He stood five foot eleven inches and weighed one hundred and ninety pounds. There was not an ounce of fat either. He was never seen without a cigar stuck out of the corner of his mouth. But his smoking never seemed to bother him. His lungs were like a set of iron bellows. He seldom smiled but inside of that mask was a gentle man. Some people often mistook the look of concern and concentration for indignation and worry. His face had lines of steel but seldom did he frown. His eyes were dark as was his hair. Whenever he talked to anyone, he would always look them in the eyes because his would seem to bore through theirs like piercing lasers. He became a legend without ever trying. It was locally understood that if he came looking for you for some dastardly deed that had been committed, then you were better off to confess and own up to it than be interrogated by him and come under his scrutinizing stare.

For thirty years, Mos Jalbert lived and breathed being a game warden. He was conscientious and fair; although there would be some who might say otherwise. He loved his work, and again, some would say to the point of neglecting his family. He was a loner and preferred to work by himself. He stood completely straight and his shoulders never sagged, even after being out for several days. Many people mistook his look of concern for anger or a frown. It was true that he seldom smiled in public, but maybe it was because he always had a cigar clinched between his teeth. But he liked a good joke as well as the next guy. Some were even played on him in his career. No one ever took his word or warning lightly. His voice might ring out across a field at night and warning a poacher if he was taking the deer to feed his family. Then he'd say, "Take it all!" Hair would stand up on the backs of many a night hunter's neck.

Mos had developed this system for curing the occasional poacher who only took to feed his family from letting the dastardly deed become anything more than helping to put food on the table. The courts, he had found, never took a personal look at a man's need or reason for taking an illegal deer. All were consequently treated the same in the eyes of he law.

His nemesis and friend, an odd and unusual parody, was Jason Smith. Through the years, they each had developed a respect and amity for the other. Mos had no qualms about pinching Jason for a fish or game violation, then sitting down at Jason's table and having a cup of coffee when invited. Jason, on the other hand, had no qualms about getting away with some caper especially if he could see an opening.

It had been said, in fact on a regular basis, that he was so mean that he'd pinch his grandmother and laugh. That wasn't so.

He had no reservations about arresting anyone who intentionally violated the law. But it was also known that he had given many a man a break, especially if he'd been caught getting some meat for his family during hard times of unemployment. Mos' only comment would be, "You'd better take it all and use it, and don't let me hear about it around town." As soon as that was said, he'd back off into the shadows and disappear.

There were several memorable characters in his career and probably by far the most memorable and colorful was the infamous Jason Smith. As much as Mos Jalbert was the symbolic game warden, Jason was the legendary poacher. He was Jeff Coongate, the notorious outlaw with a big heart that was made of gold, in Edmund Ware Smith's "The One-Eyed Poacher."

Mos and Jason had developed, through the years, an unparalleled friendship. It could be acquainted to a house cat and dog. At first, they'd be at each other's throats, trying to dig and claw at the face of the other and then eventually settling into a routine kind of understanding. It was tolerance first, then friendship.

There were others, too, like his neighbor Larry Bottel who reminded him of a timid mouse, but who could shoot a deer's eye out in the dark. There were Lucas Hanley, Henry Carter, and Arnold Parker; they were all good men.

* * * *

The hypnotic effect of the tires and the highway was sending Mos into a deep trance-like state. He became oblivious to the traffic, although he maintained a constant sixty miles an hour speed and managed to maneuver in and around other vehicles. This trance that he was in was taking his mind to the other side of reality or what we in the physical world call reality. Here, maybe by coincidence or perhaps fate, he was traveling back and beginning to relive his early years of life at the same time Jason was doing the same thing.

Mos was born in a small cabin in the outskirts of Eustis, in the western part of Maine. It was 1933 and he was christened Maurice Jalbert after his grandfather who still lived in Woburn, Quebec. During his early childhood, everyone kept remarking how much he resembled his grandfather in both looks and temperament. Because of that, his love for his grandfather, and the plain fact that Maurice sounded like a sissy's name, he and his grandfather shortened their name to Mos.

His folks, Renald and Kathryn had moved from Canada shortly after they were married to look for work. Even across the border, the depression was having its affect. Renald went to work for awhile in the woods, but that soon came to a close when the crews couldn't get their wages. The parent company had collapsed because of the depression and the contractor was unable to find another market.

About that time, a group of politicians got together in Augusta. It was said later that perhaps they had a personal interest, but regardless of the real reason, these politicians petitioned the federal government in Washington. The Civil Conservation Corp or CCC, and was asked to devise a plan to construct a road capable of sustaining vehicle traffic from Route 27 into the area of Jim Pond Township. This group of politicians hoped by opening the woods to that area that the sporting camps on King and Bartlett, Deere Pond, and the Chimes would become more accessible and survive the depression. There was also a desperate need of financial help in this area and the CCC would employ many of the unemployed.

The work was hard but at least it was work. It lasted until 1935 . Several miles of road had been built and the sporting camps did survive. After the CCC work ended, Renald got another woods job working for a local contractor to supply softwood, spruce, and fir for the paper mill in Livermore Falls. Renald worked six days a week and only came home after work on Saturday. These were hard times and he knew that as long as there was a job, he had to work in order to support his family.

By the time Mos was eleven, Renald moved his family to the gatekeeper's camp at the end of the CCC road where Foster's land began. He had gotten his wife the job as gatekeeper while he worked for Stratton Lumber Company on Foster's grounds. Foster Manufacturing Company had purchased the land in 1940. Instead of cutting softwood, their main concern now was supplying white birch to the pick mill in Strong.

Since the gate had to be tended through the November deer season, Kathryn had to tutor Mos herself and then each year, he would have to take an examination to see if his studies were equal with the other students. During the summer, Mos worked as a cabin boy at King and Bartlett Sporting Camps. He soon developed a dislike for the rich fancy-pants as he came to call them. He hated their high-winded ideas of themselves. It was a job and more often than not, he'd get a large tip from them. So he bit his lip and kept quiet.

One summer during his twelfth year, he asked Mr. King if he could go home that night because it was his mother's birthday. "Sure, kid. Do you need a ride?"

"No, that's okay. I'll walk to the hauling road and hitch a ride with one of the truckers." That night, his father was late getting home from work. When he did get home, he was carrying a burlap bag with something in it.

"What's in the bag, Dad?" Mos asked.

"A little deer. I shot it after work this afternoon. I need you to help me dress it out." They carried the deer out back and while his father dressed it out, Mos couldn't help but think that what they were doing was wrong. "Dad, isn't it against the law to shoot a deer now?"

"Yes, son, it is. But these are hard times and we need the meat."

Mos thought about what his father said and supposed that these hard times justified poaching a deer. After they had finished and the deer was hanging in a tree away from the camp, Earl Landean, the local game warden, stopped at the gate.

"What brings you out here so late in the day?" Renald asked.

"Hear there were a bunch of fish hogs at the King and Bartlett camps. I might walk around the cuttings, too," Landean added on purpose so that Renald would know that he already knew about the deer. He didn't come right out and say it, but both Mos and his father knew what Landean meant.

Times were hard and Landean knew that this wasn't the first deer Renald had poached and probably wouldn't be the last either. But Mos was surprised with Landean's aloofness. How could he be so cool about it and at the same time, be so cunning and indirect by telling his father, "I know." That experience would stay with him through the years to come and in time, he, like Landean, would often use the same cunning wiliness.

Mos laid awake most of that night waiting to see when Landean would return. The gate was normally left open after nine at night and all he had to do was drive through. But he never came through and by morning, Mos' curiosity was getting the best of him. Where was Landean and why hadn't he come through last night? What was he doing?

Mos told Mr. King that he would be back the next morning after breakfast, so Landean and his reason for being there were soon forgotten. He caught a ride with another truck and was back at the sporting camps in time to start his day's work.

No word was mentioned from any guests of seeing the warden, so Mos figured it was best to keep still about it. He wasn't sure what Landean was up to and he didn't want any suspicion laid on his father.

The next day, it rained and after breakfast, the group from New York City returned to their cabin much to Mos' displeasure. He hated to be interrupted while he was working.

"You fellows aren't going fishing this morning?" he asked.

"No, it's too wet," one of them answered.

"Too bad, they'd really bite today. The best time to fish is when it's raining."

"Well, maybe, but we already have more than we're allowed."

Mos' ears perked up with that reply. He began to wonder if Landean was still in the area and if he should tell him. *Ah, what good would it do? Probably the warden's gone by now and if he were still around, how would I find him?* he asked himself. *But I sure would like to see him walk through that door.*

No sooner had he thought that than the front door opened and there stood the all-elusive Landean. There was water dripping from his hat and his dark growth of whiskers. It was obvious that he hadn't been home for awhile. Had he been out there all that time? His appearance would surely indicate that he had. To do that, he must have had a good reason. Then suddenly the answer was clear—the New Yorkers had just said they had more trout than they were allowed. But...but how did Landean know?

"Hello, warden," the New Yorker said. "Won't you come in?"

"Nice day. I'm surprised you fellows aren't fishing," Landean said.

"Maybe this afternoon if it stops raining. Want a cup of coffee?"

"Don't mind if I do." Landean wasn't paying any attention to Mos as he sat down and continued talking. "How long have you boys been up?"

"Four days. We got in on Sunday."

"How's the fishing been?" Landean asked.

"Oh, pretty slow," the New Yorker said. Mos looked at him, knowing he was lying and wanting to say so. But he knew that if he did that he would probably lose his job.

"How long you staying?" Landean asked.

"We're leaving tomorrow. Hate to leave in a way. It's so peaceful here."

"Yeah, that it is. Got any trout to take back with you?"

"No, that is, not yet. We've eaten everything we've caught so far."

Mos tried to get on with his work, but he found it very difficult. Here was the warden, obviously apparent that he'd been in the area for some time, now talking to these guys as if he didn't know anything. Was Landean just playing with them? Or could it be that he was just here by accident? But the game continued.

"Have you tried any of the other ponds around: Felker, Everett, or Joe Pokam Ponds? They're all good fishing."

"No, we stayed here."

"What fly did you find worked the best?" Landean continued to question.

"A royal coachman. We couldn't tie them fast enough," the New Yorker said. Mos heard that admission, but Landean apparently missed it as he sat there drinking his coffee.

Landean stood up and walked over to the sink and put his cup down. "Well, boys, thank you for the coffee."

"Anytime. Hope you didn't think that we had broken the law." Mos couldn't believe what he was hearing. Those lousy flatlanders.

"No, but I'm not done looking yet. If you don't mind, I'd like to look in your cooler outside." They all went outside, even Mos. He wasn't going to miss this for anything.

"Right over here," the New Yorker said as he lifted the cover. "See, not much in here but butter and beer."

"Yeah, I can see that. Is this your only cooler?"

"Yes."

"What about the one over there in the brook?" Landean asked.

"Almost forgot about that one. There's not much in it, just some meat."

"Well, if you don't mind, I'd like to have a look."

They all walked over and Landean opened the cover. Mos noticed that the four were pretty nervous. Probably it was full of trout. But when the cover was pulled back, it was empty. There wasn't anything in there at all. The guy that had been doing all the talking exclaimed, "Gawd-damn, they're gone!"

"You saying you had some trout in there?"

"No...no, just hot dogs and some...some hamburger."

Landean started laughing and said, "Oh, come on. I took those trout out myself before I came over to your cabin. There weren't any hot dogs or hamburger either."

"You can't prove those were our fish," the New Yorker said. Mos knew he was right, but how could Landean prove it.

"Yes, I can," he said as he pulled a slip of paper out of his pocket. "You, sir, I called the noisy one, at 4:30 yesterday afternoon, you put forty-one trout in this."

Next he said, "You, sir, I called the black jacket and red cap, at 6 :30 in the evening, you put thirty-four trout in this. You, sir, I called green cap, at 2 :15 in the afternoon, you put forty-nine trout in this. You, sir, I called short and green cap, at 11 :15 in the morning, you put twenty-six trout in this."

All four of them just stood there with their mouths hung open, including Mos. Landean had stayed there all this time, watching and he knew exactly what was happening.

After everything was all over and the four New Yorkers had gone back to their cabin, Mos asked Landean, "How'd you know?"

"I didn't at first, but when it threatened to rain yesterday, I knew the fish would bite, so I stayed around. Then one by one, they committed themselves."

"If you already knew, then what was all that about in the cabin?" Mos asked.

"Well, I had enough already to charge them but I wanted to see if they would lie to me. They did, so I had a little fun with them."

"Then you did pick up on what they said about the royal coachman?"

"Yeah, I was all ears then."

"How long have you been out here?" Mos asked.

"For two days, since I saw you at the gate," Landean said.

Landean left and Mos went back to work in another cabin. All day as he worked, he kept thinking of Landean and how he had purposely toyed with those fools. They thought they were pulling one over on him and just as they thought he was beaten, Landean surprised them. He had toyed with them the same way he had toyed with his father. Except now, would he arrest his father? He thought about it for a minute and then decided that he probably wouldn't. There had been a difference. The laws had both been broken, but there was that margin of difference.

Mos went to sleep that night with deep admiration for Earl Landean and what he had seen in those last few days.

Two years passed before Mos saw Landean again. But during those years, Landean was very much alive in Mos' thoughts. He thought and dreamed constantly about the mysterious game warden that could appear or disappear, it seemed, at will. Although he didn't see the warden for two years, stories and tales of his exploits circulated throughout the woods and crew camps. It seemed as though Earl Landean had become a legend. At least to Mos, he was legendary. Whenever anyone stopped at the gate after returning from town, Mos would always inquire if there were any new tales about the warden. "Where is he? What's he doing now? Why hasn't he been in?" At the sporting camp, Landean's job was made easier by Mos. He retold the story of how the warden had mysteriously appeared in the doorway on one rainy day and nabbed four fish hogs from New York. He had become an idol to Mos. He made sure that each new sport heard the story. More than anything in his life, he had decided he wanted to become a game warden like Landean.

Then one day while he was spending some slow time with his mother at the gate, one of the truckers stopped and hollered to Mos. "Hey, Mos, I heard the warden has two fellows under arrest at Spectacle Pond. He's waiting for an airplane to fly them out. Thought you might like the news."

"Thanks, Sam. Thanks a lot," Mos said. He was back, but how did he get through here without being seen? Mos couldn't figure that one out, unless he'd come in by plane. But then there would have been some stories about someone flying because planes in those days were not that common. If he walked in from another direction, he would have had quite a hike. Mos' admiration and wonderment of this man was increasing with each feat and each new story. "I'd like to be a warden, I think. Except I don't know if I'd like to be out in the woods in the dark for all hours of the night."

* * * *

There were stories and rumors circulating that Flagstaff, Deadriver, and Bigelow villages were to be torn down and the area would be flooded with water. After school let out in the summer of '47, Mos went to Flagstaff to see a friend, Duluth Wing. "Hi, Dude. What are you doing?"

"I'm getting my gear together. I've been hired by the forestry service to man the lookout tower on Bigelow Mountain this season."

"When do you leave?" Mos asked.

"The day after tomorrow."

"Dude, what are all these stories about Flagstaff, Deadriver, and Bigelow being flooded?"

"Yep, they are. The work's supposed to start this summer. I saw some of the Central Maine Power Company people here yesterday."

"What's going to happen to all the people and the buildings like the school, stores, and cemetery?" Mos asked.

"Everything's to come down. If it isn't hauled away, then it has to be burned. The cemetery is to be moved to Stratton. Each grave will be dug up and the caskets and headstones will all be moved."

"How much of the woods are going to be flooded?"

"Seventeen thousand acres in all. There are crews out there now cutting and burning."

"It seems like an awful waste to me," Mos said. "What's it all for anyhow?"

"Central Maine Power Company needs more water to generate electricity at the Wyman Dam in Moscow. They plan to build a dam at Long Falls and back the water up and flood this valley. It'll then be a reservoir for the hydroelectric dam. When the water table drops too low in Wyman Lake, the gates will open and the water from here will flow into Wyman."

Mos was quietly thinking to himself. He had a difficult time understanding how at the flick of a finger, someone could come in and say, "Look, you'll have to move because we're building a dam and flooding your village."

The fact was that the company surveyors had started work during the twenties and plans were being laid for the construction of the Long Falls Dam well in advance of the initial starting date. People were paid for their farms and property, and then allowed to buy back the buildings and tear them down and move them to a new location. Some did this and some simply took the money and looked for a new life elsewhere.

People understood that the dam was being built to benefit the whole and not just a few. But this did little to still the emptiness and loneliness as people took a last look at what was once home. There were no demonstrations, sit-downs, or trouble. There was none of this about the water destroying a rare and precious flower, or the deer and small animals might drown. People of Flagstaff, Deadriver, and Bigelow understood that this was the law and their parents had brought them up to respect it and to work with it. So building by building, the towns were leveled and the people started roots elsewhere. Some went to Eustis and Stratton, and some were so unhappy that they left and hoped to never return.

Dude Wing's father had a team of horses and had hired on to twitch logs and brush to the fires. Mr. Wing told Mos, "I think, Mos, that I can get you a job, if you're interested, digging up graves and headstones."

"Sounds gruesome," Mos said.

"Yeah, but the pay's good."

"How much?"

"Twenty-five dollars a grave. That is, twenty-five dollars for digging it out and putting it in a new hole in another cemetery."

"How many graves are there?" Mos asked.

"Don't know for sure, but they all have to go."

That summer, Mos lived with the Wings and Dude climbed to the top of Bigelow Mountain. Each day as he sat in the tower, he could watch the work progress as the buildings came down and the land was cleared.

The next summer, Long Falls Dam was started and men from all over the area came to work. There had never been so much work in the area before. People were excited about the new project, even those who were forced to leave.

The project was completed a year later and the gates in the new dam were closed. Mos felt a disquieting sense to his being and as a lonely gesture, he decided to take a canoe trip down the Deadriver to the newly completed dam. "It'll be the last that I'll ever canoe the river again, Dad. You're working in the Spring Lake area, aren't you?"

"Yes," his father replied.

"Can you pick me and the canoe up after work on Friday?"

"It might be late."

"No problem." It was settled then. He would take a last trip down the river. He set off the next day. This wasn't his first trip downstream. He knew the river well and the history surrounding the soon to be buried villages. He settled in his canoe and dipped his paddle noiselessly into the water. He let the current carry him along. He guided the canoe with his paddle. It never occurred to him to ask someone to go with him. He was very comfortable being alone in the wilderness. He had no fears of the unknown, the animals, or of getting lost. Once, when he was only seven, his father was away working in a lumber camp and his mother was busy hanging her wash, when he and Fred, his pet dog, went out for a walk behind the log cabin. It was the middle of July and the weather was very warm.

He and Fred were having so much fun running and playing together that he forgot about going home. They came to Deadriver and Mos decided he wanted to go for a swim. He took his clothes off, and he and Fred waded out into the middle of the river. The current was swift, but the water only came up to his belly. After awhile, Mos had tired of splashing in the water. Mos put his clothes back on and then laid back on the riverbank, using Fred as a pillow.

He watched some fish jumping for bugs and birds were flying above him. He had completely forgotten that he should be on his way home and that his mother would be worried. He fell asleep with the warmth of Fred next to him. Darkness came and Mos was still asleep.

Mos awoke the next morning. He stood up and stretched, and said, "Come, Fred, I'm hungry. Let's go home."

Kathryn was up all night worrying about Mos. When he wasn't found by supper, she had word taken to her husband. Renald left for home immediately but it was almost midnight before he got there. There wasn't much he could do until morning.

At the break of day, Renald left the cabin and started searching the woods between there and the river. After an hour of searching under blow-downs and in bushes, he heard laughter and a dog barking. He knew it was Mos and Fred. He waited for them. They were coming towards him. Mos saw his father standing in front of a fallen tree with his hands firmly planted on his hips. "What's the matter, Daddy? Why do you have that funny look on your face?" Mos asked, not understanding the concern and worry.

Renald tried to explain to Mos that he shouldn't have gone off to the river without his mother because something terrible could have happened. Mos replied, "But, Daddy, Fred was with me. We weren't doing anything wrong."

Renald knew he had to punish Mos for wandering off like that. He needed the discipline, but he didn't have it in his heart to spank him. Finally he told Mos that until such a time that his mother decided, he wasn't to go out of sight of the cabin.

That lasted for two years. Then one day, he and Fred decided to go fishing down at the river. He had fished further down the river than he had planned and darkness overtook him before he could get back. Again, Mos and Fred spent another night on the riverbank. From then on, Renald gave up trying to discipline him about going alone in the woods and down to the river. Even for a small boy, Mos had an uncanny sense about the woods. He wasn't afraid of the darkness or of being alone in the woods. Renald knew that he would be okay, but that didn't comfort Kathryn any. She still worried about him.

Even now that he was almost grown up, his mother would worry about him being alone on this trip to the forgotten villages.

* * * *

That evening, he pulled his canoe ashore at the familiar spot at Flagstaff, where he had always done the same in the past. Only there wasn't anything there now except for the burned rubble. Even the forest was gone. This was progress he decided, but he wasn't happy about it. "Damn it! There's so much history here." He was right. During the American Revolutionary War, General Benedict Arnold had traveled this watershed on his way to Quebec City. He was standing on the very shore where Arnold had made camp almost two hundred years earlier. The rain had spoiled some of his provisions and he made camp there while he waited for the rest of his army to catch up. Arnold had erected a staff on the top of his tent roof and from that, he flew the continental flag.

In 1849, only a mere hundred years ago, the village of Flagstaff was incorporated and it became a town with almost three hundred residents. The Bigelow village was named after Major Bigelow who served with General Arnold on that excursion and that was the site where he and his men had made camp. The Deadriver village was named after the river, Deadriver, which was named because of the seemingly calm water.

"Oh, well," Mos sighed as he watched the sunset's reflection on the water. "That's progress, I guess."

As darkness crept in, Mos built a fire. He threw on more dried wood than he needed. The flames shot high into the night sky. Fiery embers disappeared far above him. Some fell and singed his bare arms. He sat down on the sandy soil and leaned back against a log. His thoughts drifted, much like the fiery embers were drifting upwards from the heat of the fire. He wondered if his friend Dude could see his fire from on top of Bigelow Mountain if he were in the fire tower.

Then he thought about his father and how he had worked hard all his life and still had to kill an illegal deer on occasion to put meat on the table. Landean never bothered much about his father's poaching. He just figured he was a hard working man and just a little down on his luck.

His thoughts then drifted closer to home. He began thinking about his early years and how different he was from other boys his age. None of his friends would ever take a trip like this alone. Being alone had never made him feel uncomfortable. He felt as at ease in the woods alone, even at night, than most people would feel at ease in their own yards. He enjoyed the time alone and the stillness. It was something his mother never understood about him.

He put some more wood on the fire and laid out his bedroll. He was careful not to let any embers fall on his blankets. He lay down and clasped his hands together under his head and watched the stars above him. He soon fell asleep and the fire died to a few smoldering coals.

* * * *

He started his senior year of high school that year and not wanting to spend his entire life working in the woods felling trees like his father, he earnestly began to look for future careers and possibilities. There were any number of things that he was interested in, but he mostly wanted to leave and be on his own and make his mark and say, "I've been there." He wanted to be a game warden like his friend, Landean, but he wasn't old enough yet. He would have to wait another three years before he could even apply.

By April of '51, he still wasn't sure what to do with himself. One day, an army recruiter came to the high school. The Korean War was still being fought and the military needed good men

That evening at the supper table, Mos said, "Dad, I enlisted in the Army today." He waited for a response. Renald finished chewing what he had in his mouth before speaking. "Might not be a bad idea. I hear the Korean War might end shortly. If that happens, you may not be sent overseas at all."

"Even if it does, Dad, I'm still going. I need to see for myself what's out there. I've got to be myself."

"When do you leave?"

"In June, after I graduate."

Renald knew what Mos was talking about. He needed to find his own niche in life, but he knew his son and knew he would have a hard time with the army life. His son had a large stubborn streak in him.

* * * *

Mos was a victim of his own incorruptible character. He wasn't arrogant or impertinent. It was more like he was willing to be ostracized, a castoff, in order to demonstrate that he was right. He would go to extremes at times to prove his point. He was stubborn. This attitude often times caused trouble for him with his folks and at school, and it was beginning to trip him up during his first week of basic training.

Mos had long ago forgotten that his real name was Maurice. Everyone had called him Mos since the day he adopted it from his grandfather. The very first day of his basic training, the new recruits were in formation outside and the drill instructor was calling off names to make sure that everyone was there. "Maurice Jalbert," the sergeant said. Mos kept quiet. It was not intentional at first because he never heard his name. The sergeant had said "Jalbert" with the last part of his name sounding hard, like "Jal... bert." Mos was French and he had always been called "Jalbert" pronounced "Jal...biere."

The sergeant went through the rest of his list and then came back to Maurice. "Maurice Jalbert." No reply. Now Mos' character was apt to get him in trouble again. He was French and proud of it. His name was Mos (Jalbiere) and that's how he was going to be known. It was stubbornness, but for him it was a sense of character...his character.

The sergeant tried again and finally walked over and stopped directly in front of Mos. "I've called your name three times and you have not answered. You are the only boy here who hasn't answered to some name, so you must be Mr. Jalbert."

With an even voice, Mos said, "No, sir, my name is Mos (Jalbiere)."

"Oh, an arrogant little piss, huh! Well, I'll break that troublesome attitude before I'm through with you."

Mos spent the first half of basic training on K-P and other less meaningful duties. The last half was spent in the brig for striking the drill instructor after Mos was taken off K-P duty. The sergeant singled out Mos for other meaningless jobs by saying several derogative remarks about the French. That was enough. Mos swung once and caught the sergeant off-guard, sending him backwards onto the parade ground. The sergeant was more angry from the humiliation than anything else. The entire company laughed, further humiliating him. Mos spent the next four weeks behind bars.

Needless to say, he didn't graduate with the rest of the company. How could he? He never made it to the rifle range or any of the other aspects of the training. But he did gain the respect of the sergeant and all through his second attempt with basic, the sergeant called him Mos (Jalbiere).

Mos was interested in the training and did very well. By the end of his three-year enlistment, he had been promoted to Staff Sergeant. But he had had enough. His overseas tour had taken him to parts of the world that he would have never seen otherwise. But just the same, it was time to go home and find a pretty French girl to marry. The only thing he wanted now was to become a game warden. It was his life's ambition. It was late August before Mos received his final discharge. The bad time in the brig didn't count towards his enlistment.

Mos and his father went on a fishing trip to Blakeslee Pond that first weekend he was home. The fishing was great and the fresh air and wide-open outdoors were all better than he remembered.

While in the army, Mos had almost forgotten about his friend, Earl Landean. He had been too busy with his present life to remember those formable years. Now as he and his father were sitting on a log next to the cook fire eating fresh trout, Mos had a suspicious feeling that they were being watched.

Nonsense, he said to himself. *There's nobody here but us?* he said questioningly, trying to bolster his own confidence. But the feeling persisted and eventually Landean stepped out from behind a cedar tree with a two-day growth of whiskers.

"How's the fishing?" he asked as he walked towards them.

"Not bad," Renald replied. "We got a good mess of trout."

"Jalbert, isn't it?" he asked and before either could answer, he continued, "I haven't seen either of you around for a few years now. Mos, I heard that you joined the army."

"Yeah, I'm all through now. I got home two days ago."

"What are you doing now, Renald? Haven't seen much of you either," Landean asked.

"I worked for awhile at Spring Lake, but now I'm working over in Lang Township. The money's better and so is the wood."

"What are you going to do now that you're out of the army?" Landean asked Mos.

"I'm not sure. I will go to work somewhere," Mos said. "Want some trout? They're fresh and the coffee's hot, too."

Landean helped himself and then sat down on another log across the fire from Mos and his father. After he had finished eating, he said, “Could be, you know, that I might be needing me an assistant to work with this fall.” He left it at that and poured himself another cup of black coffee.

Mos just sat there and didn’t know what to say. His eyes just kept getting bigger and bigger.

“Me? Yahoo! Yes, Jesus Christ, yes! When?”

“Next week on September first,” Landean replied with a smile. He looked at Renald and he was smiling, too.

Mos was deputized six days later and was given a uniform shirt and the traditional red warden jacket. It was to be clearly understood from the beginning that Landean would call for Mos when he needed his assistance and not the other way around. There was no training required. The commissioner had said, “Here, your job is to assist Warden Landean. He’ll tell you all that you’ll be required to know.”

The first time Mos assisted Landean, they had left their vehicle in on an abandoned woods road and walked crosscountry to an old apple orchard. “I received a complain this morning of a deer being shot here.”

“Who called?” Mos asked.

“Can’t say. The caller was anonymous. He said it has gone on for the last two nights.”

Mos wasn’t prepared for his new job. In fact, he really didn’t know what to expect. If he had assumed that working with Landean would be like a social gathering where you sat around and talked, he would be sadly mistaken.

When they arrived at the orchard—that is before stepping into the clearing—they stopped and listened. When Landean was sure that no one was around, he pointed to the far side and said, “I’m going to work my way around to thc other side. I think that’s where they are coming from. I want you on this side in case they make a run for it when I jump them. Stay in the shadows and be quiet.” That was all he said before he disappeared into the darkness of the night, blending into the shadows and becoming a part of the environment himself. Mos stood there watching and listening, but Landean had vanished almost as if he had never been there. But Mos knew he had because he had followed him here. Then it occurred to him that he was no longer a mere spectator. This was for real and those they hoped to apprehend would have rifles. This wasn't a game any longer. A shiver went up his back and down to the soles of his feet. He moved quietly, staying in the shadows, until he had a good vantage point of the whole orchard.

The next morning just before the sun came up, Landean noiselessly stepped out from the bushes behind Mos. "You had enough? Let's go before we get caught in the daylight."

Neither of them said a word until they were back inside Landean's car. Then almost as if he had been reading Mos' thoughts, he said, "You can't expect to catch someone every ight. But the night wasn't wasted either. We know they hunted Monday and Tuesday night, but not Wednesday. Most poachers will work themselves into a routine. But just in case they don't, we'll come back here every night until we catch 'em."

"What if someone shoots a deer in another field?" Mos asked. "Will we stay here?"

"We can only be in one spot at a time. We know two deer have been taken from here. Chances are, whoever is doing it will come back. By staying put and working this field and catching the fellows, we'll do more to deter further poaching than jumping around each night and ending up with nothing. Are you cold?"

"No, not now. I was for awhile. My muscles are stiff from standing all night."

"Tomorrow night, better put on some warmer clothes and if you're going to be a warden, bring a thermos of coffee. It'll keep you awake and warm. Besides, when you get bored, it will give you something to do."

Two nights later, shortly after midnight, two surly shadowy figures entered the orchard. They had walked past Landean and never knew he was there. In fact, all Landean had to do was extend his arm and he could have touched them both. But he waited. They had not violated any laws yet. One carried a spotlight and the other had a lever-action rifle, probably a .30-.30 Winchester. He stayed hidden in the shadows and watched the two figures work their way quietly along the edge of the clearing. The orchard wasn't large but in the darkness, a foot hunter could easily slip by.

He had told Mos earlier not to jump too soon. "Wait and be patient. If they shoot anything, chances are they'll drag it out the same way they came in. If they do, I'll jump them and that will be your signal to come over. If they run on me, they'll probably cross the clearing towards you. Better to take the one with the rifle just in case you can't handle them both. I won't be far behind in any case."

All that night, Mos had been going over what Landean had said, trying to figure a game plan of attack if they came his way. After many futile attempts, he finally settled on waiting to see what would happen. When the two figures came into the clearing, they were out of Mos' sight and since they were being quiet, he had no idea anyone else was there. The two poachers quietly stayed in the shadows, waiting for their scent to disperse and let all remain quiet. An hour went by and Landean began to wonder if the two were still there. If he tried to move and locate them, they would surely be alarmed if they were still there. Better wait, he thought.

Another hour went by and suddenly a light flashed across the orchard immediately followed by a rifle shot. Landean's patience had paid off. Now they waited a little longer. Mos, on the other hand, was shaken practically out of his skin.

All was quiet again after the shot and the light had been turned off. Mos strained his eyes in the direction of the shot, but he couldn't hear or see anything. If they were still there, they were being awfully quiet. His first thought was to go running across the orchard and catch the no good bastards before they got away. But he remembered what Landean had said about staying put. Besides, if they were still there and he went running across the clearing, he might get shot. *No, better to wait for Landean*, he thought. *I'd better play it safe.*

What seemed like an eternity was actually only about fifteen minutes. Long enough, however, for Mos to empty his bladder twice. The adrenaline was running through him so fast that he couldn't help it.

Landean was waiting patiently, but he too had to empty his bladder. His excuse would be the coffee, but in all honesty, after twenty years of chasing poachers, he still got just as excited as the first time he had apprehended a night hunter.

He could see movement now coming towards him. He waited. Shortly later, he could see two shadowy figures and they were dragging something. He waited until they were about four feet away. He turned his flashlight on and stepped out in front of them. "Game warden! Hold it! You're under arrest."

The one with the flashlight froze in his tracks. His eyes were growing larger and larger by the moment. He was speechless. The one with the rifle dropped his hold on the deer and bolted out across the clearing towards Mos.

When Landean hollered "Game warden," Mos' heart jumped into his throat. He immediately started out on a dead run to where Landean was and then stopped. He could see something moving and it was coming towards him. He crouched down low and waited. "Stop! Game warden!" Mos hollered at the same time as he tackled him and knocked him to the ground.

Mos was agile and strong, and had no difficulty subduing him. Since he was only an assistant warden, he couldn't legally arrest him, nor did he have any handcuffs. While he still had him pinned to the ground, he said, "If you behave yourself, I won't handcuff you. Make any trouble and I'll lock these around your wrists so tight that it'll take a cutting torch to get 'em off again."

The bluff worked and he relaxed. "Okay, okay. I won't give you any trouble."

Mos released his head and arms and stood up, picking up the rifle at the same time. They walked across the clearing to where Landean was. His light was still on. The man was still in a state of shock, unable to say anything at all.

The closest lockup was in Farmington and that was a long ride. The sun had just come up as they were getting back into their car at the jail. "How about some breakfast? I think we've earned it," Landean said.

"That's all right by me," Mos replied, half asleep already.

When breakfast was finished, they started the long drive home. Landean had bought a new '54 Ford car just the month before and the ride was excellent. In those earlier years, game wardens had to provide their own vehicles. Mos was exhausted and he laid his head against the back of the seat. But he was so excited that he couldn't relax. "Earl, don't you ever get tired?"

"Yeah, I sure do. About the last week of deer season, the odd hours we have been working and the sleepless days only goes with the uniform. You get used to it after awhile, though."

"I suppose." Mos started reliving the last few hours in his mind again. Mos had not known that anyone else was in the orchard until they had fired. Then his senses came alive. It was almost as if he was a part of the scene and the event. His hearing was more acute and he could almost see through the veil of darkness. Although he had been excited and adrenaline was surging through his body, he remained calm and the thought of fear or being afraid never entered his head. "Earl, do you ever get afraid? I mean...like tonight, you didn't know who those men were or how they would react to being caught. Do you ever find yourself hesitating a little too long because you're afraid?"

Landean didn't answer immediately and Mos could tell that he was pondering on it. When he did answer, it wasn't what he expected. "How did you feel out there, Mos? Were you afraid?"

"No, I guess not. There wasn't time for that. I was excited though. Hell! I was gawd-damned excited!"

"That's how it is with me, too. When I see something

happening, all my thoughts are concentrated on how to best handle it. I won't say there haven't been times though that things haven't been a little ticklish. But not until it was all over and as I thought back on the possibilities did I become concerned. You'll never get used to it, Mos, but you'll learn to be patient. You have to learn to be, if you're going to do this job."

"All poachers aren't as cooperative as these were, are they?"

"No. Some of them you have to fight, but only a few though. Most of them will give up once they're caught. That is until they ome to court, then they've manufactured quite a story.

"There are three types of poachers, Mos. The first is someone who does it to feed his family. This type will generally keep quiet and not brag about it. The second type is no more than a common thief. He kills for the sport of killing. He steals from everybody. The third type is somewhat less notorious than the second, but he still does it for kicks to see how much he can get away with. I sometimes have compassion for the man who takes to feed his family, but not for the others."

"Don't you get concerned with working alone and maybe coming up against a group that you call thieves or the ones who do it for the thrill. Can't they be dangerous?"

"Yes, but there's one thing I've learned since I've been a warden. Most people are a little timid of the darkness. I've seen cases where the bigger and meaner the culprit is supposed to be, the more afraid of the dark he is. Most people respect the fact that we live most of our career in the woods and the darkness and most of the time alone. Very few people feel comfortable alone in the woods whether in daylight and least of all, in darkness. "The most important thing to remember is that you must remain in control at all times. Once the violated is controlling the situation, then you're beaten."

"How do you accomplish that? By being tough?" Mos asked.

"Each situation will require a different tactic. With some, you'll have to be domineering, while others a little brazen.

And with a few, you'll have to have a little sympathy and understanding. You'll never know until you have made the initial contact. When doing this, it's best to catch them off-guard by either making light conversation or perhaps by saying something like, 'Hey, fellows, that's a nice mess of trout.' There are times when just scaring the living hell out of them works best. There's no hard and fast rule. You'll learn as you go along."

Mos wasn't aware of it yet, but those few days with Warden Earl Landean had set the forge for his mold. He had seen how a true game warden carries himself and reacts to situations and the patience that was required. But most of all, there were those few words of wisdom that were spoken on the return trip to Eustis.

* * * *

Mos spent everyday, as it turned out, working with Landean. He was a good pupil and Landean enjoyed his company. During those few weeks, Mos had developed a greater appreciation for his new friend for what he did and for what his job entailed. He knew now that he wanted the whole thing and not just to be an assistant. Landean was watching Mos very closely during those weeks. He thought of Mos as his friend. After that night in September when they had arrested those two poachers in the apple orchard, he had formed a very favorable impression of Mos. He got excited about catching poachers, without losing his cool or his patience. He definitely enjoyed the work and didn't mind the long hours. He was very capable. "Mos, there's a new warden school coming in spring. Would you be interested?"

"Would I? I guess maybe I would! How do I apply?" Mos said all in one breath.

"Well, it just so happens that I have an application. It's in the glove box. Yeah, that's the one. Fill it out and send it to the address at the bottom."

The last week of deer season finally came and Mos now understood what Landean had meant. Snow covered the ground, it was cold, he was tired, and he'd had his fill of hunters. He'd had enough. As they were on their way home the last night after finding a hunter, Landean said, "Mos, you'll have no problem with the training. What you get out of it will depend on how much effort you're willing to give. It's not difficult, if that's what you really want. Remember two things: first, find a good woman who won't squawk too much about an empty bed or that she'll have to re-warm your supper for you. Second and more importantly, when you're assigned to a district, don't go in demanding respect. People won't like it. Don't expect people to respect you until you have earned it."

* * * *

The training was at Camp Keyes in Augusta. It wasn't exactly what Mos was expecting. The instructors were game wardens, not professors. Landean was one of the instructors and this gave Mos a chance to talk with his friend. Even though they were friends, Landean didn't show any favoritism in his class.

Before he had left for warden school, Mos took his money that he had saved while he was in the army and bought a new '55 Ford. It was like Landean's but newer and fire engine red. This was his first car and he was proud of it. Instead of going home on the weekends, he generally would go for a ride to the coast in his new car until he took a fateful trip one weekend to Sherbrooke, Quebec. Originally he had planned to go only as far as the White Mountains in New Hampshire. It was an ominous beginning. He realized it or rather he sensed that this wouldn't be just an ordinary drive. When he got as far as the White Mountains, he kept going. Some invisible force to go to Canada drew him. By the time he arrived in Sherbrooke, it was really late, so he got a motel room. But it was useless. His mind was traveling a thousand miles an hour, racing out of control. He was excited and he didn't know why. Finally, he got out of bed, got dressed, and went out into the night air. It was early spring, but the nights were still cool. He walked along the sidewalk one way and then turned around and walked the other direction.

As the sun came up, he was sitting in a café, drinking coffee and eating a pair of moufflet. He was not tired but puzzled why he was there in Sherbrooke. The answer had to be there because the urge to keep going the night before was gone now.

When he had finished his petit dejeuner, he went back to his hotel room. He showered, shaved, and put on some clean clothes. Later that afternoon while window shopping, he met a young lady doing the same exact thing. "Bonjour," he said.

"Bonjour," the girl replied.

They had coffee together and spent the rest of the weekend together. On his return trip to Camp Keyes, all he could think about was the beautiful girl he had met in Sherbrooke. He was in love. He returned to Sherbrooke every weekend.

Renée came from a similar background as his own. Her family lived on a small farm in the country. To supplement his income, Renée's father worked in the woods during the winters. She was a quiet, reserved woman and Mos found that strikingly appealing. She never put on airs and was never overly concerned about other people's affairs. She was not a shallow person but entertaining and fun to be with.

Renée's family liked Mos and he was readily accepted in the family. One weekend, after several visits, Mos and Renée talked about getting married. She didn't fully know what a game warden was or what Mos would do for work as a warden. But that only mattered a little. They were in love with each other and any place he chose to live would be fine with her.

She came to his graduation and that same weekend they got married. At the graduation, Mos was told he was being sent to Patten and that he had to be there and be prepared to go to work by June fifteenth. That gave he and Renée three days to get married, pack what they could, and find a place to live. The honeymoon would have to wait.

* * * *

Slowly, Mos' conscious mind awakened. At first he didn't realize where he was. Then little by little, reality began to focus and he remembered that he was on his way to Augusta to sign his retirement papers. He looked around and suddenly realized that he was already in Augusta. "How in hell did I get here? I don't remember." He had been daydreaming about his life and how his destiny had been forged, so he was totally oblivious to everything else.

"Hello, Mos. Long drive?" Chief Warden Elma Ingraham asked. "You look awful melancholy. Are you having second thoughts about retiring?"

"Hi, Elma. No, I've just been daydreaming."

It didn't take long to say that he was all done. There wasn't many around that he knew anymore. He was the oldest warden. The others had all retired earlier. It would all be over officially at midnight. Mos Jalbert would once again return to a civilian life. He had spent the better part of his life as a game warden. Now he would have more time for Renée.

"Someone from the division headquarters will be around in a few days, Mos, to pick up the rest of your gear. Any plans for the future?" Elma asked.

"No, not really. I want to spend a lot of time with my wife, Renée, and I'd like to visit with Earl Landean," Mos said.

"Who did you say?"

"Earl Landean; he's a retired warden where I grew up," Mos said and then said to himself, *How could you know him anyway? He was before your time.* With a handshake and a last goodbye, Mos left the Augusta building and headed for home. But first he had to stop for gas and some lunch.

As he signed the gas slip, the attendant handed him back his state credit card and he suddenly thought how strange it would be not to use it any longer after thirty years. *Well, at least I won't have to put up with the off-hand remarks and jokes about using it for myself or to fill someone else's car.* Finally he was on his way north again. *How strange*, he thought, *to suddenly be so happy.* And he was. He had just retired from a career that for the last thirty years had demanded more of him to the point of not seeing his wife and family. But during that career, he had accomplished exactly what he wanted. He didn't actually work at the job, but rather he lived it. He became the job. But now that was over and it was time to get one with the rest of his life. What would he do? Would he become just another statistic and succumb to a rocking chair and die prematurely of a heart attack?

These thoughts were quickly erased from his mind as he could hear Landean saying, "Don't demand respect...earn it." He had revered Earl Landean, from his early childhood at King and Bartlett camps to the present. Landean had been his mentor from which he had forged his own standards and his own principles.

With the thought of Landean in his mind, the hypnotic effect from the tires easily sent him back again to those early years of his career.

* * * *

Mos and his new wife Renée didn't have any time for a honeymoon. There were two days left in which to find some place to live in the town of Patten. Their first order of business was to get a mailing address. "Here you go, sir," the postmaster said as she handed Mos two postal keys. "Your box number is thirteen."

"Thank you. It sounds auspicious, like a warning."

"Think nothing of it. Where will you be living?"

"Don't know for sure yet. We haven't had time to look around," Mos said.

"There's a nice place for sale up the road a ways. It belongs to an old timer. I hear that he wants to sell out and move back in the woods. You might try him. There's also an apartment available behind the hardware store, right here on Main Street."

"Where's this place for sale that you were talking about?

Maybe we'll go see the gentleman and look it over."

"About three miles out on the left. It's a white house next to the brook. It's just beyond Larry Bottel's place," the postmaster said.

It was just what they were looking for, only it would be a month before they could move in. They rented the apartment in the center of town until then.

Mos was anxious to go to work and prowl the hills and rivers, arresting violators of the fish and game laws. Like all new officers just out from their training, Mos was no exception when he said, "By God, I'll give these poachers a desultory taste of hell. I'll show them I'm nobody's fool."

That's how he went at his job at first. He came up with some good cases sure enough, but he was taking everything he found. There was no color, only black and white to the laws. Either they were broken or not. There was no in-between; no room for common sense or judgement. He was young and he was eager.

He worked long and diligent hours, but the locals were beginning to hate him. Most of all, his wife could sense the changing attitudes. Nobody spoke to her as they met her on the street and most just seemed to ignore her. Mos wasn't as sensitive. Generally nobody saw him until it was too late and they had too many fish or an early deer. He didn't care or maybe he just didn't know how the townspeople felt about him.

He worked every day. He was always putting his job before Renée. In desperation one rainy night as they lay in bed, Renée said, "Mos, we've got to talk." She told him about listening to people talk about him and how hated he had become. That he wasn't only doing his job, but rather his attitude about it and the people in the area had to change.

He listened, but only half heard what she was saying. He brushed it off as trifle. "Nonsense," he said, "It's just that I'm doing my job, that's all."

"No, that isn't all," she protested. But he wasn't listening to any of that foolishness. It was time to sleep.

He was out of bed the next morning before daylight and on his way to Nesowadnehunk Lake. It was fly fishing only and this was the last big weekend of the summer.

Once there, he unloaded his canoe and pushed off into the cool air. It was still early and the campers were probably still in bed since no one was fishing yet. The only evidence of life besides himself was a family of loons after their morning breakfast. The water was calm and the fog was just beginning to rise off the surface. "God, how I like this," he said out loud. Just then he noticed two men in a canoe, paddling towards a driftwood cove. "Hah!" he said with enthusiasm, "suspects."

The two fishermen quietly set anchor and began casting behind an old stump. Mos was watching the activity through his binoculars and at the same time, he could hear a voice inside his head. It was Landean's voice and he was saying, "Don't demand their respect, Mos. The townspeople won't like it. Earn their respect and it will be easier."

Landean had been his mentor and he listened to those spoken words, it seemed like only yesterday. From that moment, he began to change his attitude and brazen tactics, and he began to treat the people like he would want to be treated by a game warden. This didn't mean he became soft by any means, only that he wasn't so flamboyant about what he was doing. He treated people with respect and little by little, the townspeople began to respect him and they were talking with Renée once again. She was pleased. By this time, their first child had been born. They had a boy named Emil Michael Jalbert.

That fall while checking deer hunters in the Pleasant Lake area, Mos came across two out-of-state hunters apparently going home. They had all their gear packed away and their rifles were stored in carrying cases. Their clothes were clean and not the usual kind worn on a hunting trip. It was only Wednesday but they were obviously going home. This perked Mos' curiosity and he began to listen to what wasn't being said. Then he remembered watching Landean as he talked with the New Yorkers at King and Bartlett. As he approached their pickup, he candidly looked in the back and at their camping equipment. It looked as if things had been loaded hurriedly.

"Hello. Don't tell me you're calling it quits and going home already?"

"Yeah," the driver said, "we didn't have much luck. Never saw a thing. You sure you have any deer here?"

"Where did you hunt?" Mos asked.

"Oh, behind where the old lumber camps used to be by the brook."

"I'd like to see you licenses please."

"Yes, sir. Any problem?" the driver asked.

"No, just a routine check. I ask to see all hunters' licenses. You know," Mos began, "I was hunting back here once in the same area you probably were. I never saw so many deer tracks. It had snowed the day before. Early that morning, I saw this big buck and I fired. He dropped out of sight. I walked over and by the time I got there, he'd jumped up and ran off. I followed his tracks until it was dark and I never did lay eyes on him again. Saw other deer, but I kind of hated to leave that one to die."

"We hunted here three days ago." *Three days ago,* Mos thought, *was Sunday. One bad slip.*

"We saw deer everywhere but couldn't get a shot off." *Second bad slip,* thought Mos.

"Did you see anyone else back in here?" Mos asked.

The passenger started to say "Yes," Mos thought, but the driver cut him short and said, "No, we didn't see anyone at all." *Third slip,* thought Mos.

While Mos was talking with the two, he could occasionally smell the odor of a recently used outhouse and decided that one of them probably had a gas problem. It was happening too frequently and the pungent odor reminded him of a time when he had eaten too much deer liver and he had the farts for two days.

This man has been eating deer meat. Mos was sure of it,

along with the other information he was getting. "I'll play along a little longer," he said to himself.

"Did you see anything of a wounded bear?" Mos asked. There wasn't any bear except for what he was making up. "Earlier this fall, someone wounded one back in here and now it has become a problem to the camp owners on the lake."

"We didn't see any, but Joe here said he talked to one fellow who did." *Another slip. Earlier they said they hadn't seen anyone else.*

As Mos looked at the licenses, he walked to the back of the truck. There in plain sight was blood and hair. He was satisfied now. "Would you step out? I think perhaps I'd like to see what you have under all this stuff."

Reluctantly, they began to unload and there in the bottom was a six-point buck. It was cold to the touch and so stiff that the leg joints wouldn't bend.

"This looks pretty good, considering how you didn't have much luck or even see anything. Now I want the truth and we'll stay right here until I'm satisfied that I've got it," Mos said as he sat down on the tailgate.

"Oh, I almost forgot. Joe got this deer just this morning," the driver said, even though the deer was stiff and cold.

There was no smile or change in his voice as Mos said, "I'm not satisfied."

"Okay, okay, I'll tell you. I bought it this morning."

"Who did you buy it from?"

"I don't know his name. He said he once worked in here, lumbering several years ago. Said he was almost caught by a warden one Christmas day. He drives a red Chevy pickup," the driver admitted. "You going to arrest us?"

"That depends." Mos paused before continuing, "Depends if I get the rest of the story. Is he still here?"

"Should be unless there's another way out. He was driving into the head of the lake, I think he said."

"How much did you pay for it?"

"Fifty dollars."

"The deer is too stiff and cold to be today's deer. Did he come in this morning?"

"Yes, he said he shot it on the way in," the driver said.

"How did you pay him? I mean, what were the bills?"

"Fifty...one fifty dollar bill."

"Well, I guess you fellows were pretty honest this time. I'm satisfied that you're telling me the truth, so you're free to go. I'm going to take the deer," Mos said and grabbed the deer's hind legs and pulled it from the pickup. Mos left the two to reload their stuff and he headed towards the head of the lake. He had heard enough, so he figured he knew who he was after. It had to be Jason Smith. He had heard about the camps at the head of the lake. But those were before he came to the area. He knew Jason and his father had worked there and he knew that Jason wouldn't be above the law to sell a deer to an out-of-stater. Now he had to find him.

He didn't go more than a mile before he came across the red Chevy pickup parked beside the road. It was the right one and it belonged to Jason. There was no rifle but there was a partially empty box of .308 shells on the seat. He looked around and said to himself, *Have to wait. There's no other way to do it.*

He backed his car back around the turn to get it out of sight, then he found a comfortable spot behind a cedar tree where he could see Jason's truck.

Unbeknownst to Mos, when he started his car to turn it around, he wasn't the only person around. Jason had been out on one of the twitch trails he had used years ago. In fact, he had been hunting in the same swamp where the ole buck had given him the chase that day. Well, he heard the motor start and was naturally curious. Instead of storming right out to his truck, he waited at the edge of the trail, behind some trees. He heard the motor stop but didn't hear a door open or close. *That's strange,* he thought. But in a few minutes he understood why. There, walking up the road, was the warden. He watched instead of stepping out to greet him like most people would have done. He watched as the warden hid behind a cedar tree. *Hmm, two people can play at this game, ole fox. I'll just wait until you leave.*

Mos still didn't know Jason was anywhere near. He didn't hear him and couldn't see him. He blended in too well with the forest with his green jacket and wool pants. He waited and waited. All the time, different possibilities were going through his head of why Jason was there and what he was up to now. He thought for sure he would catch him red-handed at something.

Jason, too, waited and waited. He had lost sight of the warden as soon as he dropped behind the cedar tree, but he knew that he was still there. The thought that perhaps the warden had learned about him selling the buck to those two guys never crossed his mind. *What in Christ is he up to? This is a salty one. Perhaps I've underestimated him.*

Jason waited and darkness crept in. Soon he couldn't see the cedar tree and he began to think that maybe he had mistaken and the warden wasn't hiding there or that he had left long ago. He waited another hour before stepping out from behind the trees. His rifle was unloaded and he walked towards his truck. But before he got there, he saw the warden. He was standing in front of his truck, leaning on the hood.

"Hello, Jason. A little late, aren't you?" Mos asked.

"Yeah, by gee-hokey. I wasn't sure if I'd get out or not. I wounded a buck a while back and he led me on a chase all through the swamp. He got me turned around a little. What brings you out this way?" Jason asked, trying to change the temporal situation.

"Just checking. I heard something about some poaching going on out this way."

"Is that right?" Jason sounded genuinely surprised. "Did you find him yet?"

"Not sure yet." Now it was Mos who wanted to change the tempo. "Did you see anyone else in the woods?"

"No, I was the only one."

"I met two out-of-staters going out. Said they were going home because they didn't have much luck."

"Oh, is that a fact," Jason said, trying to play it cool.

"Heard you shot a six-point buck earlier." Mos purposely left it at that to see what Jason's reaction would be.

"Is that so?"

God, this is like trying to get blood from a turnip, Mos thought. "Yeah, I've got that six-point buck in the back of my car. I took it from those two fellows. Now I'm going to ask you for that fifty dollar bill in your pocket."

"Here," he said as he fumbled in his pocket and pulled out the money. "Suppose now you're going to arrest me."

"No, but I'm going to summons you for selling a deer."

"What's the fine?"

"I'll recommend to the court that it not be any more than what it was sold for," Mos replied.

Jason put his rifle in his pickup while Mos wrote out the summons. "That's fair enough. I spent a lot of years in here. There were fifty-six men at these camps once."

"Where were they?" Mos asked.

"Oh, well they're all gone now. They were just up the road. There's nothing left now but a clearing." Jason went on telling Mos about the days of the woods crew and the camps. He had an audience and Mos was genuinely interested.

"I've heard a lot about you, Mos. Some of it was good... some not so good. I guess it's time I get home. Jerri might start to think I've been arrested. Need a ride?"

"That's okay. My car is just around the corner. Thanks for offering." Mos walked back to his car, feeling good about catching Jason. He was smiling from ear to ear. "He's not a bad fellow," Mos said to himself as he started his motor.

* * * *

Mos had started smoking. He tried a pipe at first, but he

didn't like the hot juices in his mouth. Then he tried cigars. There were some brands that had a nice aroma but these too were hot. Then one day a fellow warden asked if he would like one of his. "Sure, what is it?"

"It's made in Honduras. They're quite mild."

Mos never inhaled. He couldn't; the smoke hurt his lungs. But he still smoked. In fact, he was seldom seen without one clenched between his teeth. He smoked for something to do more than anything else. He didn't particularly like the taste the tobacco left in his mouth, but he found that chewing on a cigar relaxed him and he wasn't so tense.

The following year in September after Mos had caught Jason for selling the deer, the warden in Sherman Mills had received several complaints of someone night hunting off the Cold Brook Road in Sherman and had asked Mos to help him.

"Who is it? Do you know, Andy?" Mos asked.

"I'm not sure but I think it might be Jason Smith from over your way. I don't know who the other fellow is."

They met early that evening but as it turned out, they were in the wrong spot. About ten o'clock, there was one shot fired but it was further north. They sat there the rest of that night and towards daylight, they agreed that perhaps the next night they ought to move a little closer to where they had heard the shooting.

Jason, by this time, was living regularly at his home in Patten and traveled back and forth to work every day. This was hard on the deer population around town and it kept Mos busy with a lot of sleepless nights.

Well, Jason had a friend...Clyde Walker. Clyde was having trouble with his business and his wife was about to have a new baby. If it wasn't for the deer that he and Jason jacked every night, he wouldn't have any meat to eat and store away for the winter. "Jason," Clyde asked one day as he was standing around his shop watching him work, "I know where there's a nice bunch of deer. You interested?"

"Might be. Where are they?"

"You know where my old farm is on the Cold Brook Road in Sherman?" Jason nodded his head. "Well, just down the road from that a ways is the old schoolhouse. Behind that is an open clover field. Deer come in every night and feed."

They agreed to meet at Clyde's house at dark and have a little drink before going out. "Might as well leave your rifle here, Jason. I've got one made especially for jacking."

Clyde handed it to Jason and he turned it over and over, looking at it. It was a .33 Winchester with iron sights, a flashlight for spotting clipped to the barrel, and a smaller light clipped just behind the rear sight so he could see it in the dark.

Clyde had a notorious reputation for being a crack shot, especially at night even if the deer were running. He was proud of his rifle and because he liked Jason, he let him do the shooting that night. "Here, Jason, try her out tonight and see how you like it."

"I don't mind if I do," Jason replied.

Mos and Andy had left their car next to the field that Clyde had been talking about. They were on foot on top of the knoll when Clyde drove in around the old schoolhouse. From the knoll, they had no idea that there were deer in the field below them. They were lying down and out of sight. "Surely they'll come up here and hunt these back fields," Andy said.

That had been Clyde's intention, but as he swung the headlights into the clover field, there were deer lying down not more than fifty feet from them. Jason had the rifle loaded and out of the car before they stopped. Jason snapped on both lights and fired three shots. Three deer were dead and the others ran off.

To Mos, that first shot was just like turning on a light switch. It later became publicized that whenever Mos saw something happening or heard a shot at night, he'd take a deep draw on his cigar because of the adrenaline flowing through his veins. Of course the end glowed just like a beacon. This was an alarm to watch for.

The switch had been thrown with the first shot and Mos, with his long legs, was racing down the field towards the damned poachers. Andy was shorter and fell in behind Mos. He tried hard but he just couldn't keep up.

After that first shot, Jason saw the red beacon and knew all too well what that meant. If he didn't do something fast, ole Mos would have him locked up in jail before the night was over. "Jesus Christ, Clyde, here come the wardens! Two of them! Stay in the car! I'll grab these deer and throw them in back!" He grabbed the first one, a nice buck, and threw it in the back. Then he ran for the other two. No sense in letting them go to waste. They were both small does and he took them together, threw them in the back, and jumped in on top of them. "Let's go! Get the hell out of here!"

Mos was still a good hundred yards away and as the car started to swing around, he realized that they would probably escape his irrefutable wrath. He pulled out his .38 and shouted, "Stop or I'll shoot!" He pointed the revolver in the air and pulled the trigger.

Clyde heard the hollering and then Bang! He drove his foot to the floor and the car took off hell bent for election, down across the field. Each time Mos fired, the car seemed to buck on its own and leap into the air. By the time Mos had fired the third shot, Clyde and Jason were back on the paved road and going.

Clyde had a relative who lived close by and had told them, "Any time you boys get into trouble, feel free to come here if you like." Tonight they managed to escape on their own so Uncle Sandy's help wasn't needed. The deer were unloaded and in the cellar before Jerri knew what was happening.

"What have you got down there, Jason?" Jerri wanted to know.

"We've each got a deer and one to give away." It might have made more sense and probably would have been less expensive if they had kept the third deer for themselves, but there weren't any freezers in those days. The only way of preserving the meat was to can it and that took time; enough time for the other deer to spoil. "Better give it away so it won't spoil," Jason said.

They were nervous for about two days, wondering if Mos and that other warden would come looking for them at their homes. By the third day, both Clyde and Jason were feeling kind of smug about it and decided to venture out again that night. The moon was full, so they could foot jack without a light.

In the meantime, Mos and Andy had spent every night in those fields. By now, they knew every inch of it. After that first incident when Clyde and Jason had gotten away, they had decided to use that same hiding place for their car in order to eliminate the possibility of making any more tire tracks. They were in the field each evening before dark, thinking perhaps they'd be more likely not to be seen.

So that's how it was on that third night after the previous caper. Mos and Andy were standing in the shadows along a small field not too far from Clyde's old farm.

Clyde picked up Jason at his house that night, but before leaving, Jason insisted that they have a little warmer upper first.

"Just in case, Clyde, that it might be a cold night."

"We'll have the luck of the Irish with us tonight, Jason. Just you wait and see."

Clyde left his car at his old farm. It was abandoned and falling in. They walked through the woods to the clover field and there was just one deer there. It was a huge buck. It started to run, but Clyde up and fired and the deer went down. It was a running shot and it caught the buck right behind the left ear and broke its neck.

"Well that was pretty good, Clyde," Jason said.

"We'll walk back across the orchard to my car. We're apt to get a surprise there, too." Surprise they would but not quite what they were expecting. When they got to the outer edge of the orchard, Clyde stopped and waited. "It's all clear," he whispered, "you snap the light on and I'll shoot."

Jason snapped the light on and it shined right in Mos and

Andy's faces. They weren't more than thirty feet away. Clyde ran out around Jason and in the excitement, he got the barrel of his rifle caught in the crouch of an apple tree and there he was. He backed up, trying to free his rifle and one of them, he never knew for sure which one, hit him across the knee with that damn big flashlight that they carry and that was the end of Clyde.

Jason, on the other hand, saw what was happening and he took to running in the other direction. He plowed through some alder bushes and lost his hat. He kept on running though. He would come back for the hat later. Right now he had a Jesusly lot more to worry about.

He remembered Uncle Sandy's offer and turned in that direction. He ran like the wrath of God was behind him. There was a building sitting off to one side and he decided that would be a safe place to hide. He opened the door and bolted in, but before he could close it, he was carried back outside on the back of a very excited and a very big pig. The first pig had knocked him over and when he stood up, the second pig went between Jason's legs and he rode out on it backwards. He didn't go far before he fell off. Worried now more than ever that Mos must be close behind him, he ran to the next building. He could see that there was chicken wire all around it, but he was so excited that the wire never registered the implications.

He opened the door to the hen house and was immediately attacked by a bunch of frightened hens. There was no other choice, so he had to go to the house. He didn't bother to knock. He opened the door and ran in. "Jason, what brings you around? Where's Clyde?"

"The wardens have him! Sandy, I need a place to hide. Can I stay here until morning?"

"Sure...sure thing. Might be best though if you waited in the cellar. My boy is sick and I'll be up with him for awhile."

"Thanks, Sandy." He opened the cellar door and started down the steps. The light was dim and he was all the way down before he saw it. It was the biggest dog that he had ever seen in his life. His nose was curled up and he was showing his teeth. The eyeteeth had to be two inches long, Jason thought, and he must weight at least two hundred pounds. He inched his way around him and found a shelf along one wall that went partway to the ceiling. He lay there for the night and every time he tried to move, that damn dog would stand up and show his teeth.

It was four in the morning before Sandy came downstairs. "What are you up there for, Jason?"

"That's got to be the biggest and meanest dog that I've ever seen."

Sandy laughed and affectionately scratched behind the dog's ear and said, "Oh, he won't hurt you. He only looks mean. Come on upstairs and have some coffee."

"Thanks, Sandy, but I'd appreciate a ride home."

"Okay, let's go," Sandy said.

It was still dark when Jason got home. Jerri was up. "Where have you been?" she scowled.

"Now don't get excited," he said and he sat down and told her the whole story. She laughed so hard that her sides were ready to cave in. She stopped laughing though when she looked out the window. "The wardens are here, Jason, and they have Clyde."

"Looks like they've got me this time. Better go out and so they don't go looking around in here." He put on his jacket and reached for his hat that wasn't there. Once outside, he said, "Good morning, boys. What can I do for you?" Mos stood there, holding Jason's hat in his hands.

"We've got Clyde right on the spot, Jason. I've got your hat but I can't prove that you were there. But I do know that you two poach together regularly. I'll tell you what we'll do. If you give yourself up and come in, I'll see that the court goes easy on you. That goes for both of you. If you don't, well...Clyde could get thirty days in jail and a two hundred dollar fine. What will it be, Jason?"

"I'll come in. What about Clyde? You going to haul him to jail?"

"No, you can get out here, Clyde," Mos said. Clyde opened the door and limped to the house.

"You boys like some coffee?" Jason asked.

"Thanks, but we're not done yet. There's a deer we've got to find and take care of," Mos answered.

"If you boys get any extra meat, I could sure use some," he laughed and waved goodbye.

After that caper, Jason had a little more respect for Mos Jalbert. "I'll have to find a way to outfox him," he said.

"Better leave him alone, Jason," Jerri said. "Haven't you had enough?"

* * * *

Jason's family was growing rapidly and to make ends meet, he had to spend more and more time working. He was sometimes as far away as Washington County and Brownville. Because of this, he didn't do much poaching close to home. He didn't stop by any means, but at least he wasn't a constant thorn in Mos' backside.

Mos was beginning to appreciate Jason, too. He couldn't condone his poaching, but through the years, he began to understand that it had at one time meant the difference between eating and not eating. Then he remembered his own life and that one day in particular when he had helped his father with a deer and Landean had stopped by not long after the deer had been taken care of.

Because of that understanding, he was inclined to occasionally offer a little clemency with two conditions: "Don't ever let me hear that you wasted even one mouthful of meat. If it gets back to me that I was lenient or soft and let you off, well, it will backfire and I'll come after you."

No one ever took that warning lightly and they were so afraid that they never mentioned it to their wives. It was such a well-kept secret that it was rumored through town once that the warden was slacking off and not arresting or even catching any jackers. The sources of these rumors were explanation enough and seldom were they ever believed. Because it was a well-known fact that Mos never slept at home and that he and his wife weren't seen together, some people began to believe that he and his wife had parted ways. If you were poaching, whether you were hunting or fishing, you kept a vigilant watch over your shoulder because sooner or later you were bound to meet up with Mos Jalbert.

It was true, however, that Mos didn't spend much time at home. There were times when he couldn't remember what his wife's perfume smelled like or how comforting it was to lay beside her in bed. They had another baby, a girl this time. When she was born, a neighbor had to take Renée to the hospital because Mos was at Matagamon Lake searching for a drowned fisherman. He didn't know until Re'ann was two days old that his wife had had the baby.

Renée was one of those unusual and very special women who understood and deeply loved her husband. For some unknown reason, Mos pushed himself at his work, always trying to do it all and never looking for excuses. She didn't understand it completely, but she did respect her husband's need and she supported him. He was doing what he enjoyed and there'd be that day when he would retire.

Jason had his turn or misfortune and bad luck. His equipment had broken down and before he could get it fixed and working again, the land company laid everyone off. He had repair bills to pay and no job. There were mouths to feed at home and no money to buy groceries.

Night after night, Jason went out on foot from his house. He didn't have enough money to buy gas for his truck. Each night, Mos was there watching, making sure the deer wasn't wasted.

For several months, all Jason's family lived on was deer meat and biscuits. One night on one of those escapades, Jason shot three deer. Mos was there again and watched Jason dress them off. A voice sounded in the stillness of the night, "Use that,

Jason, and don't let me hear that you sold any of it." That was all that was said and there wasn't another sound as Jason finished his work. But he knew the voice and respected the warning. He watched as the red glow disappeared.

That winter, Jason had gotten a contract from Sherman Lumber Company and was cutting in the Swift Brook area. Jerri had also gotten a job as cook in the high school in town. Jason's creditors were understanding and only compounded his interest instead of repossessing his equipment. Actually, what would a bank do with a crawler tractor?

Jason was working seven days a week, trying to catch up on his payments and put a little away for his family. In spite of his poaching ways, Jason was a family man and he cared about the well-being of each and every one of them.

One Saturday in early December, Jason was working alone and while he was twitching a load of logs out, he noticed a set of snowshoe tracks that headed for Swift Brook and crossed his twitch trail. At the time, he didn't think anything of it. *Probably just a beaver trapper,* he thought.

At the end of the day, he parked his crawler and cleaned the snow from around the lags. He looked around for the returning snowshoe tracks but couldn't find any. Still, he wasn't concerned. The town was closed to trapping so probably whoever it was they were being careful not to be seen. He got in his pickup and started for home. He went only a quarter of a mile and found Mos' car. *What do you suppose the ole fox is up to now? He probably hid in the bushes all day hoping to catch me shooting a moose,* he said as he shrugged it off and went home.

Mos had his snowshoes strapped on and had started towards Swift Brook. He had gotten word that someone had set some beaver traps and that area had been closed to trapping. He heard Jason's tractor coming and hurried across the road and out of sight. Jason wasn't a trapper and Mos wasn't actually suspecting him. When he heard Jason's tractor coming towards him, Mos ran for cover out of habit.

He waited behind a spruce thicket until Jason had unhitched his load and was on his way back for another load. Then he snowshoed onto the brook and headed upstream. He hadn't gone very far when he came to a beaver colony. And sure enough, someone had traps set. He unfastened his straps and stepped out of his snowshoes and set them aside. He brushed the snow off the ice. The ice was black and not too thick. He knelt down to look through the ice to see if he could see a trap. He could see one all right. The water wasn't deep either. As he was reaching for his axe to chop away the ice, the ice suddenly broke and Mos fell in. Instinctively, he reached out to break his fall and when he did, he caught his left hand in the trap. The jaws of the trap closed around his thumb. Panic started to rack through his body. He made himself calm down. He took a deep breath and tried to compress both the trap springs. He could compress one but not the other without using two hands. He tried standing on one spring while reaching down with his free hand to compress the other side. He couldn't reach the spring without lifting his foot. He tried to unfastened the trap. It was wired solid and he couldn't break the wire.

In desperation he knew he had no other alternative but to cut his own thumb with his knife. He had taken his gun belt off back at his car and had put it in his backpack. His backpack was out of reach beside his snowshoes. The water was only to his knees but he knew when the cold started to set in later in the afternoon he'd probably freeze to death. No one knew where he was. He had told Renée he would be home later in afternoon.But when he didn't come home, she would only think that he had been delayed or something—a fresh blood trail in the snow or a shot echoing down a valley—but she wouldn't worry. There had been many times through the years when he had to stay away from home. His only hope now was Jason. Would he be curious enough to follow his snowshoe tracks? Probably not.

Mos could do nothing but wait. The sun was setting below the tree line. Jason would be stopping work before long. Mos listened intently to the noise of Jason's tractor. He would try hollering but he would have to wait until Jason shut the engine off. He could hear the chainsaw. "He must be at the yard," Mos said aloud. The saw stopped. Then the tractor's engine stopped. Mos hollered again and again. His throat hurt but he kept hollering for help until he knew Jason would have left for home.

Mos sat on the ice and thought, "What a way to die." The sky had clouded over and fog was setting in. A warm front was coming in from the south. For Mos, it might be a chance of survival for the night at least. The trap had been set in front of a stump. There was dry grass around it and some dry sticks. He gathered together as much dried grass as he could and broke away dry sticks and dug at the stump for dry splinters of wood. The dry grass ignited like a kerosene wick and soon the dry sticks were burning and snapping. Little by little, the stump started to burn. As the snow around the stump melted from the fire, the water soaked into the dry wood. The stump smoked and smoldered, but it was burning. What a relief. Mos had almost forgot about his hand in the trap.

For now at least, he knew he would be okay. The warm southerly air blew all night. The temperature rose steadily. Except for his legs and his left arm, he was quite comfortably warm. He knew in the morning when Jason saw his car still parked in the same spot that he would know that he was in a fix and would come looking for him. Any woodsman would do the same. Mos knew there was a wide streak in Jason's character that would make him concerned about his wellbeing. Even if Mos was a damned warden. Behind that mask, Jason cared.

Morning came and with it, a new hope that he would soon be out of this fix. The sun was above the tree tops and it was still getting warmer. It was unseasonably warm. Mos listened for the sound of Jason's snowshoes coming up the brook or for his tractor starting up, but there was nothing. As long as the weather remained warm, he knew that he would be okay. For awhile that is. He wasn't sure how serious his thumb was. He had lost all feeling in that hand. If the cold was to settle in at dark, in his condition, he knew he could not last until morning.

During the long day, thoughts of his family and especially of Renée were constantly running though his mind. There were moments when he felt guilty for spending so much time away from home. He had seldom ever had the opportunity to go to his son's little league games or watch his daughter perform in the school play. He had been called out that evening to deliver a death message to a party that was staying overnight in an ice fishing shack on a remote lake. But most of all, he was feeling guilty for not spending time with Renée.

Doubts about Renée's devotion focused then at the forefront of his thoughts. Had she really been happy being married to a man she seldom saw? Or was she only pretending for his benefit? She never complained about his absence or about anything for that matter. *She deserves more,* Mos concluded. "I wouldn't fault her if she were to pack up and leave after this. I couldn't blame her," he said out loud. He decided that he wasn't being rational.

The snow was turning to slush on top of the ice. It was getting so warm. Darkness came and the temperature was still unseasonably warm. Mos tried to revive the fire but there wasn't anything within reach that he could toss on the smoldering stump. There wasn't much left of that either. He was tired and hungry. He knew he could fall asleep easy enough, but he didn't dare to take the chance of slipping into the water any further. If he got any wetter, he wouldn't survive even a warm night in his difficult situation.

He sang out loud, then talked to himself to keep from falling asleep and slipping in the water. When that got boring, he howled like a coyote. Off in the distance, a coyote answered. Mos howled again and the coyote continued to answer. He kept this up for awhile as the coyote kept getting closer.

By daylight of this day, Mos was exhausted and an excruciating pain was working its way up his left arm. He was alive though and he knew he couldn't survive another night.

* * * *

The next day, the weather warmed up so that he knew he shouldn't be driving over the softened woods road. It would rut it up too bad. So he stayed home and caught up one some needed work around the house.

The next morning, the boss at Sherman Lumber called and asked Jason not to use the road again that day and to spread the word to his crew. He did and then went down to the gas station to fill his fuel barrels. "Hey, Jason, heard about Mos?"

Harry asked.

"No, what?"

"He hasn't been home now for two days."

"So, that's not too strange with him being a warden," Jason replied.

"I suppose, but his wife expected him home two days ago."

Jason paid for the fuel and started home. But he didn't go very far before he stopped right in the middle of the road. He had a funny feeling; pins and needles were sticking into his flesh. It started in his toes and worked all the way up his spine. He thought about what Harry had said and then he remembered the snowshoe tracks that headed for Swift Brook but didn't come back out. Mos' car was parked near the woods yard. Without further hesitation, he turned around and drove to his wood yard near Swift Brook.

Mos' car was still there and it hadn't been moved. He knew that Mos was in trouble. Jason left his truck parked in the road and began running, following Mos' snowshoe tracks. The warm weather had softened the snow and the going was tiring, but Mos was in trouble.

It was strange when one looks at it and even to Jason in his later years, why had he been so concerned about Mos' isappearance and the possibility of him being in a bad fix. There was a bond that had formed between the two—the poacher and the warden. It was an unusual kind of bond, but nevertheless, it was there. Never in Jason's life though would he ever admit to anyone that Mos was his friend. "Nonsense," he'd say, "I would've helped anyone."

The snowshoe tracks went out onto the stream, but by now, the ice was too soft to risk it. He followed along the bank. He felt okay as long as the tracks were visible. He was getting tired, but he kept the pace, never breaking his stride. He followed the stream around the next bend and stopped in his tracks. Up ahead, only about a hundred feet or so, was a man standing in the water. The ice or what was left of it, was up to his knees. He couldn't see his face but he'd know that silhouette anywhere. He'd seen it enough to know that it was Mos. He was alive but why in hell was he standing in the water.

He walked carefully along the bank, trying to be quiet to see what Mos was up to. When he was beside him, he stopped. Mos was just standing there bent over with one arm in the water.

It was strange. "Hey, Mos, are you okay?"

Mos lifted his head and said, "I'm not standing in this water because it feels good. I got my hand caught in a beaver trap."

"Jesus Christ! How long have you been here?" Jason asked as he started out into the brook and then stopped.

"Two days."

Jason looked at Mos and hesitated. "Two days, huh? You must be in some kind of a fix if you've been standing in that water for two days. Well, it would have killed most men by now. You're a sultry one."

"You going to just stand there and gab or are you going to help me?"

"I'll help you, but first you've got to promise that once you're out you won't tell a soul that I came all the way in here to help a gawd-damned game warden."

"It's a promise," Mos replied. Jason knew Mos was good for his word. He broke through the ice but he wasn't paying much attention to the water. When he reached Mos, he could see that there was a number thirteen beaver trap locked around Mos' fingers. He reached into the water and compressed the springs while Mos pulled his hand out.

"Can you move your arm?"

"Yeah. It's starting to pain some but it's okay. It's my fingers that I'm worried about."

"How about your feet and legs? Can you walk?"

"Well, I'm cold and wet but I think they're okay. The water actually kept me from freezing. Thank God for the warm weather though," Mos added.

"Come on, I'll give you a hand getting out of here."

Jason supported Mos around the shoulders and helped him to shore. "You want to walk out or I can build a fire to warm you up?"

"By the looks of my hand, I'd probably better get the hell out of here and to a hospital." His hand and fingers were swollen and turning blue. The thumb had deep gashes on both sides from the teeth on the trap. The other fingers had luckily missed the teeth.

At first, Mos stumbled and fell down, but slowly, as the circulation came back to his legs, he was surprisingly agile. By the time they got back to Jason's pickup, he was even cracking jokes and laughing. "If you don't mind, Jason, I think I'd better go to the hospital in Millinocket."

"Okay, but hang on because this road is rough."

While Mos was in the emergency room, Jason called Renée and told her what happened. "He'll be fine, Renée. The doctors are going to keep him here for a couple of days so they can take care of his hand." For the most part, it wasn't too serious. The thumb though—was doubtful if they could save it. He'd be there for awhile anyhow, so Jason left and went home.

Almost a week later, Mos knocked on Jason's front door. In surprise to think that a warden would be calling on him and be out of uniform was too much for Jason. "Holy gee-hokey, Mos! Come in."

"I came by, Jason, to say thanks for helping me out back there."

"That's okay; think nothing of it. Have some coffee?"

"Sure, why not."

"Mos, how in hell did you ever get yourself in that mess to start with?"

"Wasn't too hard. I got word that someone was trapping Swift Brook and it's closed. Well, when I found the trap, I knelt down on the ice to see if I could see through the ice to see if there was a trap in it or if someone was just playing games. Before I knew what was happening, the ice broke around me and I went down. I caught my left hand in the trap and it closed on my hand. It didn't hurt much but I kind of got a sickening feeling when I realized that I couldn't get out. My axe was out of reach and I couldn't compress both of the trap springs with one hand. It could have been worse if the temperature had dropped during the night."

"How's your hand now?" Jason asked.

"The hand is okay, but they had to take the thumb. Not all of it, just the top half."

After Mos finished his coffee, he stood up and thanked Jason again. "Think no more of it," Jason said. "But don't think for a minute that this will end my poaching."

"I'd be disappointed if it did," Mos replied and they both laughed.

After that, people sometimes called him stubby, but never to his face. He was Mos Jalbert and would not be called by anything else.

Because of what Jason had done for Mos, word was circulating throughout the area that Jason could probably do just about anything, fish and game wise, that he wanted and get away with it. After all, Mos owed his life to Jason, so why wouldn't it seem reasonable that Mos wouldn't give Jason a break?

But that wasn't quite the truth for either of them. Jason had his pride and he didn't want any peripheral treatment. He would do what he had to do without favors from the law. Mos also had a similar attitude. He was first and foremost a game warden. If

Jason chose to break the law, he didn't feel compelled to treat him any differently that he would the next fellow. He realized that if it hadn't been for Jason, he probably would have died there, anchored to that trap. He felt a special fondness for Jason, but no, he wouldn't be compromised and he would soon have the chance to prove it.

Jason wasn't out to prove anything. It was more from the force of habit. But he was careless that day and Mos had gotten the better of him.

He had been on his way to work one morning and he had one of his sons with him. He had been cruising timber on the Webber grounds, preparing to start a new contract. He had stopped at Fifield's Variety for lunch. He'd left the house in such a hurry that morning that he'd forgotten to take anything to eat. That was his first mistake. It was early but Fifield was generally open for business for the woodcutters who got an early start. It was daylight but the wrong time of the year for legal deer hunting.

He hadn't driven but a short distance when a nice buck stepped into the road by the Crommett Spring. He stopped from instinct and almost decided not to but then he remembered seeing Mos' pickup in his driveway and felt pretty sure that the ole fox was still in bed. He didn't give it a further thought. He stepped out with his rifle, already loaded, and shot it in the neck. It dropped right on the road. Fearing that he might be seen by other woodcutters if he took the time to dress it off, he and his son loaded it into the back of the pickup and kicked some dirt over the blood.

Well, that shot echoed through the countryside and retired Game Warden Kevin Lewis had just moments earlier walked out of his camp on Lower Shin Pond and onto the porch and was relieving himself when he heard the rifle shot. It sounded like it came from the CC road. Kevin got dressed and went out and looked in both directions on the CC road. He didn't see anything, so he went to Fifield's and asked, "Ralph, did you see anyone go by about fifteen minutes ago?"

"Yeah, Jason Smith and his son stopped for lunch. Why? What's up?" Ralph asked.

"Oh, nothing. I was just checking. Ralph, can I use your phone?"

"Sure, but you'll have to use the one in the house. This one is busted."

Kevin called Mos and told him that he was sure Jason had just shot a deer and that he hadn't come back through yet. "If you want to catch him, Mos, I'll give you a hand and watch the road until he comes back. If he did shoot something, he'll surely have it with him."

Mos got there as fast as he could and met Kevin at Crommett Spring. They talked it over and plans were made. With their pickups hidden, they were prepared to wait all day if they had to. They were determined to catch him red-handed.

And it did take all day, too. Mos was in such a hurry that he didn't have time to take a lunch. It was almost dark and his stomach was growling. The next vehicle around the corner was Jason's. Kevin and Mos jumped into the road and stopped him.

Mos gave the pickup a quick inquisitive glance as he walked over to Jason's door. "What's up, boys?" Jason asked.

"Oh, nothing much. Would you mind stepping out for a minute?" Mos asked.

"No, not at all. Help yourself," Jason said.

Mos picked up his rifle and smelled the barrel. "You fire this today, Jason?"

"Yes, as a matter of fact, I did. About three or four hours ago I shot at an eagle and missed it."

"You ole bastard; wish you had hit it."

"What's this all about anyhow, Mos?"

"Someone shot a deer this morning."

"Is that right. Hope you catch the reprobate," Jason replied and as an afterthought, added, "Here, look in my toolbox if you want." He opened the lid, knowing full well that the deer was on the floor of the body, wrapped in his raincoat with tools piled on top.

Jason thought he had just about pulled it off when Mos walked to the back of the pickup and there on the bumper was a spot of blood. "Well, what's this? Looks like deer blood to me. Maybe we ought to have a closer look."

He found it and when he looked up, Jason was smiling. "Almost got away with it, ole fox."

"Well, look at it this way, Jason. With all the game that you haven't been caught for, this probably won't cost you more than a nickel a pound."

Jason couldn't help but laugh and say, "If this cost me more than a tenth of a cent a pound, I'll be surprised."

Mos grumbled and said, "I wish you had a moose with it."

There were no hard feelings. Jason had been careless and he was old enough to accept the responsibility of his own actions. The ribbing he got from his friends was worse than the fine. But the stories stopped though about the warden going easy on him because Jason had saved his life. Maybe in the long run the fine had been worth it.

Mos chuckled to himself as he drove home that night. But he knew deep in his heart that Jason would be laughing too and that the fine wouldn't do anything at all to slow down his poaching. It would only be a lesson—one that would make catching him again more difficult.

All of his working hours weren't spent chasing Jason. In fact, he never deliberately laid for him. The times that he happened to catch him, he had only been in that spot because of a complaint of poaching or he just happened to come upon him. That is, of course, except for the time Jason had been caught for illegal possession. There was so much illegal hunting going on then that he couldn't single any one of them out and lay for him. He prosecuted enough poachers to keep the others wary and constantly guessing to his whereabouts and looking over their shoulders. He had made a reputation for himself and slowly, people began to respect him and even a few, like Jason, considered him a friend.

He often remembered what Landean had said about earning respect and not demanding it. Now after fifteen years of service, he began to understand what Earl had been saying. Often times, even though Mos was at home, people naturally assumed that he would jump out of the bushes at any moment. They believed he was everywhere or that there was possibly more than just one Mos Jalbert. No one wanted to be his next victim.

* * * *

During his early years as a game warden, Renée was always concerned about his prolonged absences. She knew his work often required unusual hours, but she worried about him working alone all the time. No matter what he was doing, he always seemed to be alone. *What if he gets hurt? There won't be anyone to help him*, she found herself asking. He was always alone no matter if he was roaming some field at night or he was on an extended canoe trip, checking fishermen. She never really understood what drove him to seclusion and the absence of human companionship unless it was for the simple fact that he preferred it that way.

"Mos?" she asked questioningly, "Why is it that you always work alone? I know other wardens sometimes work together, but you never do. Why?"

"I do sometimes when I need it," he replied. "Most of the time I just prefer to be alone. I accomplish more that way."

That didn't ease her worry though. Her fears had come alive again when Mos had gotten caught in the beaver trap. "What if Jason hadn't been working that day and hadn't seen your car? He was the only person who knew where you were."

His answer was less than comforting. "But he did. Besides, that'll never happen again."

Finally she resigned herself and her worries to the fact that regardless of the risks and dangers, her husband would still do what he had to do. The only comfort she found was knowing that he was very woods wise and capable.

One day a friend asked Renée, "Doesn't it bother you that your husband is gone so much?"

"It used to but I've gotten used to it," was her only reply.

It is often said that a man's home is wherever he hangs his hat. In Mos' case, he could be called the exception. His home was actually outside in the grandeur of the wilderness. He became synonymous with the mention of anything minutely connected with the outdoors or hunting and fishing. The home that he came back to was his family's, Renée's and their children. He made the major repairs, but the decor and sense of well-being was not his and he understood this.

There were times when her house was more like a menagerie than a home, especially in the late spring and early summer. Mos was forever bringing home abandoned fox pups, raccoons, and even a skunk one day. "But sweetheart," he protested, "it's too small to smell."

"I don't care! It stays in the garage."

Her favorite were the birds. They were so pretty and intelligent looking. They were masters of the sky. Mos had brought home a great horned owl that had been attacked by ravens. Owls and ravens are mortal enemies and two or more ravens can kill a bird, even as fierce as an owl. Renée named it Henrí. When Mos asked her why Henrí, she replied, "He just looks like a Henrí."

The ravens had torn the flesh away from under his wings and pulled his feathers out. Renée put a tether on one leg and set him on a perch in the basement. The next morning around four o'clock, their cat started crying and wanted in, so Mos got up and let it in and methodically opened the basement door like he always did and went back to bed.

When the cat had finished eating, she went downstairs into the basement like she always did, not knowing anything about the owl. But during the night, the owl had freed itself from the tether and was perched on top of the woodpile. The cat saw the owl just in time and ran up the stairs and hit the door so hard that it closed and the cat went tumbling back down.

Mos heard the commotion and instantly realized what had happened. When he went downstairs, the owl was chasing the cat around the basement. He laughed so hard that Renée woke up and came to see what was going on.

He brought home hawks, robins, and even a seagull that later died from loneliness. Every time he brought something home, Renée smiled to herself because she fully understood this was only an extension of her husband's love for everything.

Yes, there were times of loneliness and isolation from others, but she had her children and they both idolized their father. She was quite proud of him, too.

Sometimes in the grocery store she would overhear two women talking in the next aisle and talking about how the warden had done this or that and he had caught their husband or someone else they knew. There were other times when someone would come right up to her and say something like, "Your husband is the only one who's doing anything." In one particular situation, after Mos had spent three long days and nights looking for a seven-year-old boy, the boy's aunt had come up to her and said, "You know, Renée, I don't care what people say or think, but I'm glad you and Mos live here. I think he does a great job."

There were hard times and lonely nights, but she wouldn't have had it any other way. She was proud of her husband and whatever he did was okay with her.

* * * *

He came to a stop and wondered why. Then he slowly began to understand that he had been reminiscing again and his mind had been far away, lost in his thoughts of the past. He was at a stop sign on U.S. Route 11 . He only had a short ways to go now. The trip from Augusta was erased from his memory. He didn't care. In his mind, at least, he had relived those wonderful years again. "And now it's time for another chapter in my life," he said to himself as he pulled away from the stop sign.

There was hardly a field or apple tree along the roadside that he couldn't relate to some dastardly deed. He knew every house and if there were hunting trails through the woods in the back of them. All had surely heard of Mos Jalbert. His name rang synonymous with the law. People had begun to call him at all hours of the day and night about legal problems. He was a policeman, sheriff, and game warden all rolled into one. People trusted and relied on Mos and he always tried to help.

Before going home, he decided to drive around the Happy Corner Road. It was a famously known night hunting stretch of fields and apple orchards. He stopped in front of the old church and got out. It felt good to stretch his legs and put some circulation back in them. He walked around the building and in back there was the same rock that had cost him a night hunter many years ago. He had his fire engine red Ford that night and when he saw flashlights in the field down over the hill, he quietly drove around the back to hide his car. Only he didn't know about the rock. The two foot jackers had heard the crunch of metal and left without further ado. There was red paint still on the rock. *I wonder who they were*, he thought. He never heard. Apparently they didn't do much talking because no one ever heard about the rock either. That was the only time in thirty years that he had ever used a church to hide behind. Maybe there was something gospel about it. He wasn't sure, but he wasn't going to push it. He sometimes used a headstone in a cemetery to hide behind, but never again behind a church.

He got back into his pickup and drove slowly along, enjoying everything he saw and marveling at the changes there were. "Funny how I never noticed before," he said to himself. But there were changes. There was a farm at the corner. *How many different people tried to make a go of it there?* he wondered. He couldn't remember. The last couple were from out-of-state. They lasted only a couple of months. The cold winter and deep snow had changed their mind.

The farm was vacant now and he left his pickup in the yard

and walked out into the back fields. How many sleepless nights had he spent there? For all his efforts, the number of poachers that were caught were few. He never could figure it out. Deer died there, but he had an exasperating time trying to catch the culprits. “Oh well, that’s over with now.”

He looked at his watch and decided he had better start for home. Today his wife was expecting him for supper and he didn’t want to worry her. He didn’t stop anywhere else but at each mile post along the way, he’d say to himself, “Caught ole Danny here.” Or “that’s where I almost got myself shot.” Or “this is where I got those fellows with the moose.” For Mos, this drive held a lot of history.

As he drove by Jason’s house, he noticed that Jason had driven his pickup up to the garage door and not backed in. This was a comforting feeling because in the past, Mos had learned that whenever Jason’s truck had been backed up to the garage door, it usually meant he had something to unload and that usually meant that a deer or moose had died.

He was home early today. *Strange*. Then Mos chuckled and said, “You ole rascal, what are you up to now.”

At his own house, Mos parked the pickup in its usual place and Renée greeted him at the door like she always did. Unless it was one of those long nights when Mos wouldn’t get home until the wee hours of the morning. “How was it, dear?” she asked.

“Not much for thirty years of service. Just a handshake and ‘I’ll see you.’”

“Was there anyone there that you knew?”

“That’s odd,” he said, “you know, most of the fellows are just names and faces now. On the way back, I concluded that I am the last of the old timers. The rest of them are just young kids. Even the chief warden came on long after I did. You’ve heard me speak of Landean, haven’t you, Renée?” She nodded her head. “The chief warden never knew him. You know, it’s strange how things change and you’re not even aware of it.” Mos’ problem was that he was always too busy, so wrapped up in being a game warden to ever notice the changes. They were there for everyone to see.

Mos went into the living room and sat down in his favorite chair. It was next to the window so he could see who was driving by. Renée went to the cupboard in the corner of the hallway and mixed a drink for herself and Mos. "Here, Mos," she said. He stood up as she handed him his drink and she offered him a toast. She held out her glass to his and said, "Here's to you, Mos. Thirty good years and one hell of a game warden."

They drank and in the back of her mind, she was drowning in tears. She knew how important it had been for Mos during his last thirty years to be the best that he could possibly be and how much he enjoyed being a game warden. She hoped he wasn't retiring because of her and then later regret it and shrivel up like a dried prune and just sit around and wait as if death was just around the corner. *Oh, God, I hope he's doing the right thing,* she thought.

"Just think about it, Mos," she said on a lighter note, trying to sound happy, "you won't have to worry about Jason and his silly pranks anymore."

He didn't reply because he knew he would miss those times most of all. That was what had made his job so interesting and so much fun. It had become a game and the only way for him to score a point was to catch the culprit and get them to court. The poacher scored if the got home safely with his bounty. But Mos and Jason had their own game in which no one else was allowed to play, not even Jerri or Renée.

Neither of them actually ever came out ahead unless you count the time that Jason had gotten Mos out of the trap. Then who was ahead—Mos for having his life or Jason for saving it?

"Supper will be ready in about thirty minutes. Why don't you lay down and take a nap?" Renée said as she headed for the kitchen.

In a few minutes, Mos came into the kitchen. "I thought you were going to take a nap?" Renée asked.

"I couldn't keep my eyes closed. Have you heard from Emil or Re'ann?" Mos asked.

"Re'ann called after you had left this morning and said that she and the baby would be up on Sunday. Why don't you go sit down and relax?"

"I can't," he said. "I think I'll go upstairs and pack all my old uniforms in a box and look around and make sure everything is ready so when they come to pick up the truck and the rest of my things."

"I did that this morning, Mos. Besides, supper is ready. Go wash up."

When they had finished eating, Mos started clearing the table, putting the dirty dishes in the sink, and the milk and butter in the refrigerator. Renée was worried. She had never seen Mos looking so melancholy before. "Mos, why don't you go out for one last night. Besides, you're officially still a game warden until midnight."

That was just like turning on a light in a dark room. It made all the difference in the world in his attitude. "You wouldn't mind?" he asked.

"Why should I, you've been doing it for thirty years. Besides, when I lay awake in bed tonight, I'll relax by knowing that this will be the last."

He put on his night-hunting clothes as he always called them, grabbed a handful of cigars, and kissed his wife.

CHAPTER 3

The Last Caper

When removed from the picture, one sometimes can see the overview or completeness of something, thereby gaining some sort of understanding. That night as Jason was leaving from his house for a last night-hunting caper, Mos was preparing to leave to work a last night hunter before his retirement became a reality. If looked from an objective perspective, the observer might have assumed that it was fate that Jason and Mos had both decided to retire on the same day and that each of their wives had suggested that they go out night hunting and go to the same field.

If asked if Jason had any beliefs in a given destiny or fate, he probably would have scoffed at the idea and said, "Is that so," or "it might be." If the idea of fate had been asked of Mos, he probably would have said, "Don't believe it. I do what I have to." Each in his own right was too stubborn to ever admit that perhaps there was something more to it than just mere coincidence.

Jason methodically took his favorite rifle, his .308, named as the "bad news rifle" by his family because once something was focused in the scope and the crosshairs were centered on the target, it generally died and became the next meal.

He took a clip full of cartridges and a small light. As a second thought, he returned to the garage and in the corner, underneath a pile of junk, he lovingly picked up a half-gallon of whiskey. He wrapped it in his jacket so that Jerri wouldn't suspect what he was doing.

He had all the essentials, so he drove to the Clark Road to the Stacey Farm across from Weeks Brook. He turned around in the farm yard and then drove back to the brook and left his pickup behind some bushes on the south side of the road. Instead of rushing right into it, he stepped out and walked around his truck, relieved himself, and took a drink. Not until he was satisfied that he was alone did he finally don his hunting apparel and load his bad news rifle.

The field that he had in mind, he had successfully hunted on numerous occasions in the past. The field was on the north side of the road and followed a brook back for the better part of a mile. It was almost to the town line. Someone several years ago had planted apple trees at the furthermost end of the field. The field at this time of the year would be second growth clover and green grass. The combination of clover and apples made it a deer sanctuary.

Jason always remembered the lesson that his father had taught about staying in the shadows if you don't want to get caught and you'd better go alone and don't tell anyone.

The moon was just coming up. It wouldn't be in its full phase, but with his scope, there should be sufficient light. He took his time. There was no need to hurry. The sooner this night was over, the sooner his night-hunting days were over. That didn't mean that he'd never poach again; it only meant that this was his last night-hunting caper.

The night air was warm and he was enjoying himself immensely. He stopped to listen to the stillness of the night when he had walked about halfway up the field. The only sounds were that of a screech owl and a lone coyote off in the distance. He pulled his rifle up to his shoulder to scan the field with the scope. On the further edge of the field he could make out four deer that were feeding together. It would have been an easy shot, but tonight he wanted the granddaddy, the king of all bucks. He knew he was coming to a pile of apples at the very end of the field.

Jason had just seen the huge buck the season before and had patiently laid plans to get him. During the winter, he made snowshoe trails through the woods and cut down cedar trees for the deer to feed on when the snows became too deep for easy traveling. In May, he had salted a burlap bag and hung it in a maple tree. When it rained, the water would soak through the burlap and into the salt and eventually it would seep out onto the ground. The ground underneath looked like a D-9 bulldozer had turned around because the ground was pawed up so hard. Just a week ago, he had taken a bunch of apples up and those were without a doubt mostly gone by now.

Jason knew he could get big money for the antlers that ole buck was carrying. And just once, once in his life, he wanted a rack so he could taunt the ole coot on Silver Ridge.

He continued up along the edge of the field, stopping occasionally to listen. When he reached the very end of the field, he found his blind and waited patiently for the buck to appear.

* * * *

During his second year as a warden, Mos had cleared a footpath from the corner of his property up along Larry Bottel's back fields and across Ryan Hanley's property at the top of the hill. Ryan was known for poaching a little, along towards September, in his own back pasture. The footpath eventually stopped at the Stacey Farm in the back corner of a large field.

Historically, this was a poaching area and Mos figured that the only way he was going to catch anyone there was to make it appear as if he were at home. He would leave his vehicle in the open and turned the yard light on. Even Renée would help out. She would put on one of Mos' uniform shirts, red jacket, and hat, and stand by the window, watching the cars go by. Mos would hike along this path and work on foot. This way he could keep an eye on his neighbor, Larry, at the same time.

During the winter, while poaching and fishing activity was at a slump, Mos would put on his snowshoes and go for a walk along this same footpath. When he came to the Stacey fields, he found another and slightly older snowshoe trail. That's all it took to arouse his curiosity. The trails didn't seem to have any definite direction and as he was about to overlook it as someone just out for a hike, he found the first cedar tree chopped down and picked clean by hungry deer. He followed the trail in a wide circle and found several more fallen cedar trees. Was someone doing this to help the deer out or was it done to entice the deer so they could shoot it? But winter deer that have been feeding on cedar generally taste like cedar, so that would cancel the efforts of a poacher.

He watched the small cedar thicket for the rest of the winter and nothing happened. Then in the spring when he found the salt lick hanging from a tree limb, his suspicions were rekindled. He kept watch on the salt lick faithfully every night for a month and nothing happened.

He was dumbfounded and soon forgot about it. No, he didn't forget, he just set it aside. But he wasn't yet aware of the apples. If he had been, that probably would have, without a doubt, postponed his retirement until he caught the culprit who was responsible.

It was dark as he walked up across Bottel's line. He waited momentarily to see if by chance Larry might be out and around. He took a last drag from his cigar and then crushed it under his boot and then lit another.

Even though it was dark, Mos had no trouble finding his way along the trail. Years ago, he had cleared away all the low-hanging limbs that might hit him in the face or scratch against his clothes and make a noise. It was almost like a garden walkway in the park.

He took his time because there was no real hurry. If someone were going to jack those fields, it probably wouldn't be until after eleven o'clock. Mos knew enough about the area and the people so he could anticipate when something was going to happen. *No need to hurry. If I hear a shot, I can get there from here easy enough before they dress it off.* He knew from experience that whoever it was that would be hunting there would be doing it on foot. Since it was about a mile walk to the end of the field from the road, the deer would have to be dressed off so they could drag it out.

How long would it take a new warden, right out from training, to learn these finer points of being an effective warden? Mos had learned, but those were years when you could do warden's work and not have to worry about someone breathing down your neck all the time.

He stopped at the brook, laid on his stomach, and took a drink from the cool stream. There was only a short distance to go now. He could almost see the clearing in the skyline. Caution started to prevail and he proceeded like a cat stalking its prey—one foot at a time.

From the brook to the very edge of the field, Mos had even gone to the extreme and hand raked the path free of any debris that might make the slightest sound and give his presence away. He stole along the path, listening with each step. In front of him, about fifty paces away, was a huge deer standing broadside in the path, watching him. Mos stopped to watch the deer and when he did, the deer jumped and ran down the path towards the field.

All was still except for the pounding hoofs on the ground. And then, only seconds later, the air was filled with a cannonlike rifle report that echoed only briefly and then all was quiet again.

Mos waited; patience being the better part of valor. He'd learned long ago not to go running straight into trouble. "Wait and be patient," Landean had said. While he waited, he urinated. "It always happens," Landean had said. And to this very moment, every time he heard a rifle shot, it had.

There were no sounds at all. Perhaps the shot had missed and the deer had escaped. Not likely though. Whoever it was knew what he was doing. He would be a seasoned poacher and not easily caught.

He waited for what seemed like an eternity. But after about a half hour, he quietly inched his way to the edge of the field.

* * * *

Jason had never known that Mos had discovered the fallen trees and salt lick. He never surmised that Mos would walk to these fields through the woods from his own house. He never anticipated that Mos would be anywhere around on that particular night.

The deer that Mos jumped was the illusive granddad buck that Jason wanted so badly. So naturally, when he saw it running, there wasn't time to think about what had caused the deer to run in the first place. He only had time to pull his rifle to his shoulder and squeeze the trigger. The bullet took the deer at the base of the neck by the forward shoulder. The deer dropped and died without another sound.

Normally Jason would have waited like Mos was doing and not rush in. But this was no ordinary deer and he wanted to get a good look at it. He emptied his rifle and threw the empty shell and remaining bullets far into the woods. This was out of habit and not a spur of the moment reaction. The deer lay there, quiet and still. There was steam already rising into the air where the bullet had entered.

Jason counted fifteen points and said, "The spread must be at least two feet." He wasn't long dressing it off. After the belly was laid open, he reached in with both hands and tore the stomach muscles, and pulled the stomach and intestines out without leaving a bloody mess. He had all he could do to drag the deer. There was no way that he could ever expect to get it to the road. He dragged it to a clump of bushes in the field and covered it with leaves and started back across the field to get his rifle.

He hadn't gone far when panic seized him and he froze in his tracks. At the edge of the woods directly in front of him was the unmistakable glow of a cigar—Mos Jalbert.

Terror ran up his back and then down to the soles of his feet. But experience had taught him not to panic. Play it cool, he thought to himself. He left his rifle where it was in the field and walked towards the glowing cigar. He knew what was there, so there wouldn't be any surprises.

Jason knew he wouldn't have any blood on him but he wasn't so sure about hair. His knife was lying on the ground by his rifle. Mos really didn't have too much on him, or did he? If it hadn't been so dark, Jason would have seen the smile on Mos' face. It wasn't a rueful, sinister smile, but rather one of satisfaction. An eloquent way to end his career. He had his old adversary with his hand still in the cookie jar. He had been an antagonist from his first day as a warden right to the end. He had also been a friend.

He'd have to do some talking in order to get himself out of this fix. "Nice night for a walk, isn't it, Mos."

"Yes, my friend, that it is. It's obvious why I am here. What brings you to this little corner of the world, Jason?" Mos asked as if he didn't know.

"You know, it's a funny thing. Just this morning, my doctor advised me that I should get more exercise. I've been feeling poorly lately. The wife told me to get out of the house right after supper. There are a lot of memories in this field and I thought I'd saunter around awhile and reminisce about the ole days when I used to poach...a little."

"You ole rascal, Jason, you've shot more illegal deer and moose than I've arrested people in the last thirty years," Mos stated and they both laughed.

Jason was feeling a bit nervous and probably rightfully so. Mos had him dead to right and was only toying with him now like he did when he was caught for selling that deer. The conversation they were having now helped, in an odd sort of way, to pacify him and keep him from saying, "Jesus Christ, Mos, are you going to arrest me or not? Or are you going to toy with me all night?" But he kept quiet and tried to play along.

"It seems to be quite a coincidence that you just happened to be here, Mos. If someone had seen me walking up across this field and complained, I doubt you'd had enough time to get here. Were you waiting for me, Mos?" Jason asked.

"No...I'm not a firm believer in coincidences and I don't rightly know why the two of us should come here together of all nights." He meant that since he signed his retirement papers and they would take effect at midnight. He absentmindedly looked at his watch and it was 12 :03. Three minutes into his retirement. "No, I wasn't waiting for you, Jason. In fact, I just got here," he lied.

Jason' didn't catch what Mos had said about "...of all nights." He knew wherever Mos had been when he shot that buck, he had to have heard the shot. But he was acting like nothing at all happened.

Mos unzipped his wool jacket, removed his badge, and slipped it into his pocket. Then he sat down on the ground, using the trunk of a maple tree for a back rest. "Sit down, Jason, that is if your doctor won't mind. I'll tell you a story and why I'm really here."

Jason accepted the offer and found a similar tree to lean against. *Oh boy, here it comes*, Jason thought.

"I just retired, Jason." He left it at that before continuing. He wanted to see Jason's reaction.

"Is that so? When did you do all that?"

"Yeah, it's a fact. I was all done at midnight."

"Then what brings you out here? If, as you say, you're all done."

"Same as you, I guess. After supper, Renée told me to go. Another coincidence?"

Jason was confused then. "But how in hell did you get here?"

Mos snapped on his flashlight and pointed it behind him. "See that trail? It goes to my house."

"Well, Jesus Christ! How long has that been there?"

Mos didn't have to answer. The presence of that trail answered one of the mysteries about Mos Jalbert and how so many of his friends had been caught in this same field.

Mos looked at Jason and in the glow of his light, he could tell by the expression on his face that he didn't have to explain any more. He only smiled and Jason smiled back. "Why you ole fox," Jason said. It suddenly occurred to Jason and he exclaimed rather vividly. "By Jesus Christ! It was you! You were the thieving son-of-a-whore who took them, weren't you? It had to be you! This here trail explains it!"

Mos laughed so hard that his sides hurt. He thought his head was going to split open from laughing. Mos knew exactly what Jason was referring to. "Yeah, I took 'em," he confessed.

Jason laughed with him. "Wait until I tell Larry where those two deer went. He'll shit green apples from now 'til Tuesday." Then he said a phrase coined by Larry, "and I'm a *poooor* man." Jason laughed so much that he rolled over onto the ground and Mos thought he might have busted a gut.

"What was that you said?" Mos asked. As soon as Jason could stop laughing, he said, "You want to hear a funny story?"

"Sure, why not. I'm not in any hurry."

"But first, this calls for a celebration. I mean your retirement and you not being a game warden anymore. I've got a half-gallon of Wild Turkey whiskey in my car. If you trust me to go get it, I'll bring my pickup back up along this here road and we'll have ourselves a drink."

"If you trust me to stay here," Mos replied.

There it was—he knew. He knew about the buck. *Oh, hell, why not,* he thought, *I'll only be a few minutes.* He didn't trust Mos enough to just walk over and pick up his knife and rifle. No, I better leave them there. I can come back for them later.

While Jason was gone, Mos got up and walked about a bit. He felt his age in his muscles and he knew he had made the right decision to get done. By the time Jason got back, Mos had a fire going and enough wood piled along side of it to last all night.

Jason walked over to the fire and handed a cup to Mos. "Looks like perhaps you intend to stay here awhile." He filled each of their cups, set the jug down, and raised his cup to offer a toast. "Here's to you, Mos, and may you enjoy your retirement. I know I will." They laughed and then they drained their cups. Jason refilled them.

This time it was Mos who raised his cup to offer a toast. "Here's to you, Jason, an amiable adversary. Thank you again for saving my life." They drank that cup and then sat down on the ground before they fell.

"Now you were going to tell me a story. I'm as curious as hell," Mos said.

"Back a few years ago," Jason started then settled into his storytelling pose. He took a deep breath and another drink of Wild Turkey. "Larry and I used to poach together some. We also hunted in the daylight. Well, by Jesus Christ, he stopped in the house one night and said, 'Jason, I know where there's three deer coming regularly. They're handy to home, too.' I said, 'Is that right?' He said, 'Yeah.' He said he'd come just after dark and we'd go get them. After supper, I went up. He said, 'Now we'll lay our plans in good shape.' We went upstairs and closed the bedroom door and we lay on the bed so we could see your house. You were just leaving in your state vehicle. You went by Larry's house and I said, 'There, Larry, we're all set, but he's one foxy fellow.' He said in a whisper, 'Now, boys, we'll want to talk low. He has awful ears, you know.'

"We went outside—Larry, Henry Carter, and I. We no more than got started and ole Larry stopped and pointed his nose in the air and began sniffing. 'Smell that, boys,' he said. 'Smell what?' I asked. 'Cigar smoke,' he answered.

"I said, 'By Jesus Christ, Larry, we all saw him leave.' Larry was convinced that you'd come back down the hill with your lights off. He said there was a change of plans. 'We might have been overheard, so we'll have to detour.'

"We lined it up across the field and down to your place. We could see that your truck was gone, but Larry insisted we check your garage. Henry and I stayed on the side hill while Larry went down. He couldn't see in the window so he reached up and grabbed the windowsill to pull himself up. When he was about halfway up, a car came down over the hill and lit the back of your garage and him up, too, just like daylight. He let go and fell over backwards into that Christly wet hole and he came up spewing and sputtering, covered with that green, slimy shit from head to toe. 'Jesus Christ,' he said, 'I'm going to get pneumonia out of this! I'll have to go back and change my clothes.'

"We went back to his house and he changed his clothes. Before we left, he told his wife to turn the yardlight off and keep the kitchen door unlocked. Well, we headed for his back pasture finally and my sides ached from laughing so hard that I didn't know if I could hit anything or not.

"Larry was so nervous by then that he forgot to be cautious. He snapped the light on and there in the middle of the field were three nice deer. Their eyes glowed like red hot coals. Just as I pulled up to fire, they began to run. I fired three shots and the first deer took two jumps and laid down in the field. The other two dropped just behind the fence. I started to fire at the first deer again because it was trying to get up. Larry saw what I was about to do and he grabbed the rifle barrel, pulled it down, and said, 'Oh, Jesus no, Jason! We've rattled everybody's cupboards from here to China!' He took out his big skinning knife, put it between his teeth, and started to crawl on his stomach towards the deer. Henry and I were laughing so hard that probably ole Sharp could hear us from his place.

"Well, anyhow, when Larry got to the deer, he grabbed its ear and brought his knife down to stab it in the throat. He almost stabbed himself. After the third try, he said, 'We'll come back in the morning. It will bleed to death.' The other two he said wouldn't go far. 'They're as good as hanging in my garage. We'll come back in the morning and get ole Mos to put a tag on them for us. We'll put one over on the ole fox.'

"We headed for his house and when we got there, the lights were all on and the door was locked. It was just the opposite of what Larry asked his wife to do. He started jumping up and down, 'Jesus, Jesus, ain't this awful! A man caught in his own dooryard! I am a poor man!'

"By then, Henry and I were laughing so hard that tears were streaming down our faces. Larry started banging on his door. 'Open this door! Open this door!' Just then his son pulled the curtain back and said, 'Is that you, Daddy?'

"'Snap off this light and open this gawd-damned door!' Even after we were inside, he kept sputtering about being caught in his own house.

"He told us to come back at daylight and we'd go get the deer. Well, we did. The first one was dead all right, but the coyotes had eaten everything except the front shoulders. The other two were gone. Someone had drug them off." Before continuing, he looked questioningly at Mos who had a broad grin on his face. "It was you, wasn't it?"

Mos was quiet during the oration. He was just listening to a comical poaching caper, as Jason would have called it. But after he had finished, Mos couldn't for the life of him, hold it back any longer. He burst out laughing and slapped the ground with his hands while trying to tell Jason that he had taken those deer. "Only I didn't know there was a third one or that you were involved."

"Where in the devil were you?" Jason asked and he too was laughing.

"Maybe I'd better start from the beginning and tell my side of the story. Larry's suspicions that night were warranted but I didn't know how he knew I was on to him unless he was simply paranoid because he knew what he was doing was wrong."

"You mean that you knew we were going out that night?" Jason asked quizzically.

"Not exactly but I knew it wouldn't be long before he did. You see, I also knew that there were three deer coming out just after dark. But Larry wasn't sure if I did or not. Over the years, Larry had unconsciously exhibited a routine whenever he was about to do some poaching. It took me awhile to catch on, but when I did, I turned it around and used it against him.

"Every time that I had gotten wind of some illegal deer or fish that he'd taken, he always came to see me a few days before it would happen. Then I discovered that he was only coming down to find out what I was doing or where I might be working. He tried to be discreet and ask something about fishing on a particular brook or if I had heard shots a few nights ago at someone's house. He came to me to see where I had been.

"Well, he'd been down to see me two nights before this went down. A call came in and I had to leave before we did much talking, but I knew he was up to something. He's awful clever that way.

"When I saw the upstairs lights come on, I knew he was up there to see if I was home or not. I left purposely, hoping that he would see me leave and feel safe enough to go out. Since the deer were coming out behind his house, I figured that was the logical place to look for him."

"Did you drive by with your lights off?"

"No, that was probably nothing more than his nerves. In fact, I walked in on this trail. Only I didn't get there until it was all over. I'd just started in on the trail when you apparently fired. I heard the shots. I waited for hours by the edge of the field and it wasn't until the sun came up that I discovered that I was almost standing on those two.

"I had to be somewhere else early that morning, so I didn't wait for him to come back after the two deer. I didn't want him to get away with it completely. So I took them to my place."

It was Jason's turn to laugh now and Mos joined in with him. "And I'm a pooor man." They laughed some more. Jason filled their cups again and Mos threw a couple of sticks on the fire and lit another cigar.

"Cigar, Jason?"

"Yes, I don't mind if I do." They were both silent for a while and probably thinking along the same lines. How unusual their friendship was. Not only now at this moment, but all through the years that the two had known each other. Their background and childhood were very similar. They were both brought up around the lumbering business' and spent most of their adolescent years in the woods.

Mos was thinking of Landean just then and something he had once said. "Not everyone who poaches, Mos, is bad. There's a lot of good people wherever you go. Don't look for just the bad, look for the good." He was right. Most of the people he had come in contact with throughout his career were good people.

"Jason, you know what I've appreciated most about you through the years?"

"What's that?"

"You seldom ever wasted anything you shot. If you couldn't use it, you gave it to another family."

"My father started me on that. He called it 'giveaway meat.' That reminds me of a couple of stories. One of them is quite comical. I'm not ruffling any of your feathers am I?"

"Not at all. I'm enjoying this."

"Well, you know it was a well-known fact that if at anytime you needed some meat, all you had to do was drive up the north road a ways and you'd have your pick. Well, one day I had to go to Washburn to see an uncle, so I naturally took my rifle just in case, you understand."

"Naturally."

"When I got to the first McMannus place, there was a spike horn feeding under an apple tree on the lower side of the road. I just couldn't pass it up. There wasn't time to take care of it then, so I dragged it into the woods and went to see my uncle.

"I told him if he'd come down and help me with it that I'd give him half. He didn't want to get caught, so he said no.

"It was already dark before I got back to where the deer was and when I turned into the road there, my headlights picked up a reflection from taillights. I figured right then that it was a warden, so I never went near the deer. I got out and walked around some. In no time, I saw this red jacket step out from behind a spruce tree and another one was coming across the road.

"One of them I'd met before—Maurice Gordon. Nice warden, yes, sir. The other one I never did know. Well, Maurice asked what I was doing and I told him that I'd seen the tops of the spruce trees and decided to see if there was enough to cut and if someone might get a permit to lumber. The other warden looked my car over pretty good and looked at my rifle and smelled the barrel. 'How long ago did you fire this?' he asked. I told him about an hour and forty-five minutes ago. He just grunted and put the rifle back. Maurice said that I probably wouldn't be able to get a permit and wondered if I'd mind leaving. I said, 'No, not at all, boys.'

"I hated to go off and leave it, but what else could I do? I never shot anything just to kill it. I always tried to use it.

"I never figured out how those two knew that there was a deer there. I hid it amongst the trees."

"They were probably down on Tracey Brook checking fishermen when they heard the shot," Mos replied. "Once the deer was found, they probably would have laid on it until it had rotted, waiting for you to come back. I once laid on a moose for three days. They had gutted it out and put a stick in the rib cage to open it and then piled fir boughs over it. They came back at midnight on the third day. There were four of them."

"The other story is a little more comical. You'd better have some more Wild Turkey first." Jason poured each of them some more. "I always felt bad about this caper but after we shot the moose, we honestly couldn't have helped it."

"Well, you've got me a little more than curious. Come on, out with it," Mos said.

"Before I start, I'll say it again—I hope your feathers don't get ruffled."

"Come on with you," he coached.

"Well, one day I drove over to see Lucas. I had borrowed a cable cutter earlier and decided to return it with a new one. I had broken his. Well, we had a couple of drinks and Henry showed up to help Lucas with something. I can't remember what it was now, but anyway, it was about supper time and we all decided to ride up the north road and get us some meat.

"Henry made some excuse about his wife needing the car so we couldn't take his. 'That's okay, Henry,' I said, 'We'll follow you home and you can leave yours with your wife.' Lucas took his rifles.

"We went all the way to the Oxbow turn and never saw a car or deer for that matter. That is until we started back and then they were everywhere. Each time we'd stop, a car would come along and the deer would leave.

"I began to think that one of us was a jinx. We got all the way back to Knowles Corner and we saw a cow moose standing right in the middle of Harris Bog. I stopped and told Lucas to shoot before anyone came along. He jumped out and the first bullet caught the moose in the forward shoulder. 'Give her another one!' I shouted. He did and that moose reared up on her hind legs and I shouted, 'Give her another one, Lucas!' That shot went right behind the head.

"We could see she was going down. Lucas put his rifle behind the seat and then we hid my truck on that gravel road and the three of us circle that bog. Once we were at the end of it, I told Henry and Lucas to stay put and that I would wade out to it and cut the legs and loins out. There was no sense of all three of us to be out there. It might attract attention that way.

"I thought I could see where she went down and I started out. In some places, the water was clear up to my belt buckle. It wasn't all like that though; some of it was pretty good walking. Well, I got to the place where I thought she'd gone down, but there wasn't any sign of her anywhere. I looked around and all I could find was a large mud hole with moose tracks coming in but none going out. Then I saw some hair and blood on the water. The water was riled up, too.

"When she had reared up on her hind legs, she must have sunk out of sight in the mud. That's why we thought she was down and couldn't see her.

"I knew the boys wouldn't believe me. I called them to come out and when they got there, neither of them could believe it. Henry said, 'Maybe we better get out of here before we get caught.'

"'Caught for what?' I said. 'There's nothing here but us.' We all agreed never to say anything to anyone. We figured nobody would ever believe us. Nobody ever has until now, so I'd appreciate it if you keep it under your hat. I'd hate for the other boys to find out that I said anything, especially to a warden. Well, you're not ...a...you understand, don't you?"

"Sure. Did you ever go back to see if maybe she might have come back to the surface?"

"I thought about it once but I didn't know if you ever found out about it or not. If you had, I didn't want to be found looking around there."

"No one ever said anything to me about it or that any bones had ever been found. It's probably still there if she didn't come to the top," Mos chided.

Mos moved just a little so he could lay straight out and stretch his muscles and rest his back. He lay there and looked at the stars and was only a little surprised at himself because of the caper. Then he began to laugh out loud as he thought about how the other wardens would react to his being there with this ole rascal, especially since he had the goods on him. But he wasn't a warden any longer. He felt the stump of his thumb he had left and said out loud, "An eloquent caper."

Jason, by this time, had stretched out too. "Did you say something? What are you laughing about?"

"Oh, I was just thinking about the other wardens and what they would think with the two of us here." He didn't mention the deer that he knew Jason had shot. There wasn't any need. "And then I was thinking about how you're always calling one of these excursions a caper. Then I thought of 'an eloquent caper.'"

Jason laughed with him and then said, "I like that; it has a nice ring to it."

Both were quiet then as Jason laid there. As he looked at the stars, his thoughts changed to the man beside him. He had, for thirty years, represented the law. He was the protector of game. He, Jason, through his childhood and the necessity to survive, had taken illegal game to eat. This had set the trend throughout his life. Even though Mos had taken Jason to court on numerous violations, there was something about him that inspired a mystic sense of being. What drove him and forced him to the extremes to enforce the laws? Why did he seem to find so much enjoyment? Was it the fact that he got pleasure out of seeing people humiliated and suffering from hunger? He thought about that for a minute and then decided that wasn't the case at all. Hadn't Mos let him go on numerous occasions when his luck was against him? He had done the same for others, too. At times, Mos had become the provider himself. There were rumors once that Mos would hear of a family in desperate need of meat and shoot a deer to give to the family. He would claim that it was a nuisance animal or a road kill. Mos never talked much about that and if asked, he always denied it.

Mos, in Jason's mind, was a peculiar fellow. It wasn't that he was physically or mentally different from anyone else. Mos just cared about other folks and about what he was doing. That was the difference. Mos was just Mos Jalbert, forged from his own mold.

"Mos?" he asked questioningly. "What is it that has driven you so throughout the years? What was it that kept you out there, hours on end, and days at a time? Like tonight even?"

"You know, Jason, I've often wondered about the same thing. The only answers I can find was the excitement and suspense. It was more or less the same as you, like when you pull the trigger and the deer drops. The suspense of being out here in the dark and hunting. It's the challenge. You like to hunt and so do I. I've found it a whole lot more challenging to hunt man. And I suppose that I just like the outdoors and what I do."

"Were there ever any times when you wished you hadn't been a warden?"

"No, but that's not to say that there were never any trying times either, like spending the night out in the cold rain without seeing anything or spending an entire day in subzero weather, watching for something when I could have been home where it was warm. Sometimes on the weekends and holidays, when families should be together and do things, Renée would always go without me. I think that's what was most difficult."

"People around here didn't think too much of you at first, when you first moved here. You had a big chip on your shoulders. Then it was like you changed overnight. What happened?" Jason asked.

"I just remembered something that an old friend once said. I've got a story for you," Mos said. "You might enjoy it. This all happened quite a few years ago. Me and the warden from Sherman had caught six fellows night hunting on Bates Hill in Moro. There were three fellows in the cab and the other three were in the back of the pickup. One of them had a shotgun with buckshot, another had a rifle and scope, and a third one had a bow and arrow. We arrested all six and took them and their truck to jail in Houlton."

"Did they give you a rough time where there were so many of them together?" Jason asked.

"No, surprisingly they were very cooperative."

"They weren't night hunting," Jason interrupted. "They were just out there for a good time."

"We left them at the jail and headed back to Bates Hill. We wanted to look the area over. There was a new warden in Houlton, and he was a young fellow by the name of Roland Pelletier. He had heard the traffic on the radio and had driven over to Bates Hill to wait for us to return.

"As we went by the town line, on the Line Road, I shut off my lights. Well, Roland was watching and thought perhaps someone was hunting the York Fields, so he headed towards us with his lights off, too. The fog had rolled in and it was difficult to see anything. Well, we met halfway...I mean, we met almost head on. There was a big crash and we all got out and looked our vehicles over. Roland had just gotten a new Dodge pickup. He tore one of the fenders right off. No one was hurt, we all stood around laughing."

Jason laughed and said, "I see you fellows can get in some pretty good scrapes, too."

"They went for a trial and after everyone had testified, the judge asked one of them if he had seen anyone at all night hunting on that road. You had to be there to appreciate it. This fellow was a little slow and a little simple. He said, 'Nobody but us.'"

They each laughed over that and each required a call to nature. Mos put some more wood on the fire and Jason filled their cups again.

Mos leaned back against the tree and Jason sat on a piece of wood next to the fire. "What was your most hair-raising experience, Jason?"

Without any hesitation, Jason answered, "The time you and the other warden came to the house with my son, Kenny. I had had a little too much to drink that day, so I laid on the couch to sleep it off. I woke up and saw the two of you standing in my driveway with Kenny. I thought at first that I was having a nightmare. Then Kenny came in and said, 'It's okay, Dad, they only want me. I told them I'd give them the rest of the moose if they left you alone.'

"By crying-eyed Jesus, man, you almost gave me a heart attack. I had three deer and three moose quarters hanging in the cellar. I thought I'd bought the farm until Kenny explained that you only wanted him.

"What tipped you off, Mos? How did you know that Kenny had that moose?"

"I received a complaint from someone who drove by and saw him burying something with his skidder. After Kenny left that afternoon, I dug it up and found he had buried some moose meat. It had been nicely wrapped in white freezer paper and labeled. I could have gotten a search warrant, but I already had enough on him to stick. But what I couldn't figure out was why he buried it? It was all cut and wrapped."

"That moose must have been dying. The meat was rotten.He took right care of it, too. Jerri told him one day to get rid of it all. It smelled the house up really bad. No one would ever cook it, let alone eat it. Kenny did that moose a favor by shooting it. Jerri was at the neighbors when you pulled into the dooryard. Because of all the meat we had hanging, she thought you were going to take her and the tenderloins that she cut and wrapped. She didn't care if you took the rest, just leave her tenderloins alone," Jason laughed.

"That's strange," Mos said. "I've never heard of such a thing. I've seen meat so tough that a dog couldn't chew it but never one that was rotten. I wonder if it had that moose disease that kills them?"

"I don't know, but it smelled awful and you couldn't cut the gravy," Jason replied.

"We've seen the best of it, Mos. The woods, the game, the fishing, everything. It'll never be the same."

"I agree with you, Jason. I don't think the next generation will have any idea of what the woods and the game were like."

"When we were young, poaching was almost a necessity of life. We didn't have welfare or food stamps. We worked and if we needed meat, we took only what we could use. I never shot deer or moose just for the sport of killing something. But people today have changed. Even those who hunt legally are different. They do it for the thrill. And those who poach, do it only for the thrill of it and don't take care of it, those are the bastards that I'd like to see caught." Jason was getting excited and he was almost shouting. "I've got no use for that kind of a poacher. He's not a poacher, but a thief."

"Did you ever see any of the giant white pine in your days, Jason?"

"No. I saw some nice trees but not the size that you are talking about."

"I found some old pine stumps once. They measured between six and seven feet," Mos said.

"Where was that?"

"It was on the upper end of Grand Lake Sebois. I was looking for an Indian village that was supposed to be on that end somewhere, when I came acrooss these two old rotten stumps. The trunks weren't there, so I assumed they had been cut down and taken. I found two boom anchors, too. Someone had handhewn a cedar tree and bored a four-inch hole through it to anchor a boom chain. I found one on each end of the cove."

"I cut up there one winter. It had some of the nicest spruce you ever did see. We used horses then. We twitched onto the ice and piled them there. When the spring break came, they were floated downstream to the East Branch. There were lots of snow in that country. There were big deer, too."

"I think there's a story there, isn't there?" Mos asked.

"Yeah. It was an inhuman son-of-a-whore."

"Who are you talking about?"

"Not who—it was an inhuman deer. It was the last week of deer season. The snow was already very deep. Everyone had a deer except for Sheridan.

"He had a small crawler and was doing some bulldozing for us, making twitch trails for the horses and loading ramps. He was too busy to hunt, so he asked me if I'd get him a deer. I said, 'Sure, it won't be any trouble.' At least I thought it wouldn't be. Well, it was easy enough to find the ole son-of-a-whore, but it just wouldn't die. Even after I had it's heart laying in my hand!

"When I left camp that morning, I took my rifle with me and I no sooner got to the woods and this nice eight-pointer jumped into the trail and stood broadside. It was an easy shot. At least I thought it was. I aimed just in front of the front shoulder and squeezed the trigger. He fell, but when I walked up to it, it jumped up and ran off. There was blood and hair everywhere, so I knew I had hit it good. Well, I followed it for a ways and took another shot at it. He fell again. I aimed for the same shoulder where his heart should have been. It was still alive when I walked up to him. Instead of shooting it again like I should have done, I was going to cut the throat. Every time that I would make a swipe at it, it would shake its head and kick the knife out of my hand. After about the fourth try, I succeeded and began to dress it off. I pulled the stomach and guts out then I reached up into the chest cavity and his heart was still beating. Even after I cut it out and had it in my hands, it was still pumping. I threw the heart as far as I could. That inhuman son-of-a-whore is probably still beating! That is, if the ravens haven't got it."

Mos was beginning to feel the effects of the whiskey and he became sleepy, but to maintain his image with Jason, he forced himself to stay awake. He was feeling a little devil-may-care and infirm of purpose as he said, "Jason," he paused on purpose before continuing. "You know what would taste good right about now?"

"What's that?"

"A little venison to roast over the fire."

"Yeah, it would be good at that, but we'd have to shoot us a deer unless you happened to bring some with you." *He knows, gawd-damn it, he knows! But what is he going to do? He's retired now*, Jason thought nervously to himself.

"I've got a couple of sandwiches in my pack if you're hungry." Mos turned and rummaged through his knapsack and handed one to Jason. "I'm hungry. How about you?"

They ate their sandwich in silence and Mos washed his down with a hot cup of coffee. "Want some of this?" he asked.

"Mos, do you think there's as much poaching going on now as there used to be?"

"In all honesty, it's hard to say. Back when I first came here, those who did poach did so primarily to feed their families and it was all done close to home. But the woods now have been opened up so and exploited that the fellows can range further and I may not hear about it at all. It's done for different reasons now, too. The typical poacher himself has changed and the deer have changed also.

"To answer your question, no, there probably isn't as much poaching now. But it's wider spread and the deer are spread out more, too," Mos added.

"Back when I was poaching...regularly, there were a lot of deer everywhere. They were around the farm lands and wood operations. The deer seemed to be tame then. But now, when they're scarce they're smart. Looks like Mother Nature's way of protecting them," Jason said.

"Maybe," Mos replied, "any of that Wild Turkey left?"

They filled their cups again and Mos continued. "I've got a story for you.

"This only happened a few years ago. It was back when I was working that commercial meat ring. I had been walking around the old fields and clear cuts at the base of Mt. Chase, in there where Haines had cut a few years back. I'd come out into this clear-cut and was working my way back to my pickup when I saw a reflection through some trees. I looked through my binoculars and saw that the sun was shining on a vehicle parked on a side road off the mountain road." Jason shifted uncomfortably because he knew what Mos was talking about. "I circled around the open cut and came up behind it and when I did, I saw that it was you. You were just sitting there. That made me curious, so I sat there and waited to see what you were up to. After awhile, Bert Laudin drove up behind you and you laid your head down on the door like you were asleep. Bert walked over to your side of the truck and you acted like you had just woken up. I was too far away to hear what was being said, but I guessed you'd been watching for a moose to step out of that swamp and into the road."

"It was a good thing for me, I guess, that Bert came along. You had it figured about right," Jason admitted.

"I've got another story for you, Mos." Actually, he could sit there for the better part of a week and tell stories without ever repeating himself. "You almost had me on this one. I was almost ready to give up before I saw an opening.

"Remember back some years ago on the Poorman's Retreat Road when you caught me coming out early one morning? You said you were trying to catch a couple of fish hogs."

"Yeah, I remember that. You mean you had something after all?" Mos asked.

Jason laughed and said, "Yeah, it was more like three deer."

"Hah! How could that be when I didn't see any?"

"Well, maybe I'd better start from the beginning. I hope you haven't' got a tape recorder in your pocket." Without waiting for an answer, he continued. "I was on my way back to work that morning when I came around the curve where the spruces are now and there were seven deer. I stopped and they just stood there. I loaded my rifle and stepped out, and they still stood there. I shot three of them. I didn't dare to wait around and dress them off because I knew you had been in there trying to catch me. I stuffed the two yearlings in the box in the body of the truck. The other deer was an eight-point buck. It was a nice deer. I had to put him in front with me. I had a raincoat and some old newspapers that I laid over the top of him, but you could have still seen it if you had gotten out of your pickup and walked over.

"Well, I left there and was burning it back to my house when I met you by the old schoolhouse. I said to myself, 'I'm screwed right here. All he has to do is look inside.' Jesus, I always liked you, Mos, but I sure wasn't glad to see you just then. I decided I'd better let you do the talking. Maybe someone had called you and maybe not, but I wanted to see which way you were leaning. When you came right out with 'Ha, ha, I know what's the matter. You've got some meat, don't you?"

"Well, by gee-hokey, I was honest. I said 'by Jesus, you're smart, aren't you? I shot three this morning.' I saw a slight opening when you said, 'Oh, bullshit, don't tell my any of that. Just tell me the truth for once.' It was worth a try, so I told you that the skidder wouldn't start and that the starter switch was gone.

"Well, I burned it across the Winding Hill Road and threw

those deer in the cellar and grabbed a new starter. Of course, there was nothing wrong with the one I had. I was afraid that you might try it just to see if it would start.

"When you showed up again just as I was finishing with the starter, I almost had a heart attack. Then, you ole fox, you wanted to run the skidder for me for the rest of the day! Jesus, then I knew that you must have found something. By Jesus, I was so nervous. Before the afternoon was over, I was sure that you knew about the three deer," Jason ended.

"I suspected something and that's why I said I'd always wanted to run one of those skidders. I thought maybe I'd find something. But I didn't. I did get those fish hogs though. One had one hundred and ten trout and the other one had a hundred and fourteen. They got the book thrown at them, damn it! I hate a gawd-damn fish hog, at least when they poach that bad," Mos said.

"Yeah, that's right," Jason concurred. "They shouldn't have been that greedy. Say! I've got a fish story for you. This one happened before you came here. Steed was the warden then. Did you ever know him?"

"I was only here two years before he moved. He must have been a hard one. He always talked about how much he liked his work. Even when I was talking to him about something, he would get excited and try to help lay a plan. I think he kind of missed it when he retired," Mos said.

"Yeah, he liked his job all right; about as much as you do." Jason laughed and then he told Mos about the time Steed had almost caught him that Christmas morning and how he did it only to teach him a lesson.

"He sounds a lot like Earl Landean," Mos said.

"Well, back to my story. Did you ever know Acer McDonald?"

"No."

"Well, he probably moved away before you came. He used to work on the roads here and then shortly after this fracas, he moved to Connecticut. Anyway, he wanted me to go fishing with him into Pleasant Lake. He needed a four-wheel drive and I had one. I told him that I couldn't because I was working the next day. He said okay and that he'd get his wife to drop him off at the mouth of the lake road and he'd walk in.

"He got as far as Pickett Mountain Stream and sat down on the bridge and had a beer. Then he decided it was an awful long walk into the lake. He threw his line in by the bridge and pulled out a couple of fish and thought that was pretty good.

"About a hundred yards up the brook around the first bend where the pool is, Acer threw in his line and zip, zip, zip, he pulled in a few more. That night when he stopped back at the house, he had about a hundred and twenty nice trout. He gave Jerri and me about forty. You see, we had a pretty big family by then and he knew that we could use them. We had a good feed, too!

"Well, he said, 'Tomorrow night I'll have another good mess when I come out here.' He got up about daylight and headed in. When he got back that night, he had a pack basket about this high," and he pointed to just above his knee. "It was full of trout except for a couple of inches from the top. I never saw such a mess of fish like that before in my life! He gave me over a hundred that time and that didn't lower his pack one might. That pack must have weighed nearly two hundred pounds. I had all I could do to lift it."

"I've never seen anything quite like that," Mos said. "The beaver have the brook damned up now so the trout can't get up from the lake. The water's low, too."

"Hey, I've got another fish story for you. You'll laugh so hard that your sides will hurt."

"Where was this?"

"Pleasant Lake. Except we didn't exactly go for fishing though. Lucas, Henry, Arlo Parker, and I went into the lake thinking we'd get us some meat. We took some rum, of course. You know Arlo, he could catch a fish in a mud puddle, so he took one of the boats and went fishing. Lucas, Henry, and I motored down to the Emerson spring and set up camp. We thought perhaps the hunting would be better at dusk, so we decided to make a night of it.

"While Arlo was fishing, the three of us had a little rum and when Arlo got back, he was mad because we hadn't waited for him. Well, he cursed us out and eventually he made supper. We had to clean his fish and clean the dishes too. He said, 'that's punishment for drinking without me.'

"While we waited for dusk, we sat around the fire to ward off the mosquitoes and we had a little more rum. 'Bout the time the sun started to go down, we figured it was time. So we all loaded into the boat and Henry pushed off.

"Arlo hadn't had quite so much to drink as the rest of us, so he wasn't as merry. Lucas decided he wanted to sing so he began singing I've been working on the railroad. Then Henry and I joined in and this just made Arlo angrier.

"By then, we really didn't care if we saw any game or not. We were having ourselves a good time as it was. Well, we motored down to the thoroughfare and we had wanted to go through to Mud Lake because that's where the best moose are. But the water was too low to carry us all through and nobody wanted to get out. So we started back when this jesusly big bull stepped out into the water. I had the only rifle and it was a fight as to who was going to shoot it. I allowed that whereas the rifle was mine that I was going to do the shooting.

"I had to stand up to get a good bead on it and I was having a difficult time because the boat was rocking so hard. Arlo was trying to quiet Lucas and Henry. They were still arguing over who was going to do the shooting. The next thing I knew, I was upside down in the lake. When I fell in, Henry was just standing up and he was knocked off balance and he fell in, too.

"That ole moose had had enough. His sides probably ached as bad as my head from laughing over the comedy that we made in the boat. Arlo and Lucas sat right there, laughing their asses off.

"After awhile, we made it back to camp. Henry and I were frozen. We stripped down and got our clothes dried. By then, of course, we had some more rum and our blood was circulating good, so we didn't care if our clothes were dry or not.

"The only thing that we got out of that trip was wet clothes and one feed of trout. We'd originally planned to get enough meat for the four of us.

"It was around midnight before we settled in and went to bed. By then, we'd all had too much to drink. Along about four in the morning, I woke up and stirred the fire and threw on a few more sticks. Then Lucas got up. We had a few more drinks of rum and got pretty hot again. Ole Lucas, he..." Jason was laughing so hard and slapping his leg that Mos began to laugh too. It wasn't because of anything comical, but because of the state they were both in and Jason's laughter was contagious. Finally, Jason was able to compose himself enough to finish. "Lucas, he looked out across the lake and squinted his eyes to shade them and says, 'Jason! Which side of this jesusly lake are we on anyhow? This side or the other side?'

"'Well, Lucas,' I said, 'I'm not too sure but I think we're on this side.'"

That was more than either Mos or Jason could take. Their heads hurt and their sides were busting, yet they continued to laugh. Finally, after some effort, they stopped. "You know, Mos, come morning we didn't have a thing to eat and no meat to take out with us. But we sure had us a good time."

Mos stood up and walked up the trail a ways for another call of nature. Jason reached over and put a couple of sticks on the fire. How he loved the smell of wood smoke and it especially smelled good on this occasion. He was sitting there under a clear sky with only stars as witnesses to this last caper...an eloquent caper at that. He, being the notorious poacher and all, spending the entire night drinking whiskey with a game warden and smoking his cigar. How he prayed that not a word of this ever leaked out to some of his friends. He'd never live it down. But

Mos was different. He cared about what he did and about people, even those he chased. That was the difference and after all, he said he'd retired, didn't he? Or was that just a trick that the ole fox was using to lure him into the trap. Mos was a crafty one all right, but he wasn't dishonest. If he said he had retired, then he had. This was to be his last night-hunting caper anyhow.

But the thought of that buck deer in the bushes, not even seventy-five yards from where they were sitting, still made him nervous and the fact that he didn't know what Mos' intentions were. Mos obviously knew about the deer or at least he suspected because he would have been close enough to have heard the shot. *Hell! He could have heard it from his house,* Jason said to himself. *But he hasn't said anything about hearing a shot*, he questioned himself.

He couldn't leave just yet. He didn't want to leave his rifle and knife for Mos to find. What about the deer? He couldn't just walk over and pick them up. Even if he was retired that would be too much of an insult. No, I'll wait and play his game and see what he's up to.

Mos came back to the fire just as Jason had finished his thoughts about Mos and his intentions. The timing was so close that it appeared that Mos almost knew and had given Jason his privacy with his conscience. "Peaceful night," Mos said. "I'll miss these nights I think."

"You said earlier that you had retired. You know, I more or less retired today, too," Jason said.

"You did?"

"Yeah, I'm not as young as I once was. The woods take a lot out of a man. I sold everything except my crawler this afternoon. My sons will carry on for me."

"Hope they don't shoot as well as you," Mos chided.

"I think my two oldest could probably outshoot me, Mos. My eyes aren't what they once were.

"As I was saying, I retired today and I needed something to pick up my spirits. I didn't know but what this here might cheer me up." But what neither of them heard because of the effects of the Wild Turkey was that Jason had just contradicted his reason for being out there that night. "Yes, Mos, I looked back on my days in the woods today and you know, I don't like what I see coming. These new mechanical giants are cutting the forest out too damn fast. There'll be a day when the big companies will regret it. The modern day woodcutter is just that. There aren't any more lumbermen. They faded out with the arrival of the skidders and crawlers like mine. They just don't take any pride in their work now.

"And there isn't the game around the woods operations that there once were. Most of the animals have got to have something besides these huge clear cuts. When we cut with only horses, there were deer everywhere in our works, summer and winter."

This revelation had been pestering Jason for quite some time. It disgusted him to thing that these companies could just clear the land like they were doing and not give it a second thought about a future reforestation. They didn't think about there not being any more giant pines or hardwood ridges with trees so huge that two men couldn't link their arms around it. Those days were gone and the trees went with it. Soon, the game would be gone too. Was Jason just getting old and finally realizing it? Or was he seeing a true perspective of what was happening? He had never denied being a poacher but he never let what he shot go to waste. If he couldn't use it, he saw that another needy family got it.

There was one primary difference with Jason's concept of his poaching. He knew what he was doing and that it was illegal. Each time he went out on another caper, he was prepared to accept the responsibility if he were caught. If he was caught, and there were a few times, he paid his dues without arguing. He knew when he went out that he was doing wrong and it was the warden's job to catch poachers. Jason always said, "How can you hold something against a man for doing his job?" That was his philosophy and he would try to get away with it if he saw a slight opening and then with his gift of conversation, he often times succeeded.

He never held anything against any of the wardens and would just as soon invite them into his house for a cup of coffee as well as the next friend. That is, of course, if he didn't go looking in his cellar.

"Mos, do you know Raymond Turner and his wife, Linda?"

"Not well, but I know of them," Mos answered.

"I can tell you a comical fracas that he and I got into once, but you'll have to promise not to ever say anything that would get back to him."

"That serious, huh? Okay, I promise."

"This is the honest truth. Several years ago, Raymond called me on the phone and wanted to know if I wanted to go get some potatoes. It was the end of September and most of the farmers had their potatoes dug and were letting them dry in the air. Well, way in the back of the Cunningham Farm, just off the Clark Road, was a five acre piece that had been dug and left. The crews wouldn't work on Sunday, you see. There are a few old apple trees around the edge and Raymond's wife, Linda, said she had seen some deer there on Saturday while she was working.

"Well, Raymond picked me up after lunch and of course, I took my rifle. We got up to the first field and we could look out across the other one. There were five deer standing there.

"Raymond said, 'We'd better drive around and come in behind them, don't you think, Jason? If we try to sneak down across this field, we'd have to stay pretty close to the ground and stay out of sight. It might scare 'em.'

"I thought I might try if from where we were. If I missed, they'd only run into the other field and we might get one out of there. Well, I held up on a nice buck. I put my bead right on top of his head and pulled the trigger. Bang! Down he dropped!

"We drove down alongside it and it was still kicking. We didn't think much of it at the time. The bullet hit it right here," Jason said as he pointed to his lower jaw. "It followed that jaw bone right around and came out here. We thought it was just nerves, so we threw it in Raymond's trunk and picked two bags of potatoes and threw them on top of the deer. Raymond didn't want to take the time to dress it off, so we threw him in, paunch and all. 'We can do that once we're at the house,' he said.

"Before we drove up the Clark Road, we went by to see if you were home. You weren't, so we felt reasonably safe. Well, we headed for Raymond's house with the deer in his trunk. When we went by his neighbor Joe's house, you and Joe were sitting on the porch, smoking cigars and there were a bunch of kids across his yard playing hopscotch or something. 'Well,' I said, 'if we get it out quick, he probably won't see it.' Well I reached in that trunk and 'thunk...thunk.' I said, 'Jesus, Raymond, we'd better not try her here. That son-of-a-whore is still alive!'

"'Oh, that can't be, Jason, you hit him right in the head,' he said.

"'Well, something is funny in there.' I was nervous with you being within hollering distance. He opened the trunk anyhow and the jesusly deer came to life and jumped into his yard and roared and roared, then he began to run. Well, he came by me and I grabbed one of his horns and put one foot in front of it and pushed him as far as I could. Ole Raymond, he grabbed him by the tail and twisted it and gave it hell. That deer sailed down the cellar through an open window and we had to let go or get dragged down with it!"

Jason had come alive with his story and as he told the story, his arms and hands were flying through the air, trying to mimic the excitement. Mos looked at him and saw how excited he was in just retelling this caper and he understood that this was a good part of what Jason Smith truly was all about. He was a storyteller and the best tales—were his own. All the while Jason was reciting this caper, he kept laughing. Mos, too, was enjoying it.

"Ole Raymond said, 'I don't think we were seen.'"

"'No, I don't think so,' I said."

"Crash! Crash! 'Oh, Jesus! Linda's preserves.'"

"He had barrels down there with planks across the tops of them for shelves. Raymond said later that his wife had a hundred and twenty-nine quarts of preserves. She had strawberries, raspberries, dandelions, fiddleheads, and oh my God, what else?

"Well, that deer went straight through there and upset that and all her preserves onto the floor. They were all broken! This is just as true as hell. I'm not exaggerating one bit," Jason reaffirmed.

"That ole deer then began running around the cellar and went behind the furnace. Raymond had an old tie axe and he made a pass at the deer and hit one of them big pipes. Crash! That fell to the floor. He went around again and whack! He hit another piece of pipe and put a big gash in that. Whack! Another pipe went to hell!

"I said, 'Holy Jesus, Raymond, you'll stave everything all to hell if you keep that up.' Every time that deer went around that cellar, it would break another jar or two and then it would knock down some shelves that held old cooking dishes, pots, and pans. Nothing broke though. Raymond by now was getting panicky. I took the axe and when it came around again, I hit it in the head and knocked it down. Then I cut its head off as quick as I could."

Jason was roaring with laughter now and tears were gleaming in the firelight as they streaked down his face.

"Well, sir, we just stood there looking around and neither of us could believe that one Christly old deer could do so much damage. Linda's preserves were all shot to hell, the furnace was full of holes, and there were dishes all over the floor along with soot, ashes, and blood. 'I'll get a washtub and fix some of this. We won't mention any of this to Linda and she'll never know. Maybe I can buy her some preserves somewhere and replace the broken ones and get them in here without her seeing,' Raymond said.

"I came home. The deer was dead and in his cellar, and his cellar was stove all to hell. Her preserves were all mush and you were still at Joe's, sitting on the porch. Jesus, that was a close one!"

Mos hurt all over from laughing so much and when he could finally speak, he asked, "Did Linda ever find out?"

"Oh, hell yes! She gave him the cold treatment for over a month. We had a lot of fun together like that. Well, that was no fun...it actually happened. One hundred percent!

"You were shot at once, weren't you, Mos?"

"Yeah, but he missed." They both laughed.

"Whatever happened with that?"

"Oh, he paid fifty dollars for night hunting and another fifty for shooting at me. It goes to show you how much I'm worth in a court of law," Mos laughed.

Jason laughed one of his jolly deep throated laughs and said, "Yeah, about as much as that deer!"

"You know that son-of-a-bitch he was with got away. He just disappeared that night. He was a real poacher. The fellow who shot at me was from New Jersey. He just got excited and pulled the trigger. He said this other fellow offered to take him out for a fee. He said he knew where there was a good buck."

"How'd it all happen?" Jason asked.

"The warden in Sherman asked me to come down and work a couple of nights. Someone had been shooting deer at night and leaving them in the woods. The next morning, an out-of-state hunter would pick it up, tag it, and then pay the poacher for it.

"We were on foot at the back end of this field on Silver Ridge. It wasn't long before we saw these two guys with a light. When they walked past us, we stepped in behind them and started to follow. We wanted to get the best case that we possibly could. We had only gone a short ways when they turned around and put the light on us. They must have heard us. The night air was so still. Well anyhow, one of them took off running and I made a dash for him but I tripped and fell. Good thing I did because as I was falling, the other fellow fired a shot at me. I could feel the air as the shot went by my head. It was that close! The son-of-a-bitch had a double-barrel shotgun with buckshot. If I had been a little further back, some of the shot would have hit me in the face.

"Well, Andy thought I was dead. He saw me fall and all. He pulled out his revolver, a .22 Woodsman. He couldn't find the safety on the damn thing, so he dropped it and tackled him. Andy probably would have shot him if he'd found the safety. Well, I got up and that was the first time Andy knew I was alive. I pulled him off the guy and I tackled him." Mos began to laugh.

"Andy saw what I was doing and hollered, 'Jesus Christ, Jalbert, take your mittens off! Stop pulling your punches!' I don't know when I've been that angry before."

"And all he got was a fifty dollar fine?" Jason exclaimed in disbelief. "Why I've been fined more than that for shooting an illegal deer! There just ain't no justice," Jason finally concluded.

"You know I've come to believe that myself," Mos added. "I've found through the years that my remedy for poaching was more effective than the courts."

"How's that?" Jason asked.

"Oh, sometimes with a little devilry." That's all he would say and no matter how much Jason prodded him, Mos wouldn't explain. "It was something I learned a long time ago from a friend." Meaning of course, Earl Landean.

Mos leaned back against the tree trunk and lit another cigar, and passed one to Jason. "Pass me your cup and I'll refill it," Jason said. They each took a sip and settled back to wait the coming of daylight. "You know, Mos, if I had to do it all over again, I don't think I'd do anything different. I'm not saying that I've always been proud of what I've done, but I've had a hell of a lot of fun," Jason added.

"I don't think I'd want you to be any different, you ole rascal. It just wouldn't have been the same. You were a challenge all right. But then you've pulled some pretty foxy tricks over on me, too." Then he said to himself, *but it ain't all over with yet either, you ole rascal. Before long you'll come to realize that this night will undoubtedly prove to be the most eloquent caper of them all.* He laughed silently to himself and wished he could be there when Jason discovered what he had done while he went after the Wild Turkey.

Jason swallowed a sip of Wild Turkey and puffed on his cigar. "I've got another story for you...another near scrape. I've had a dozen and with some, I wasn't so lucky either. We were cutting at Sawtelle Deadwater. It was good moose country, too. Just as I got into the yard that morning, a nice buck walked right out into the middle of the yard. I couldn't pass it up, so I shot it and loaded it in the back of my pickup. I helped my son, Kenny, scuff some dirt over the blood and I headed out. I left Kenny to run the skidder that morning. We already had four or five twitches down. Well, I headed out and just as I got to the Scraggly Road, the tailgate fell off. One side was broken and it was only tied on with a string. That's all I had. Well, I put it back on and tied it as best as I could.

"I continued on and got as far as Crommett Spring and a truck went by and blew its horn. I was sure he must have seen the deer laying right in the body and he was so high up in the cab. He could look right in, of course. I got around the next corner and the gawd-damn tailgate was just hanging there. It had fallen down again. I didn't have time to hang it. And who did I meet just coming around there, just burning it? That new warden and a little ways behind him was his boss, the one from Millinocket. They both waved and I waved back. I was sure they were going to see it. All they had to do was look in the mirror.

"I knew then that I had to get rid of it before they came back. You know my father used to live at the Crommett Field. He had a little camp there. He's dead now. Well, that sets up high there and I could look back and see that they weren't coming. So I drove out back and put the deer in the horse hovel. It was shaded and it was fairly cool inside.

"I went to town then and got my tailgate fixed. All it took was a little welding with only a little bead. That's all that was wrong with it.

"I went back to Sawtelle and got Kenny. I told him we

would skin the deer out right there and dump the guts in the bushes. There won't be anyone around. He had twitched out what we had down and some more, too.

"Well, by Jesus Christ, when we got there, every fat-assed woman from town was there picking berries. That's an awful place for berries, you know. I never thought much about it when I hid the deer in the hovel. So I said, 'Might as well take it.' So I backed up to the hovel and Kenny helped me put it in front with me. He had his own truck."

"'Where are we going to take it?' he asked."

"'Right in the middle of the garage...the door is open.' Everyone should have known about it by now.

"I don't know where you were then. I never expected to see those other two. Jesus, all they had to do was look in their mirror. The deer was right in plain sight by then. And why no one ever said a word about that, I'll never know. There were enough people who knew about it."

They each had a good laugh over that. "I've got one for you, Jason. This involves you and I don't think you ever knew anything about it. Remember back about ten years ago. I believe it was the last day of the season. There was snow on the ground and you were hunting behind the old York Farm at the end of the Retreat Road."

"I remember that day. I went almost to the last minute before I got my deer. It was a legal one, at that. Actually, it was the only one I shot all fall. I was away working and then some equipment broke down. I didn't have too much time for hunting that year." He stopped and scratched his head and said, "But how should that connect with you? It was a legal deer, one hundred percent!"

Mos laughed so hard that he rolled onto his stomach and pounded the ground with his fists. "You ole rascal, you never knew, did you? You had no idea that I was there!"

"Was where? What in gee-hokey are you talking about? And what in hell is so gawd-damn funny?" Jason wanted to know.

"The York Farm. I was there, too." He laughed some more

and tried to explain that after all this time the joke was himself and he had fallen victim of his own demise. He had created a situation in his mind and had fallen prey from his own skepticism.

"Why did you take your jacket off and put it on that stump?"

"How in hell did you know that I took my jacket off?" Jason asked.

"I told you that I was there!" Mos laughed some more.

"No special reason. I was hot, that's all."

"Maybe I had better start at the beginning. I was looking for a deer myself that day and thought perhaps that would be a likely place."

"It used to be when the fields were cut. There used to be apples there, too," Jason said.

"I was out late the night before and slept shortly before noon. After lunch, I drove across the Winding Hill Road. There were too many people around there, so I drove to the York Farm and found your pickup already there.

"'Well, shit,' I said, 'that spoils that.' Then I got to thinking. I hadn't seen you much that fall and I wasn't sure if you had tagged a deer yet or not. Anyway, I figured it would be a pretty good bet, so I followed you. After about an hour, I found your jacket on that stump, so I stopped."

Now it was Jason's turn to laugh. And he did. He roared with laughter until his head hurt. "And you waited, thinking I'd come back!"

"Yeah, that's about the size of it. I wasn't sure if you left it there, knowing I was following and knowing that I would probably wait there for you, or if you wanted me to wait, knowing I'd smell something fishy while you committed some dastardly deed."

"What did you do?" Jason asked with a smile on his face.

"I waited. I waited for you, you ole rascal, until eight that night. Finally I said, 'To hell with it,' and I went home."

They were both laughing again. Mos was laughing to himself and Jason was laughing at the whole diabolical scheme.

"I wish it had been on purpose."

Mos heard that and stopped laughing. "What did you say?"

"I said, 'If only it had been done on purpose."

"You mean you didn't leave your jacket there?"

"No...I mean, yes, I left it there on purpose, but I didn't know you would find it there and wait. Hell, I didn't even know you were there!" he laughed. "I was hot, so I took it off and laid it on the stump. I had intended to pick it up on the way back."

Mos waited patiently for Jason to continue. "I shot a doe just before sunset and dragged it back to the Retreat Road. I came out down over the hill. It was too dark to go back and look for it, so I left it. Did you bring it with you?" Jason asked.

"Nope."

"Then I guess it's still there."

Mos thought to himself, *That's okay, you ole rascal. But tonight will make up for all those devilish deeds.*

"That reminds me," Jason started, "reminds me of another story. It happened about five years ago. I was cutting a right-of-way for Huber. My boys were working with me. I've probably said it before, but there are some people who just can't seem to shoot a deer, legal or otherwise. You must have seen that with your line of work and all. They can be right in amongst them and still not see them."

"Yeah, I know what you're saying," Mos said.

"Some people would say that no way in hell could it have ever happened, but it did. You can ask my boys. Sheridan Hartley was doing the bulldozing in there. He had seven men working for him. They were coming up behind us as we cut the right-of-way that fall. They were having the damnedest luck trying to get meat. I don't understand it. Holy Jesus, I've never seen anything like it ever. You get up across Second Lake...well, I never see anything like it. There were no moose, but there were deer. Holy Jesus, there were deer!

"Well, my freezer was full and we had my garage full of deer. Me and the boys had four or five hanging in my camp behind a fir thicket. I said 'Boys, don't shoot anymore deer! We've got all we can eat now!'

"Well, this one morning, Hartley comes over to my skidder and says, 'Look, Jason, why don't you shoot us a deer and I'll buy it from you?'

"'Christ,' I said, 'I'll bring you a deer. A couple or three if you want'

"'Well, if they're that gawd-damn thick, bring us all one!' he said.

"I told him, 'Okay, I will.'

"He asked, 'Is there any dry cedar up there?'

"'Oh, yes,' I told him.

"'Well, bring one of them down, too.'

"There was a lot of dry cedar up there. There was one that must have been sixty feet long. I know it had a cord in it. That son-of-a-whore was two feet on the butt. The boys went up ahead of me. George had my skidder and I was on my crawler. Well, anyway, Kenny shot two. Mark shot one and I came right behind them and shot three! I never saw the likes of it before. Well, coming back down, I shot two more while I was on my crawler. The last one I shot was a fourteen-point buck. That baby...his rack, would be worth several hundred dollars today.

"Well, I threw those on and I cut that dry cedar. Me and the boys showed up at the yard at the same time with eight deer. There was enough for all of Hartley's men.

"'Jesus Christ! I suppose you were only fooling about getting us each one,' he said.

"Well, he was so nervous then that he shut his dozer down and went to get his men to take care of those deer before you showed up. Oh, gee-hokey, am I glad that you weren't there then. You would've had me in jail until the sun rotted and fell from the sky!"

"I wish I had been," was Mos' only comment. He picked up the last of the firewood and threw it on the fire. He lit another cigar and Jason poured the last of his Wild Turkey.

"What time is it getting to be?" Jason asked.

"Oh, a little before four. Why, are you in a hurry to go somewhere?"

"No...no, just curious. That's all." But he wished to hell that Mos would get tired and go home so he could grab his knife and rifle and throw the deer in his pickup and go home, too. It wouldn't be long now before the sun was up and he wanted to be gone by then. He said to himself, *yes, sir, that ole fox knows about that buck sure as hell and he's going to keep me here until daylight. But then what? Damn it! He's retired.*

"Jerri going to be worried if you don't' show up tonight?"

"No, she's pretty good that way. There's only been one time when she ever got angry. I wasn't out poaching either. That was back when I was a lot younger. I'd been drinking with some buddies and it was three days later before I got home." He started laughing. "It was the damnedest sight ever. It sobered me up fast, now I tell you.

"It was the middle of the afternoon and when I walked through the door, well Jesus, she was standing there with her arms folded across her chest and her hair was all done up with rollers and pin curls.

"'Where in hell have you been?' she asked.

"She never gave me a chance to answer. The next thing I knew, I was laying on the floor and she was sitting on top of me, screaming. Jesus, I decided right then and there that I'd never do that again.

"That reminds me of another story about Jerri. Now this is true, it really did happen. The other stories are true, too, of course. I wouldn't be telling them if they weren't. Did you know Jerri was a beauty queen?"

"No, I guess I didn't," Mos replied.

"Yep, she was. In fact, she was for two years in a row. In '46 , she was the Winter Carnival Queen in Island Falls. Then she won again in '47 at Patten's May Day Festivals. God she was a good looker. I never quite understood what she ever saw in me."

"It must have been that eloquent charm of yours, Jason."

They both laughed.

"You know, Mos, the truth be known, she's always been one hell of a woman. She did an awful good job of raising our children. I wasn't around much."

"That sounds familiar," Mos added. "I wasn't around much either when my boy and girl were growing up. Renée saw to most of that."

"Let's have a drink to our wives," Jason said.

The night air was changing. It was cooling off and the ground fog was beginning to carpet the field. The sky was still clear and the stars were bright, but soon the fog would lift above the tree tops and obliterate those tiny specks. Mos and Jason both moved closer to the fire and held their hands up to the flames, warming them. "The fire sure feels good," Mos remarked.

"It sure does," Jason replied. He laid his cup on the ground and stretched out by the fire. Mos did the same. For a brief moment, Jason tried to keep his eyes open and watch as the ground fog rose, covering the stars. But the effect of the Wild Turkey was too much and he was soon asleep and snoring loudly. But Mos never heard him because he too had succumbed to the effects of the drink and was snoring just as loud.

Jason began dreaming of the days of the king white pine. Everything was so vivid. He could smell the sweetness of the pine and spruce, and could almost feel the softness of the moss that blanketed the forest floor.

The early lumber crews had not yet discovered this grove. The tops of the pines were so full and spread out so wide that they prevented the sun from shining through. Everything was so clean and clear. It was the way he had always imagined it would be.

He looked down through these tops and he was amazed to see himself standing at the base of the largest of these pines, gazing up the trunk. The tree had grown straight and tall, and there were no branches until the very top. What fine finish lumber these brutes would make. But instead, they were the property of the King's Royal Navy in England and would be used as ship masts.

He heard a noise behind him and was startled to see a crew of men walking towards him. They were dressed oddly and then he realized, as he watched this from above, that these men were English and wore the clothing of the colonial days. They built a fire and put an iron rod in the coals. When it was red hot, the leader of the bunch took it out of the fire and walked towards the trees.

Jason saw himself jump between the tree and the man carrying the red hot iron. "Out of the way, stranger, unless you want this broad head branded on your chest. This tree belongs to the King's Royal Navy and anyone who dares fell any of these trees with this mark on it will be hanged! Now move!"

Jason had no choice but to move, but he didn't have to stay there and watch as the red hot iron burned through the bark, branding this magnificent tree.

From above the trees, it seemed, he watched himself run deeper into the forest. And then like a nightmare, everywhere he turned he could see men branding these giant pine trees. In complete horror, he ran faster and faster through the forest, trying to get away from this abominable scene. But there was no use, he was surrounded it seemed. But just then, everything changed.

He was still aware that he was watching everything from above, but the forest was gone and in its place was a huge grassy valley. He stood on a knoll that overlooked this valley and thought how strange it was that he had not seen any animals. There weren't any in the forest either. But no sooner had he thought this when miraculously all the animals appeared that he had known should have been there: all the little furred animals, the birds, bald and golden eagles, bear, deer, moose, and some that he had never seen like a caribou and a bull elk. What a heaven, he thought. There's some fine-looking meat. But he was succumbed with a strange and peculiar feeling. Instead of wanting to shoot them all, he just wanted to stand there and watch. He thought, how bizarre it was that they all seemed to live there in cognizant with each other. Some or all, it seemed, were natural enemies of another. Yet they didn't pay the least bit of attention to the others. As farfetched as it seemed, he was there and he was seeing it for himself for the first time.

But this place, wherever it was, was bizarre in itself. Because he was still aware that he was seeing all of this from above and at the same time he was watching himself standing on the knoll. The pine forest that he had seen earlier had been bizarre also. He couldn't believe he saw the King's men branding the trees. *No, in a place like this, I guess it isn't strange at all to see all the animals co-existing. But where is this place? I have never been here before,* he asked himself.

As he was thinking this, this scenes before him were beginning to change again. The animals disappeared first and then ever so slowly, the lush green valley started turning back to a forested wilderness. But it was not the same as before with the giant pines. This forest was like what he was familiar with. There were yellow birches and rock maple that he and his father felled for aircraft plywood during the war. Then later the huge spruce and fir trees appeared. He saw the old style crew camps with the dirt floors and low ceilings. There were men working, felling trees and others were driving horse teams and twitching logs to the yards.

There was the smell of fresh baked bread and there was smoke coming from the chimney of one camp, which he recognized as the cook camp. Still from above, he watched himself walk towards the cook camp and open the door. There seated around the table were all the men he remembered from his father's crews, when he was growing up. Jim Ryan, the Irishman, Homer T, the little French musician, Sherm, and his brothers, Beecher and George, and the little Frenchman who had climbed the maple sapling and shot through the air were all there. His stepmother, Marg, was serving them dinner.

He heard the door open behind him and when he turned to see who was there, it was Steed, the ole game warden. He walked in and seated himself down at the table alongside Homer T and Jim Ryan. No one was paying him any attention. It was almost as if he were invisible. He walked outside and back into the camp yard. The scenery was changing again. The camps disappeared and he found himself standing on a riverbank, watching the log drive. The river was full of giant white pines and on the surface of each log was the King's brand. The logs were all lined up in unison, like soldiers marching off to battle. A little further downstream, he saw a crew of men working to free a log jam at the head of some rapids. The force of the water had piled the logs higher than a man's head and as he stood there watching, he knew that the one log that had to be freed was lying at the bottom of the pile. It was a dangerous job for the man who had to walk out there on the logs and free the jam, but it had to be done. This is what the drive was all about.

Several attempts were made and each time someone would fall into the icy water. One man fell off his log on the wrong side and was immediately crushed by the other logs. No one seemed to pay any attention to this fellow who had died. They didn't even seem to care. They were too busy working. "Is this what the logs drives are really like?" he asked himself. "What became of the clamorous lumberjack who skipped from log to log, singing and dancing? This isn't how it's supposed to be." But this was how all the early drives were done. The logs were too precious to leave lying on the shore while human lives were expendable and the logs were not.

He was confused and had a nauseous feeling in his stomach. He turned away from the scene on the river and found himself looking at his own family as they all sat around a table. It was Thanksgiving dinner. All of his children were there and his wife, Jerri, was just bringing the turkey in from the kitchen. There was an incessant gnawing and an unexplainable reason that he knew he had to leave this scene behind and move along. There seemed to be an urgency to his dreams and there was something requiring his attention.

He drifted over his own house and left the gaiety and feasting behind. He was slowly drifting through the air like a fluffy cloud and he soon found himself looking at Mos Jalbert's house. They, too, were eating Thanksgiving dinner. It was just Renée and her two children, Emil and Re'ann. Mos wasn't there.

Then it suddenly occurred to him that Mos was at the Stacey Farm in the far corner of the back field. Then he remembered Mos saying something about a path that he had made several years ago from his house through the woods to the Stacey Farm. He went in search of this path.

It wasn't hard to find. By the looks of the well-worn trail, Mos had used it a lot through the years. Jason was no longer drifting through the air, but he was now walking along this path and his curiosity was getting the better part of him. It lined up over the hill and at one vantage point, he stopped to look around and realized from this spot that Mos had been able to watch Larry Bottel's house and the fields directly behind it.

"Why that ole fox," he mused. "I bet he has watched us from here on many-a-nights."

Daylight was gone now and it wasn't yet dark either. It was more like that brief period just before the sun comes up. Then he remembered that Mos had said that it was a little before four in the morning. *But that was before...before what?* he thought. He couldn't remember.

His thoughts were interrupted then as he found himself at the end of the path and watching Mos and himself, both sound asleep by the fire. Then he remembered why he was there. He had shot a big buck and had dressed if off when he had seen the red glow of Mos' cigar. The deer was left in the bushes and his rifle and knife were still in the field.

With the thought of Mos sleeping next to him by the fire, and the deer, knife, and rifle in the field, Jason began to panic. He awoke from this seemingly nightmare with a start. "Holy

Jesus Christ! That was some dream!" he exclaimed.

At the same time as Jason was looking up at the stars and feeling the effects of the Wild Turkey they had been drinking, Mos was also succumbing to the same effects and was drifting off to sleep. He, like Jason, was also dreaming.

He woke up to find himself standing on the shore of the Deadriver, watching General Benedict Arnold and his troops pole their way upstream. They were on their way to Quebec City in Canada during the Revolutionary War. Mos saw the land as it was back then, before the construction of Longfalls Dam and the subsequent flooding of the three villages. He could see Arnold's tent on the opposite shore and from it, there waving in the breeze was the Continental Flag.

He had always wanted to study more about why the dam was built and to talk again with his friend, Duluth Wing, but during the last thirty years, he had been a game warden and he had been too busy for anything else.

He looked across the river again and now on the opposite shore was Duluth and his mentor, Earl Landean. Arnold and his troops had disappeared.

Mos called out to his friends, but they could not hear him. They were too busy sifting through the beach sands looking for artifacts. They were too busy to take a moment and talk with Mos, the same as he had never taken the time in the last thirty years to stop and visit with them.

He stood there remembering the past and the times he and Duluth had shared on the river before it was flooded. He also remembered the times he had spent with Landean, those young formidable years of his youth at King and Bartlett when Landean would mysteriously appear only to disappear again.

But the scene was beginning to change and he could smell the salty air of the ocean and hear the surf as it broke on the shore. A warm breeze was blowing in his face and as the imagery cleared, he could see palm trees and a sandy shore. The water was as blue as crystal. The scene reminded him of a small south sea island in the Pacific. He walked off the knoll he had been standing on and went towards the sandy shore. How warm the sand felt beneath his bare feet as he walked along the shoreline. There were coconuts and pineapples everywhere. It was a land of milk and honey.

He kept following the shoreline, hoping to find someone so he would know that he wasn't there alone. But his search was to no avail. He was alone and he began to wish that Renée was there with him. Then suddenly he remembered that she had asked...no, she had pleaded with him to take her on a trip to the South Pacific. She had found an ad in one of her magazines that advertised a one-week trip to some island in the South Pacific at an unbelievable price.

His answer had been the same as that week when he was expecting a large fishing party at Matagamon. This group had a bad reputation and he wanted to be there. No, they couldn't go; his job came first.

Now as he walked along the sandy shore, he wished he had taken the time to bring Renée to an island like this. "She would have enjoyed it," he said aloud.

He found a hammock of grass and sat down, watching and listening to the surf roll in. The breaking surf made a lonesome, forsaken sound and to anyone else, it would have made them lonely too. But Mos was no stranger to being alone. He had been alone for most of his life. In complete honesty, there were times when he had found it rather comforting to be alone with his thoughts. But now was not one of those times. He wished more than anything that Renée was here with him. He drew his knees to his chest and folded his arms across them, making a pillow for his head.

When he finally looked up, the scenery changed again. This time he was on the shore of Nesowadnehunk Lake, watching a youngster paddle around in a small canoe. There was another day just like this one that he could remember with the same set of circumstances. But this was that same day! This was only a dream though that he was reliving—this very scene with the boy in the canoe. The wind suddenly came up and as the young boy tried to paddle back to his campsite, the wind blew his canoe up against a piece of driftwood and he tipped over. Mos tried to get up to go to his rescue, but he couldn't make himself move. Just then he saw the damnedest thing.

Out of the bushes ran a stranger towards the water, kicking his boots off as he ran. Mos took a deep breath as he recognized this stranger as himself and then he remembered that this was only a dream. He watched himself swim out and rescue the young boy and bring him back to shore. No one else had seen the canoe tip over and the boy would have drowned if it hadn't been for the fact that Mos had decided to go to Nesowadnehunk instead of spending the fourth of July celebration with his family. Maybe he had made a difference after all, he found himself thinking. He was leaving the shore of Nesowadnehunk Lake and the young boy. He was drifting through the air, heading back towards home. No, he wasn't going home yet. It was dark now, so Mos concluded that it must be night. Strange it came on so suddenly, he thought. Before going to his home, he found himself suspended over the whole town. Below him, he watched as men left their homes to go foot jacking. This was an all too familiar scene. It was familiar because all the scenes below him had been actual events. They were the times he had stayed in the shadows and watched, making sure the poacher took care of the deer and took it all. He knew these were the men he had let go; those that had been forced into it because of the need to feed their families. "Take it all, boys or I'll surely take you!" he heard himself say.

Everything was quiet now. They had all taken their deer and had gone home. All but one, that is. His attention was now shifting to the back end of a field on the Stacey Farm. He laughed as he thought of the possible consequence of this eloquent caper.

Mos woke himself from his own laughter and found that Jason had just awakened also. Mos sat up, rubbing his face and Jason did the same. "Wow, that was some dream," Mos said as he reached for another stick of wood, but it was all gone.

"Yeah, I had one hell of a dream, too. Nightmare is more like it," Jason replied.

They each sat there in silence, thinking about their own dream. But with each passing moment, the details became fainter and fainter. The fire had burned low and there were mostly just coals remaining. They moved closer to the fire in order to capture the last of the radiant heat. Jason was the first to break the silence. "Mos, what do you think of them trying to bring the caribou back again?"

"I think it's an ill-fated attempt. I think they should leave it alone. They left here for some reason and I don't think they'll stay this time either."

"My feelings exactly. It's a waste of money. The woods have changed too much to keep them here for long." Then Jason remembered part of his dream. "There was a time when the caribou lived here because there was food and habitat to support them. The giant pines formed a canopy above the forest floor, allowing moss and small bushes to grow which the caribou depended on. When the pines were cut, the moss disappeared and new growth replaced the pine groves, but they were so thick that the caribou had to move on. No, they won't stay this time either," Jason allowed.

"That was a pretty good summation. Did you study ecology or something?" Mos asked.

"No, I saw it in a dream.." That's all Jason would say about it. After a minute he asked, "Probably I've asked you before, but did you ever regret being a warden?"

"No," he said with a long pause before he added, "No, not really. I like to think though that maybe somehow I've made a small difference, that's all."

"For years, I thought ole Steed was the most infamous warden around, but after these past thirty years of yours and after listening to you tonight, ole Steed never had anything over you. Too bad you weren't around then."

Jason was still thinking about the deer and how he was

going to move it. He wished Mos would call it a night and leave for home. But he sat there, seemingly enjoying the tight situation that Jason was in. There wasn't any outward indication that he even knew about the deer, but Jason suspected that he did. Why else would he stay here all night talking, especially since he's retired and he could be home with his wife.

Mos was enjoying it, too, and he had a difficult time to keep from bursting out that he knew about the deer. He wanted to stay there as long as he possibly could to make the final effects of this caper have a lasting meaning, but he didn't want to make it too obvious either. In order to have the effect he wanted, it had to be done with dignity and finesse.

"What will you do now, Jason, since you've sold your lumbering equipment?"

"I've thought a lot about that and I honestly don't know. I'll spend some time with Jerri, quit my poaching, that is as long as my poaching wife doesn't want any fresh meat," he chuckled.

Surprised, Mos asked, "What brings this revelation to be, Jason? Are you turning over a new leaf?"

Before answering, he thought about the dream he had just had and instead of saying so directly and letting Mos make light of what he had seen, he simply said, "Oh, let's say I've seen the error of my ways. Besides, it won't be the same without you out here giving me a run, Mos. You've been a challenge, you ole fox, you know that?"

"Won't you miss the woods? I mean, you've spent practically your whole life in the woods," Mos asked.

"I suppose, but yesterday morning I sat on the shore of Mitchell Pond for awhile and reflected on my past and what I've done and I'm happy with the decision. Anyhow, I'll be free to come and go when I want. Jerri and I will probably spend a lot of time together back in the woods. "What about you? Won't you miss being a warden? That's all you've done for the past thirty years."

"No, I don't think I will. Things have changed too much

and it's just not the same anymore. No, it's time to let someone younger take over."

"It's ironic, the two of us being here tonight. I mean, I'm a poacher, no denying it, and you're a game warden. Yet, here we sit. Yesterday we both said that we've had enough and retired. It just seems kind of odd to me," Jason said.

"Maybe, but we all have to be somewhere and we can't work forever."

"What will you do now, Mos?" There was real friendship and concern in his voice.

"Well, you know Renée and I never did have a honeymoon. We were married the day after I finished my training and then we moved here. We never had the time. Now we do. I want to take the rest of my life to get to know my wife. I haven't done much of that. I also want to learn to be a grandfather. I have two grandkids, you know."

"No, I didn't."

"Yeah, I do. I want to spend a lot of time with them."

Mos stood up and stretched and looked around. Jason noticed him looking and knew it was coming anytime now. Mos knew about the deer in the bushes. But what Mos said next took him by surprise.

"The sun is almost up. If I leave now, I can be home before Renée is awake. I think I'll make love to her this morning. That'll sure surprise the hell out of her." He turned to leave and then said, "Oh, Jason...stop by for coffee sometime." He didn't wait for a reply. He started for home along the same familiar trail.

Jason sat there in total disbelief. He was bewildered. Mos had never said a word about the deer or even let on that he knew about it. But he had to have known, unless he was completely deaf and Jason knew better than that. Then why? Why did he just walk off as if he didn't know anything about it?

But the fact remained. Mos was retired and was now on his way home and Jason had his deer. He waited several minutes before he moved away from the fire. He wanted to give Mos enough distance so that he wouldn't hear him load the buck and then drive over and load the second deer. The bullet had gone clean through the buck and had hit the small deer in the neck. When he fired, he had no way of knowing that there was another deer in the field and least of all, that he would shoot two with one bullet. "Hah, I really put one over the old fox this time," he chuckled.

But Jason wasn't the only one laughing. Mos waited until he was out of earshot before he dared to stop and laugh. When he did, the ground beneath him shook like an earthquake had rumbled through.

Mos had heard Jason's rifle shot and also knew that he had probably been shooting at the buck that he had jumped just moments before. So, when Jason left to go back and bring his pickup back along with the jug of wild turkey, Mos had wandered around and found Jason's buck. He made an incision along the back with his knife. Next he removed his badge from his shirt and tucked it into the incision. "Oh, how I'd like to be a mouse in the corner of his garage when his skins that one out!"

The End

Author, Randall Probert

Randall Probert lived and was raised in Strong,Maine; a small town in the western mountains of Maine. Six months after graduating from high school, he left the small town behind for Baltimore, Maryland and a Marine Engineering School, situated downtown near what was then called "The Block". Because of bad weather, the flight from Portland to New York was canceled and this made him late for the connecting flight to Baltimore. A young kid and alone from the backwoods of Maine finally found his way to Washington DC and boarded a bus from there to Baltimore. After leaving the Merchant Marines, he went to an aviation school in Lexington, Massachusetts.

During his interview for Maine Game Warden he was asked, "You have gone from the high seas to the air. . .are you sure you want to be a Game Warden?" Mr. Probert retired from Warden Service in 1997 and started writing historical novels about the history in the areas where he patrolled as a game warden, with his own experiences as a game warden as those of the wardens in his books. Mr. Probert has since expanded his purview and has written 2 science fiction books, *PARADIGM* and *PARADIGM2,* and has written a mystical adventure, *AN ESOTERIC JOURNEY.* Mr. Probert is also currently working on another historical novel, *EBEN McNINCH,* which should be available in the fall, 2014.

Other Books by Randall Probert

A Forgotten Legacy

An Eloquent Caper

Courier de Bois

Katrina's Valley

Mysteries at Matagamon Lake

A Warden's Worry

A Quandry at Knowles Corner

Paradigm

Trial at Norway Dam

A Grafton Tale

Paradigm II

Train to Barnjum

A Trapper's Legacy

An Esoteric Journey

www.ingramcontent.com/pod-product-compliance
Lightning Source LLC
LaVergne TN
LVHW020713110826
845149LV00012B/2244

* 9 7 8 0 9 8 5 2 8 7 2 4 5 *